R

Anna Martin

Five Times My Best Friend Kissed Me

"The chemistry between Scott and Evan is very well written and I just had a great time reading this book in one sitting. I hope you enjoy this fun, lovable story."
—Three Books Over The Rainbow

"I highly recommend this to all lovers of MM romance, and if you love slow burn, there's very few that are more slow burn than this one, but are so worth the wait when the sparks ignite!"
—Hearts on Fire Reviews

My Prince

"All over a very sweet, hot and romantic story. Recommended to all romance lovers!!!"
—Reading is the new SEXY

"It's wonderful period: CHARMING and WITTY and a little dirty, with an absolutely perfect HEA."
—My Fiction Nook

Signs

"It was so perfect, and so sweet, and it swept me away so thoroughly that it left me with no choice but to give it a well deserved 5 star review."
—Watch and Word Society

"I can't praise this high enough! 6 of 5 hearts!"
—The Kimi-chan Experience

By ANNA MARTIN

Cricket
Cuddling (Dreamspinner Anthology)
Dr. Feelgood (Dreamspinner Anthology)
Five Times My Best Friend Kissed Me
The Impossible Boy
Jurassic Heart
Kid Gloves
Les faits accomplis
My Prince
Signs
With Tia Fielding: Solitude
Summer Son
Tattoos & Teacups
Two Tickets to Paradise (Dreamspinner Anthology)

ANOTHER WAY
Another Way
Of Being Yours
To Say I Love You

With M.J. O'Shea
JUST DESSERTS
Macarons at Midnight
Soufflés at Sunrise
Devil's Food at Dusk

Published by DREAMSPINNER PRESS
www.dreamspinnerpress.com

THE IMPOSSIBLE BOY

ANNA MARTIN

Published by
DREAMSPINNER PRESS

5032 Capital Circle SW, Suite 2, PMB# 279, Tallahassee, FL 32305-7886 USA
www.dreamspinnerpress.com

This is a work of fiction. Names, characters, places, and incidents either are the product of author imagination or are used fictitiously, and any resemblance to actual persons, living or dead, business establishments, events, or locales is entirely coincidental.

The Impossible Boy
© 2017 Anna Martin.

Cover Art
© 2017 Garrett Leigh.
http://blackjazzpress.com
Cover content is for illustrative purposes only and any person depicted on the cover is a model.

All rights reserved. This book is licensed to the original purchaser only. Duplication or distribution via any means is illegal and a violation of international copyright law, subject to criminal prosecution and upon conviction, fines, and/or imprisonment. Any eBook format cannot be legally loaned or given to others. No part of this book may be reproduced or transmitted in any form or by any means, electronic or mechanical, including photocopying, recording, or by any information storage and retrieval system, without the written permission of the Publisher, except where permitted by law. To request permission and all other inquiries, contact Dreamspinner Press, 5032 Capital Circle SW, Suite 2, PMB# 279, Tallahassee, FL 32305-7886, USA, or www.dreamspinnerpress.com.

ISBN: 978-1-63533-204-9
Digital ISBN: 978-1-63533-205-6
Library of Congress Control Number: 2016915097
Published January 2017
v. 1.0

Printed in the United States of America
∞
This paper meets the requirements of
ANSI/NISO Z39.48-1992 (Permanence of Paper).

With enormous gratitude to Gus and Jane;
infinite thanks to Kira, who never gave up on my impossible story
(even when I almost did);
and Lynn, who gave this book a home
when I never thought it would find one.

PART ONE

CHAPTER ONE

THERE WERE few places in the world where Stan could blend in. He'd been around the world more than once in his twenty-two years, and yet this little corner of North London seemed to be the spot for him. It felt *right*.

He'd taken the Northern line to Camden Town on the recommendation of a friend and spent hours wandering around the hundreds of stalls at the market there, buying a new leather jacket and a tartan scarf from a real Scottish person and some rings. He'd eaten in a vegan café that tempted him in with the most delicious smells. Then he'd gotten lost, taken a wrong turn, and ended up in a little pub tucked away out of sight of the main road.

It had just started to spit with rain, so he ducked inside.

This was his kind of pub—dim lighting, low tables, and parquet floor that must have cost a fortune. A huge statue of the Virgin Mary was behind the bar, but someone had painted an inverted pentagram on her cheek and created a tiny, perfectly fitting Mötley Crüe T-shirt for her to wear. The statue was adorned with multicoloured Christmas lights, even though it was April. Over the bar, a hammered, blackened copper sign proclaimed the place to be Buck Shot. There wasn't a sign over the door like most bars. Just a badass one inside.

"What can I get you?" the bartender asked as Stan nimbly slid onto one of the barstools. He was tall and lanky, his hair a thick mop that fell across his forehead, the sides shaved close.

"Um...." Stan looked over the specials, which were written in chalk on a blackboard behind the bar. "Do you have a blond beer?"

"We have a few."

"Your choice, then," Stan said.

"Sure thing."

When the guy turned away to pull a bottle from the fridge under the bar, Stan looked a little too hard at his backside. It was clad in very, very tight black jeans; his long, lean legs poured down into a pair of black Doc Martens. *Wow.*

"Three eighty."

"Sorry?"

"Three eighty," the bartender said with a smile.

"Oh." Stan fumbled for his wallet out of his own jeans, which were tight but nothing in comparison to this guy's. He wasn't used to the British currency yet and handed over a ten.

The pub was fairly quiet, although there seemed to be a steady stream of people walking in and out to smoke. The smell of cigarettes followed them back inside, mingling with the earthy smell of beer and the tang of sweat.

The cute bartender handed him the change, offered a quick smile, then turned to serve the next person. Stan sipped his beer and decided this might be his favourite place in the whole world. No one was even *looking* at him.

On impulse, he shrugged out of his battered leather jacket and pulled off the infinity scarf from around his neck. The action caused his hair to spill out down the back of his neck, the blond strands feathering out over his shoulders and down almost to his waist.

That made the cute bartender look. Stan didn't mind at all.

He finished the first pint, feeling warm and full and happy, then pulled his sketchpad out of his satchel so he could work a little while he had the next one. There was nowhere he needed to be anytime soon. Not until Monday morning, in fact.

"Another?"

Stan looked up to meet Cute Bartender's warm brown eyes. He nodded mutely for a moment, then found his voice and said, "Please."

While the bartender poured the beer from bottle to glass, Stan debated whether or not to try to make conversation with him. It wasn't normally his thing, and coming on too strong, or even at all, could be dangerous.

For the most part, men didn't like being come on to by a man who looked more like a girl. A hot girl. A really hot, slightly confusing girl. Stan knew what he looked like—he owned it.

This time he had a handful of change ready. He'd been collecting it periodically through the day, and it was weighing down his pockets.

"Can you help?" he said, fluttering his eyelashes just a tiny bit. "I don't quite know what all the coins do yet."

The cute bartender laughed and leaned in over the dark wood bar. "Sure. These are pound coins. I need three of them...." His fingertips brushed over Stan's palm as he sorted through the loose change, separating tens and twenties and fifty-pence pieces. He was wearing black nail polish, chipped around the edges. "Fifty, seventy, eighty. There you go."

"Thanks," Stan said with a half-smile.

"You're welcome, mate." He turned and deposited the money in the till, then turned back. "I take it you're new to these parts."

Stan nodded, secretly thrilled. "I just got here on Thursday, actually."

"Oh wow. From where?"

"Um, Russia originally," Stan said. He lifted the pint to his lips and took a small sip. It was good beer. The Brits definitely knew how to do microbrewing. "I've been living in Italy for the past year, though. And America before that."

"Probably why I couldn't quite place that accent. I'm Ben, by the way."

"Stan." He slipped his hand into the one Ben offered to him, finding it warm and dry, and squeezed slightly as he shook it. "Nice to meet you."

"Same."

As more people started to file into the pub, Ben's attention was stolen by those he was being paid to serve. Not that Stan minded all that much. He stayed perched on his stool to the side of the bar, sketching out ideas and designs while surreptitiously—he hoped—watching Ben work. By the time he finished his second pint, there was no use; he had no excuse to stay any longer, and he couldn't risk another drink or he'd be well and truly drunk.

He debated for long moments while swirling the last of his beer in the bottom of the glass, then impulsively tore a sheet of paper out of the pad and scrawled his name and phone number on it in looping script. After folding it twice he wrote "Ben" on the top and tucked the note under his almost-empty glass.

Without looking up or over the bar, Stan shrugged into his scarf and jacket and tucked his sketchbook carefully back into his satchel. With gentle fingers, he pulled his long hair free again, left it loose down his back, and combed it away from his face.

Before leaving, he glanced over at Ben, unable to stop himself, then lifted a hand in a wave. Ben nodded and smiled, and Stan strode out in his high-heeled boots.

"Mate," Tone breathed, Bristol audible in every long vowel as Ben unfolded the note, smiled, and tucked it into his back pocket. "Did she leave her number for you?"

Ben pressed his lips together and shook his head. "No."

Tone gave him a confused look.

"He left *his* number."

"You mean…. What the…?"

"It was a dude, Tone."

A pause. "You sure?"

"Yeah," Ben said with a laugh, unable to hold it in any longer. "He had an Adam's apple. And his name is Stan."

"I'm so confused," Tone grumbled, reaching for the mixer gun, then squeezed the button for soda. If the pub was empty, he'd direct it into his open mouth, but the boss was around, so it went into a glass. "I'm not gay, but I'd do her—*him*, all night long. That has to be the hottest guy in the whole fuckin' world."

Ben smiled to himself and moved to serve the next batch of people who had arrived at the bar. Secretly, he agreed with Tone, not that he would admit it just yet.

Being Saturday afternoon, the pub would get busy soon and stay that way for most of the night. He'd started at lunchtime and would be done by nine, giving him plenty of time to get over to band practice at Geordie's. They didn't often rehearse on a Saturday night—most of the people in the band preferred to go out and get rat-arsed instead. But Jez had some weed and was apparently in a sharing mood, so they'd all agreed to make an exception.

It would be nice to have a night off.

As expected, the crowds soon swelled in, and Ben worked steadily through the evening, his mind elsewhere.

Stan. Jesus, that man could start wars. Like a modern-day Helen of Troy. It seemed like everything had come together when his DNA was being formed—the angels were singing and created a perfect balance of cheekbones, angled jaw, sparkling grey eyes, and long, long blond hair. Like a fucking mermaid.

Ben had got stick from the other guys when he first started dating Alistair last year, even though it turned out to be a brief fling with the Frenchman that hadn't lasted much past the end of the summer. His mates didn't take the piss just because Ben was bi—they took the piss about everything. It was more to do with the fact Alistair was a poncey git who saw Ben as a bit of rough.

Well, Alistair had had his fling and slummed it with the real kids in London, then flounced off back to *gay Paris* as soon as the rain came in October. Well, fuck him. He was nowhere near as pretty as Stan.

When the end of his shift rolled around, Ben handed over to Mel with the obligatory high-five tap out and dragged Tone away from a bunch of girls who looked amused but slightly scared. Tone did that a lot. He meant well, but if the broad Bristolian accent wasn't enough, the shaggy beard and mass of curly hair gave him something of a *Stig of the Dump* look that tended to terrify the ladies.

"What?" Tone grumbled as they gathered up backpacks and guitar cases from the cellar. "I was in there, mate, I swear."

"Of course you were," Ben said soothingly. "Gotta get to Geordie's, though, before all the weed is gone."

Tone perked up at that idea and followed Ben to the Tube station with one of Ben's guitars slung over his shoulder.

The band had started out as a ragtag group of people who just got together to jam and do covers a few times a month. Ben had met them through Tone after he got the job at the pub and had mentioned that he played guitar. Not that well. His lack of skills didn't matter. Apparently, it was more a chance for the group to get together and smoke or get drunk.

In the year and a half since they started playing together, things had become more organised, and they had taken the big first step to actually playing in public. That meant needing a set, though, and not just a bunch of covers. Writing their own music was a big step up. It had caused weeks of rows.

There was still a dent in the side of Ben's head where Tone had thrown a drumstick at him, called him a "fucking Kiwi bastard," and stormed out of their rehearsal space. They had been best friends ever since.

Nowadays there were only a few places in London where the band could get together to practise—Buck Shot had a music venue attached by a big set of double doors at the back, which opened up when a band was on. During the day, or when it wasn't being used, the doors stayed closed, and Mel, the manager, let them use the stage. The acoustics were weird when the room wasn't full of people, but it was better than nothing. Plus, over half the band worked in the pub anyway, so it was easy to gather them in one place.

If the venue space was being used or if they wanted to do stuff that was only semi legal, they hung out at Geordie's mum's place, which was in Notting Hill and had a soundproofed basement. Ben had always thought Geordie—not his real name; he was just from Newcastle—lived the sort of life most people could only dream of.

Geordie's mum had won the lottery. Over sixty million on a normal Saturday night. It was crazy. The family had blown a load on a holiday to Magaluf, then set up in London so his mum could go and watch musicals to her heart's content. She had two kids at Sylvia Young Theatre School and threw her remaining millions at producers, with the hopes of funding a big hit.

For all of their nouveau-riche lifestyle, Geordie's mum was sound and didn't care that her only son was slumming around as a wannabe rock star. And she let the band rehearse in the basement. So Ben did his duty, flirted with her whenever he visited—mostly to annoy Geordie—and kept in her good graces.

"Alright, Sherrie?" Ben said when she opened the door. He leaned in and gave her a kiss on the cheek and a quick pat on the bum. He was one of the few people who could get away with it.

"You are naughty, Ben," she said with a laugh, then shooed them down to the basement, where the others were already gathered.

"Ben's got a girlfriend," Tone announced as soon as they both got over the threshold and shut the door behind them. "Well, sort of."

"Fuck's sake, Tone," Ben muttered. "I don't have a fucking girlfriend."

Geordie looked over, exhaled messily, and raised an eyebrow. "Coming back from the dark side, are you?"

"Nah." Ben held his hand out for the spliff and nodded in thanks when Geordie passed it over. "Men are so much less hassle than women."

"They don't bleed either," Tone mused. "Unless you do 'em really hard, anyway."

The group groaned in almost perfect harmony, and Summer threw a guitar pick at Tone's head. It missed by a mile.

"You're disgusting," she said.

"Tone" wasn't short for Tony or Antony, as most people assumed. His given name was Daniel, and he'd earned the nickname for his uncanny ability to lower the tone of a conversation, even when people assumed it was already at rock-bottom. They had a thing for nicknames in this band. Which was ironic, really, since they'd never really agreed on a name for the band itself. Having the Greek God of War as their moniker seemed apt.

Summer produced a bottle of rum from her bag, waved it invitingly, and said something about ice and mixers. Four heads turned towards Geordie, who stalled for a moment, then hauled himself to his feet, grumbling about being a fuckin' hostess.

"Love you, Geordie," Summer called after him.

"So, have we got any gigs lined up?" Ben asked.

Summer took responsibility for organising the gigs Ares played, mostly because she was the only one who the clubs would deal with. Ben did it sometimes, when he had time, but between working two part-time jobs and rehearsing, he didn't have much in the way of spare time.

At nineteen, Summer was the youngest in the band by a few years and had been introduced to the others via her on-again, off-again relationship with Geordie. Her singing voice was incredible, and she could strum along on a guitar, so they kept her around despite the drama. She wasn't bad to look at either—her dark hair was shaved on one side, and the rest of it fell in thick waves down her back. Slim and tanned, with her nose and tongue pierced, as well as stretchers in her ears, Summer did not live up to her sunshiny name. She was a source of constant disappointment to her mother, who lived in Stoke Newington and drove a Prius.

"Next month," she said. "Got us a slot in the venue on the seventeenth and—actually, I should wait for Geordie to tell you."

"Fuck Geordie," Tone said. "Tell us."

"She hasn't fucked Geordie in ages," Geordie said, taking the steps down to the basement two at a time. He had a bag of ice under one arm and a fizzed-up bottle of Coke in the other. He clutched a stack of plastic cups between his fingers.

Summer rolled her eyes. "I got us a slot supporting Racket City. Not first support, second. But it's at the Electric Ballroom, and it should be a really good gig. They're gonna put our names on the posters and everything."

"Fuckin' ace," Geordie said and leaned over to kiss her cheek. "Well done, gorgeous."

He started to pass the rum around for a celebratory drink, but mixing booze and weed gave Ben a headache, so he passed and rolled a cigarette instead.

"Sounds good," Ben said, then licked the paper to seal the rollie. "How long have we got?"

"Forty-five minutes. We need to pad out the set."

Their current set was about twenty-five minutes, tops, and that included the cover of "Teenage Kicks" they did to kick off every gig. They used the song to raise the energy and the atmosphere, and it was appreciated almost everywhere.

"Fuck," Ben muttered and took another drag on his cigarette. "Better get fuckin' started, then."

THE MAGAZINE had arranged Stan's flat in Bow, in a gated complex that had once, many years ago, housed a match factory. The red-bricked building in the East End of London had been split up into smaller flats, and Stan had been offered a neat, spacious one-bedroom home that was his for a year.

He'd only just moved, so some of his possessions were still in boxes, and all of those boxes were stacked in the living room. Stan kicked off his shoes, dumped his bags, and stared at the boxes for a long moment before turning on his heels and walking through to the kitchen. The green tea he preferred would help combat any lingering tipsiness from the two pints he'd just consumed.

The kettle whistled merrily on the stove when the water boiled, and he carefully deposited it into a chipped white china cup and tied the teabag around the handle. While it steeped, Stan twisted his long hair back onto itself and secured the knot with a pencil lying on the countertop. Although the weather was far from warm out, the Underground in London was close and humid, and the sweat on the back of his neck made his hair sticky.

Using the kettle as a mirror, he checked his make-up. Still perfect. Thank goodness. At least his eyeliner was supposed to be a little smudged. That was the look he'd gone for that morning—slightly tousled, rough and lost.

With a sigh, he took his tea back through to the living room and stared at the boxes some more. It was no use. He had every intention of working through his current contract, which was for a year, and possibly staying in London longer if things worked out. Of all the places he'd travelled to in the past few years, London was by far his favourite. With the way things were in Russia these days, he didn't feel safe going home anymore, even when his mama begged.

This was his life, now.

The tight jeans and loose, cut-up T-shirt he'd been wearing all day were not the right sort of clothes to do unpacking jobs in. Stan set down his tea on the coffee table—one of the few pieces of furniture he'd acquired so far—and went into his bedroom to change. Stuff wasn't any more organised in there. The only things he'd unpacked so far were his boxes of make-up and hair products, and a suitcase of clothes that was now spilling possessions onto the floor.

He knew, for sure, a pair of loose pyjama pants were hidden in this suitcase somewhere. He rifled through denim and leather and silk and soft, soft cotton, until he located the baggy red pants with the reindeer pattern. He wore them year-round. They were his most comfortable lounging-about pants.

The T-shirt was fine, and with his hair tied back, Stan could start the long, laborious task of creating his new home.

By late the following morning, it was nearly done. All his clothes had been hung in the wardrobe, the things that needed to be ironed separated out and tossed over the back of a chair. He'd get to that... sooner or later. The only thing left to do was unpack the kitchen, and he had brought very little in the way of cooking utensils with him, so that wouldn't take long.

Stan yawned, feeling his muscles stretch and move with him, then padded back through to his bedroom to change. Food was the next thing on his agenda.

The box of Twinings tea was the only nutrition he had in the house, and the last thing he'd eaten was at Camden the previous lunchtime. From his exploring, he'd discovered plenty of fresh produce available on market stalls for much lower prices than he'd been warned he'd find in the capital. Yet so many people here seemed to shop in the supermarkets. It was the same in America. He couldn't get his head around the idea.

Not wanting to make a fuss to go out for simple groceries, not when he wasn't planning to run into anyone, anyway, Stan brushed his hair and gathered it into a loose ponytail at the nape of his neck. With an oversized powder brush, he swept MAC NC5 loose powder over his whole face, then filled in his eyebrows with an angled brush and mid-brown shadow. He'd recently acquired some Benefit bronzer, which was deliciously soft and blended perfectly, so he added a little of that to his cheekbones.

A quick lick of mascara finished the low-key—for him, at least—look. Stan changed into jeans and a black T-shirt, stamped his feet into heavy boots, and tucked his wallet, phone, and keys into his pockets.

Done.

It took a few minutes to get his bearings, and he doubled back more than once after taking a wrong turn. But it didn't take long to get to the long street—Brick Lane—lined with all its Indian restaurants and suspicious-looking cafés.

Stan found a grocer that looked good. A wide range of produce was displayed in wooden crates outside the front door, and an older portly gentleman with an apron and a beard sat on a stool behind the counter, an open newspaper spread in front of him.

"Mornin'," he said, barely looking up.

"Good morning."

There wasn't a basket, so Stan loaded vegetables up in his arms, things he recognised and a few he didn't. Mushrooms, peppers, courgettes, tomatoes. Some fruit too, rustic red apples, and limes to go in water.

It fell to the counter in a tumble of thuds, and the grocer looked up at him properly for the first time. His eyes widened comically.

"I'll… uh… I'll just ring this little lot up for you," he said, and Stan smiled again, suppressing his laughter.

"Thank you," he murmured demurely.

He couldn't be sure—either he was undercharged or this really was the place to come for good-value vegetables. Not that he minded, much. The old man got a good look, and Stan got a decent dinner.

With the blue-and-white-striped bag hanging from his fingertips, Stan moved on up the road.

WHEN HE arrived back at the flat, his wrists were hurting from carrying so much stuff. It was hard not to buy in bulk, not when all of the little shops seemed to cater to a multinational community, and rice was sold in bags that probably weighed more than he did.

He felt all warm and fuzzy seeing things here that he hadn't seen in years—not Russian food, but treats and sweets from Eastern Europe that his grandfather had brought back with him when returning from one of his many business trips.

Stan had tried to find some kind of logic or order in the kitchen but couldn't, and just deposited all his purchases in whatever cupboard they fit in. The morning had exhausted him, and he was still jet-lagged from travelling.

The flat had come partially furnished, which was a blessing, and Stan curled up on the sofa with his hands pillowing his cheek, content to look out over the courtyard through the open door and Juliet balcony. Buying a television was on his list of things to do, although not a priority. He had never been one for watching TV, and moving about so much over the past few years meant it had been almost impossible to keep up with the shows he liked.

With the summer warmth streaming in through the window, he was content to snuggle down on his surprisingly comfortable sofa and drift off to sleep.

THE RINGING phone startled Stan out of his foggy nap.

"*Pronto?*" he answered out of habit.

"Hello? Is that Stan?"

"Yes. Allo. Sorry. This is Stan."

The instinct to answer the phone in Italian had obviously not left him just yet. Stan felt the blush rise to his cheeks, and he held his fingers there, cursing his exceptionally pale skin, even though the caller obviously wouldn't judge his complexion.

"Hi. Uh… this is Ben. From the pub."

"Ben?"

"Yeah. You left me your number?"

"Oh gosh. I'm so sorry. I forgot…. I was just sleeping."

"I guessed." Ben's voice had taken on a soft, teasing tone.

"I didn't think you would call."

Stan stretched out across the couch, letting his knees click and hips clunk back into place. Each individual toe could crack of its own accord—something of a hidden talent and incredibly satisfying to do.

"I've just finished my shift. I wasn't sure if you were still around Camden."

"No. I'm sorry. I live in the east of London." Speaking English, especially when his brain hadn't quite woken up yet, was proving difficult. Stan could hear his own accent, thicker due to fatigue. Ben must have been too polite to mention it.

"That's a shame. Maybe you could let me know when you'll be over here again? Or I'm working next week. If you want to stop by the pub again, I mean."

"Yes. I'd like that. And then, maybe when you finish your shift again...."

"Yeah. We could...." A pause. "Go out, somewhere?" he finished lamely.

Stan smiled to himself. He hadn't even been sure Ben was interested, and now he was flustering over his words.

"That sounds good. I'll send you a message in the week. I have to work long hours, I expect. I start my new job on Monday."

"Good luck," Ben said. The sentiment sounded genuine. "Maybe we could go out on Friday to celebrate your first week. I'm on 'til six on Friday."

"That sounds good," Stan said and smiled to himself as he scratched his belly. "I'll look forward to it."

"Me too. Catch you later, Stan."

"Goodbye."

Stan pressed the End button and hugged his phone to his chest. He had a date. And he'd been in London less than a week.

CHAPTER TWO

NEW JOB. First day. The desperate desire to prove oneself.

Power dressing was definitely on the cards, but exactly how, Stan wasn't sure.

Hair and make-up had taken a full thirty minutes, not that this was entirely unusual. After washing and blow-drying his hair straight, he'd slicked it down with a dab of serum so it fell in a glossy wave. When it came to make-up... well, he'd amassed a collection so vast it was almost silly. He had boxes of the stuff, and only used a few of those things on a day-to-day basis.

In the end, with time ticking away, he'd gone for a classic smoky eye—dark liner, grey shadow, a lighter colour in the inner corners of his eyes to make them look bigger. He'd perfected the look a long time ago.

Now he just had to pick clothes. Standing in front of his wardrobe in a pair of very tight black boxers wasn't going to get him far.

In most situations, when Stan walked into a room it caused enough of a ripple of interest, without him going wild on the clothing front. But he was working for a fashion magazine.

"Come on, Stanislav," he muttered, flicking through the rows of wooden hangers. "Pick something."

Black skinny jeans tucked into black motorcycle boots, and an oversize, white, billowing shirt that was more than a little see-through. Edgy, but classy.

He had some chunky jewellery that had been given to him as a gift, the castoffs from a photo shoot he'd worked on in Italy. Rings on his fingers, long necklaces, and a slick of gloss over his lips.

On the weekend, he'd timed how long it would take getting to the magazine's offices in Spitalfields and added an extra half hour for the early morning commuter rush. He was fifteen minutes ahead of schedule.

A massive Mulberry bag—already packed—was ready and waiting by the door, along with his new leather jacket from Camden. Stan had a mirror, just a small one, hung next to the door for a final check before he left the flat.

Perfecto. Let's go.

He arrived early—which was good—and introduced himself to the waifish girl on reception. She stared. They all did.

The office wasn't as glamorous as *Vogue Italia*, but few places in the world were. Stan looked around while he waited for his new supervisor to come down and meet him, noting with interest some of the magazine spreads in huge, high-definition shots hanging on the walls.

Where most of the big Italian fashion magazines liked the sparse-and-clean look, here things were decidedly more chaotic. The reception area looked warm and inviting, with pictures of previous months' covers in large frames on the walls. Stan already knew he'd be reporting directly to one of the senior editors, but she was yet to arrive, and no one had come to find him yet to show him around.

"Can I get you coffee?" the receptionist asked, and Stan shook his head.

"No, thank you. Do you know where my office will be?"

"Um...."

It took a few minutes of clattering about on her keyboard and a phone call upstairs for her to direct him to the third floor, where someone would, apparently, be waiting to meet him. He nodded his thanks and walked to the shiny glass elevator.

The young woman who met him on the third floor was a chaotic explosion of bleached-blonde curls and a slightly saggy cardigan.

"Hi, I'm Kirsty," she said. "Sorry it's so cold in here—someone left the air con on overnight, and it's bloody freezing. You must be Stanislav."

"Stan," he said, extending his hand for her to shake. He noted her bitten-down fingernails and forced a shudder inwards.

"Nice to meet you. I'll be your assistant. Well, I'm the assistant for everyone who reports in to Victoria, but basically if you need anything, just give me a call."

Kirsty was nice, a little talkative, and willing to show him around the large third floor that was made up of a number of smaller offices. His was particularly tiny, a reflection, he was sure, of the fact he was new.

Stan was left alone in the office, which wasn't too bad at all, on consideration. From the looks he'd stolen into the other offices, it seemed most people decorated their working spaces to reflect their personalities, or maybe just the way they worked. For Stan, the clean white walls and neat glass-topped desk would be fine.

After checking no one was around, Stan stretched his arms out to his sides and turned a full circle in his new space, letting a grin creep onto his face.

"Let's get to work," he murmured under his breath.

BY MID-AFTERNOON Stan's head was frazzled from all the people he'd been introduced to, from other creative editors like himself to the terrifyingly tall, thin Victoria—not Vicky, Kirsty had impressed on him. Never Vicky—who ran the department. The woman had long, straight, dark hair and delicate designer spectacles, and had given Stan a very visible once-over before offering him a tiny smile and shaking his hand firmly. For some unknown reason, Stan got the impression he'd met his match.

He'd also gained a new respect for Kirsty, who ran around like a crazy person trying to satisfy the whims of all the different people she worked for. She offered coffee almost on the hour, every hour. Then she was going out to collect lunch. Stan elected to go with her and learned where the best places to eat were. He got a large salad from the delicatessen that made them fresh while he waited.

"You worked for *Vogue* before, right?" Kirsty asked as they walked back to the office. She was balancing two bags full of sandwiches and refused any help.

"Yes. In Milan."

"Milan," Kirsty sighed dreamily. "I can't imagine how awesome it must be to work for *Vogue*. In *Milan*. Most of the people here are hoping to go there, not leave."

"It was good," Stan conceded, rolling his shoulders and tipping his face up to the sun. "But I wanted a new challenge. It's such a different aesthetic here—much edgier, and the styles change so quickly. You need to keep your ear to the ground, watch the street fashion, let the people lead instead of the designers. That's interesting to me."

"I guess."

"Here we can't get away with running florals for spring. Can you even imagine?"

Kirsty laughed, a bright sound. "You'd be castrated."

"Darling," Stan said, giving her a pointed look. "But yes. I want to walk around London and let that be my inspiration, not the top-down politics where it's all decided and dictated months in advance."

"I think you'll fit in well here," Kirsty said. Stan squirmed under her scrutinizing. "You're different, but in the right way."

"I'm different everywhere," Stan said with a humourless laugh.

Kirsty left him in peace that afternoon, quickly learning he didn't like to be disturbed when deep in a project. It might only be his first day, but fashion didn't wait. He was going straight in, feet first—exactly how he liked it.

BY THE end of the week, Stan had developed a routine that suited him just fine. He was the first in the office most days, usually by seven in the morning, and left early to compensate. His instant, first impression of Kirsty was, to his shame, off the mark. She was sweet and smiling and highly efficient, but a tiger underneath when crossed. Stan had decided not to cross her.

He alone of his colleagues left the office at lunchtime and took the short walk to the deli with Kirsty. It was nice to get out of the office and get some fresh air to enjoy the breeze and the sunshine that he'd been promised wouldn't last. It was with Kirsty, out of all his new colleagues, that Stan found himself starting to bond.

As for Ben… they exchanged a few messages midweek, then, on Friday lunchtime, while Stan was eating his salad and reading the *Guardian* newspaper online, his phone buzzed again.

Are we still on for tonight?

From Ben. Stan made himself wait five minutes before responding.

Yes. I hope so!

Ben texted back immediately.

Great. Do you want to meet me at the pub? I finish my shift at six, then I thought we could go out for something to eat.

Food. Stan winced and wondered if it was the best time to bring up all his issues. Probably not.

That would be nice. I don't want to make a fuss, but I'm mostly vegan.

There. It was done. He leaned back in his chair and fiddled with his phone while waiting for Ben's response.

Oh, no worries. There's plenty of places to go around here. I don't eat meat very often. Not a problem. :)

"Thank God," Stan muttered and typed a quick response, then shut his phone back in his drawer so he wouldn't be tempted to send another message.

MANAGING HIS own workload meant most of the time Stan controlled his own working hours. No one challenged him if he disappeared for a while in the afternoon, or if he loaded his iPad up with stuff and took it home to work.

Coming in early was a habit he'd picked up in Italy, one no one here seemed to share. Some people didn't stumble in until ten. By that time, Stan was on his second coffee and well into his working day.

Since he had a date, and he had been working for hours already, Stan packed up and left the office at two in the afternoon. Some people weren't back from lunch yet, and he hadn't taken a break at all.

The Tube was busy, but nothing compared to rush hour, meaning he got back to his flat with plenty of time to take a shower, carefully keeping his hair out of the water.

With soft music playing in the background, Stan dried off and lay down on his bed, naked.

This wasn't quite meditation, but something akin to it that he'd done since he was a child. His mother had often caught him and thought it was a kinky thing, at least at first, until he grew up enough to request a lock on his door. It wasn't about being sexual, or masturbation, just... existing. Being. Acknowledging one's own mortality.

And a good opportunity to decide what he was going to wear for the date.

He didn't want to go too overboard, and even though he had a new maroon lipstick he wanted to try out, this probably wasn't the right time. The last time he'd seen Ben, he was relatively low-key, and without knowing what their plans for the evening would be, it was hard to decide.

Cigarette pants—incredibly tight, sandy colour, went well with everything. A very loose, black cotton tank that hung off his slim frame. Maybe a little more eyeliner than normal. His black motorcycle boots, a favourite, and good for walking in case they ended up having to go a distance.

Stan managed to reduce the contents of his Balenciaga bag to the pockets of his jacket—a thigh-length, sleeveless, tan trench coat that had blessedly large pockets and tied with a belt around his waist.

On impulse, just before leaving the flat, he took a detour to the bathroom and found a condom in one of his baskets of beauty products. His face flushed a little as he tucked it into the back of his wallet, not sure if this was the direction the evening would take. It felt good to be prepared, though.

Ben was still working when Stan arrived at the pub, admittedly early but better than being late. He sidled onto the same stool he'd sat on the last time he was here and pouted invitingly at Ben until he noticed and came over.

"I'm early. I'm sorry."

"It's fine. I can't go until Gem gets here to take over from me." Ben smiled. "You look great, by the way."

"Thanks."

"Can I get you a drink?"

"Um...."

Stan didn't want to drink, not this early in the evening, and not when he hadn't had anything to eat in hours. He got drunk quickly at the best of times.

"Can I get a tonic water with lime?"

"Wedge or cordial?"

"Wedge, please."

"No problem," Ben said with a wink and moved efficiently around the bar to fix the drink. The booths were buzzing with people but the bar itself was relatively quiet, leaving Stan with plenty of space to lean his elbows on the slightly sticky wood and play with his phone until Ben was ready.

Gem, it turned out, was a tall girl with multicoloured hair. It was streaked with blue and pink, mostly, with some blonde peeking out through the roots.

Stan surveyed her with the critical eye he'd developed since he started working in fashion. She was too curvy for couture—she actually had curves in the first place, which was too much for some fashion houses. But her look was delicious, her proportions exquisite, and she could get some editorial work, if she was interested. Stan decided to not say anything unless he got a chance to speak to her alone. He didn't want to offend.

"Right," Ben said, appearing from the cellar that apparently doubled as a staff room. He shrugged into his leather jacket, one covered in patches, and pulled a rolled cigarette out from behind his ear. "Ready?"

"Yes."

Ben waved goodbye to his friends but didn't stop to speak to them again, and briefly put his hand on Stan's lower back as they wandered out into the cool London evening.

"Do you mind if I...?" Ben said, gesturing with his cigarette.

"Oh, no. Not at all. I'd join you, but I had one on my way over."

Ben smiled and quickly lit the rollie. "I was thinking sushi," he said, leading them off up Camden High Street. "There's a good place not far from here, and I know they do vegan plates."

"I like sushi," Stan said. "That would be nice. Thank you. And sorry for—"

He didn't finish his sentence, Ben was already waving the apology away. "It's fine," he said. "Really. I like this restaurant anyway, and there's loads of places around here where you can get good vegan food."

Stan nodded. "How was work?" he asked, wanting to move away from his least favourite topic of conversation.

"Not bad," Ben took two quick drags on his cigarette and tossed it into the gutter, where it fizzed in the last of the previous night's rain. "I was on the early, so I started at lunchtime and opened up. I don't mind doing that—there's normally plenty to do, getting the delivery out and cleaning what they didn't get chance to do last night."

"Have you worked there long?"

"Yeah. It was my first job when I moved to London. I think I stay there for sentimental reasons sometimes... but the pay isn't bad, and I get to pretty much pick my hours. If I need time off, they let me have it. And we get good bands and stuff coming through. Here," Ben said, nodding to a tiny restaurant. The entrance was only six feet wide, a door with a window that was already steamed up. He let Stan go in first.

Inside, the smell of food was thick in the air. Stan was surprised—the restaurant was much larger on the inside than what it looked like from the street. The room stretched way back, and a staircase to the side suggested space for more tables upstairs.

"Two," Ben said from over Stan's shoulder, to a young Japanese girl who smiled at them and gestured for Stan to follow.

The little table was towards the back of the restaurant, pressed against a wall with other diners either side of them. Stan shrugged out of his jacket and hung it carefully over the back of his chair—he got the impression this wasn't the sort of place that would hold it for him. Ben did the same and they shuffled into seats.

"Tea?" she offered.

"Please," Ben said. Stan nodded. The waitress handed each of them a menu, then left them alone.

A rush of insecurity swept into Stan's stomach.

"So, we can order whatever, or there's a sharing plate they do for sushi… let me find it for you," Ben said. He was babbling. To think that Ben was nervous too was reassuring, and Stan forced himself to roll his shoulders, stretch his neck as surreptitiously as he could, crack his thumbs.

Ben turned his own menu around and pointed to a sharing plate.

"That looks good," Stan said with a nod.

"Yeah? Okay."

He smiled.

"It says vegetarian, but I can check if it's vegan. I expect so. They don't label things as vegan in here."

The server returned with the tea and placed the two delicate cups in front of them. Confirmed the food was vegan. Did a double take at Stan's flat chest.

"Green tea," she said, gesturing to the cups. "No milk."

Ben nodded, and she left.

"We ask if the food is vegan, then she mentions milk," Ben said with a laugh.

"I can't have cow's milk. I'm not allergic," Stan said. "What's the word… like allergic, but it's not that bad?"

"Intolerant?"

"Yes, that's it. I'm intolerant to cow's milk, so I can only have goat's milk or soya. I don't eat cheese anyway. I do like honey, though."

"London's probably one of the best places in the world to be vegan," Ben said. "There's plenty of cafés and restaurants that are vegan only. You just have to know where to go."

"I don't know many places here yet," Stan said with a laugh. "I live quite close to Victoria Park, so I walked around there the other day. That was nice. I keep meaning to go down to Piccadilly Circus and Leicester Square, all the tourist places, but I haven't built up the courage to do that yet."

"I hardly ever go into central now," Ben said, fiddling with his chopstick. "Not if I can help it, anyway. It's mental."

"Exactly! And I don't want to be one of those horrible tourists who just stands and looks up at everything. I was like that the first time I went to New York, and you can tell the people who live there, because they just give you this *look*…."

Ben laughed. "I know the one. You'll get to learn how to do it once you've lived here for a while. It's equal parts exasperation and derision."

"I'll look forward to that."

Stan reached for his green tea and sipped. He didn't normally talk this much—not just on dates, at all, and he suddenly felt self-conscious. Under the table, where no one could see, Ben tipped his ankle against Stan's. It wasn't sexy, or even suggestive. Just nice.

"So, tell me how your first week at work was," Ben said.

Stan cocked his head to the side. "It was okay. I have a lot of work to do already, but I was sort of expecting that. I took a week off between finishing my last job and starting this one, so I have had a break this year."

"You work in fashion?"

"Yes. I'm a fashion journalist."

"As you can tell," Ben said, with a self-deprecating smirk, "I'm not the most fashionable person in the world. I have no idea what a fashion journalist does."

"No, no," Stan protested. "Fashion is fleeting, but style is forever. You have a very striking style, Ben."

"Do I?"

"Yes." Under the table, Stan knocked his ankle back against Ben's. "I like the way you look."

"Thanks," Ben mumbled. He sipped his tea to hide his embarrassment. "Tell me about what a fashion journalist does, then."

"That's not necessarily easy. My job is quite varied. I got my start in blogging. Then I moved on to working for a magazine. Sometimes that means working on shoots. Sometimes I write articles or report from big runway shows."

"You moved here from Italy, right?"

"Mhmm."

"How come?"

"I wanted to take a step back. I was working for *Vogue Italia*, and it was so high-pressure, high stress, and I wanted to work for a smaller magazine where I could make more of an impact, instead of just being one of many."

"And you're young, to have a job in a magazine like *Vogue*...."

"Is that a sneaky way of asking how old I am?" Stan said, realising he was flirting too late to take it back. Ben held up his hands and laughed.

"You got me. I'm twenty-six. There. I went first."

"Twenty-two."

"Are you serious? Wow. I mean, you were working for *Vogue* when you were how old?"

"I left St Petersberg when I was fifteen. I had a chance to go to America, so I went, then within a few months, I was interning at a magazine. Unpaid, of course. I sort of snuck into doing this. Tell me about your job."

Stan was eager to move the conversation on, away from himself. He picked up his tea again, hoping that by occupying his mouth, Ben would do the talking for a while.

"Well, I work in the pub. As you know. And I've got a little freelance job tutoring, which is mostly after-school stuff."

"You teach?"

"Tutor," Ben corrected. "I did a qualification in it, and now I go round to people's houses and help their kids cram for exams. Some parents like me because I'm young and relatable and I look like this, so their kids get on with me better than some of the stuffy old ladies that do it."

Stan laughed and leaned back in his chair, holding his cup carefully close to his chest. "That sounds like fun."

"It is. I have to stay on top of a lot of the legislation that comes out and go to seminars a few times a year to keep on top of the game. Tutoring is a big-money business now, and parents all want the best for their kids."

"What subjects do you teach?"

"Maths and English, some music, science, and history. I specialise in music, but most of the time I do maths and English. Those are the important ones."

"Music?" Stan prompted. He liked the way Ben used his hands to demonstrate his point when he spoke, fingers drawing pictures in the air in front of him. He seemed utterly unselfconscious.

"Yeah. I play in a band, guitar, and I help kids mostly with the composition element of their GCSE."

"You're in a band?"

"Yeah." Ben smiled. "You should come see us sometime."

"I will," Stan said with a nod. His next question was lost as the server returned with plates of food. "Oh my gosh," he muttered. "We'll never eat all of this."

"You underestimate how much I can put away," Ben said, rolling up the sleeves of his long, black T-shirt, revealing the black-and-grey tattoos underneath. It seemed both arms were inked, from elbow to wrist, at very least. Ben caught him staring and winked.

"Later," he said. "Food first."

CHAPTER THREE

IT WAS good sushi, and Stan had been to Japan once with *Italia*, so he knew good sushi—and more importantly, bad sushi. Ben wasn't lying, he really could eat a lot, and Stan preferred to sit back and nibble while Ben talked and talked.

And ate.

"Please, tell me something," Ben said. "I really won't shut up otherwise."

"I don't want you to shut up."

"I do."

"Okay. Um...."

"What's the magazine like? Is it different to *Vogue*?"

Stan nodded slowly and carefully selected another piece of maki, dipped it in the rich, dark soy sauce, then put it to the side of his own plate before talking.

"It's very different from what I'm used to," he said. "I've worked for a few magazines now, and they all work in their own ways, of course, but the underlying structure is the same. I know my job, and I know I'm good at it, but I feel like I have to prove myself all over again."

Ben nodded. "Even though you're established, you still need to show the new people what you can do."

"Yes, exactly. And these people are a tough crowd. Is that what you say?"

He ate his maki while Ben answered.

"Yeah. That's right." He scratched his nose, but Stan still saw the smile Ben was trying to hide.

"There's some nice people, though. The subeditor I'm working for is terrifying. My assistant is very good. Competent."

"You have an assistant?" Ben sounded surprised.

"She works for the department," Stan was forced to admit. "I'm hoping to take her with me to a shoot next week."

"That's quick."

"That's journalism," Stan said with a grin. "Things move very quickly. I think one of the reasons why they hired me is because I can get straight into the job, no hesitating or learning things new. Apart from not knowing a single thing about London. That's very frustrating."

"But why you have an assistant," Ben said reasonably.

"Yes, I suppose."

Ben insisted on paying for dinner, which Stan thought was charming, then took Stan's hand as they walked out into the rapidly darkening London streets. They wandered back to the Tube station and the pub without discussing their direction, and all of a sudden Stan found himself back where he'd started. Almost.

"Do you want to go for a drink?" Ben asked, and Stan hesitated, considering it, really considering, before shaking his head.

"Not tonight. I've been at work all day, and…."

"It's fine. I understand." Ben stepped closer. A car rushed past them on the street. "Can I…?"

The question trailed into nothing as Stan nodded, leaning forward and up on his toes to close the distance between their lips. Ben kissed carefully, a steady press of his warm, soft lips against Stan's. Just when Stan felt a flutter of disappointment that it wouldn't be going any further, Ben cupped his jaw in his hand and flicked his tongue into Stan's mouth.

This was what Stan had been hoping for. He lowered his heels slowly, bringing Ben with him so Ben was leaning down, taking control of the hot, slick slide of two tongues, gasps of breath traded from one mouth to the other.

Stan tilted his head to the side, letting Ben control the angle but kissing with an enthusiasm he hadn't felt in a long time. This was kissing like he hadn't experienced—hot and wild and a little lost.

He was gasping for breath when Ben pulled away and pressed kisses under his ear, then down the side of his neck.

"Ben…."

"Yeah?" The word was mumbled against his collarbone.

"Do you want…?"

"Probably, yeah. We should…."

"Stop," Stan agreed. "For now."

"Yeah. Fuck."

Slowly Ben loosened his grip and smoothed Stan's hair back into place, running his hand down its length all the way to Stan's waist. The action sent a shiver down Stan's spine—at least, that was what Stan was blaming his reaction on. Physics. Biology?

"Am I going to see you again?"

"I bloody well hope so," Ben muttered.

Stan leaned in and kissed him again, quickly, then slower when Ben insisted. This kiss was even longer, and Stan had to arch his back, bending to the pressure of his slightly taller partner.

"Oh wow."

Ben laughed, kissed him again, then again, then sighed. "What Tube do you need to get?"

"Um, the black one. Northern line, but going south."

"Okay. I'm going in the other direction. I'll text you, if that's okay?"

"Yeah."

Ben reached for Stan's hand and squeezed it lightly. Somehow this felt even more intimate than the kiss.

"I'll see you soon."

"Okay."

"Goodnight, Stan."

"Goodnight."

WORKING DOUBLE shifts, plus band practice, plus trying to feed the spark of a new relationship meant Ben was almost always tired. He'd gotten used to insomnia as a teenager, the result of a massive shift in his lifestyle and the stress of his parents' divorce. These days he tried to meditate every night before going to sleep, although some nights he ended up crashing out and forgetting. Smoking didn't help.

"You look like shit," Jez said as Ben stumbled into the kitchen of the North London house they shared.

"Cheers."

"I meant it in a nice way. You not sleeping again?"

Jez wasn't exactly known for his subtlety. Tall and handsome and with an incredible singing voice, he was the ideal lead singer for the band, even though his look was slightly more clean-cut than Ben and the others. Jez kept his dark brown hair in a fashionable quiff, and preferred button-down shirts to the ripped-up T-shirts the rest of the band often wore. He was one of the few people, other than Tone, who knew about Ben's family and how he'd made the leap from Auckland to London.

"Did you get a shag out of last night, at least?"

"No," Ben said, carefully slotting two pieces of bread into the toaster. It was a death trap and even touching the outside could give a mild electric shock. "I think I need to take it slow with this one."

"That sucks. Not literally, of course."

"It's alright. I'm gonna see him again."

"You sound pretty sure about that."

Ben leaned against the counter and crossed his arms over his bare chest, feeling the sticky edge against his back. The kitchen was fucking disgusting, but that's what happened when five blokes lived together. The rent was cheap and the landlord didn't bitch, and that was the best they could ask for, really.

"He was really nice," Ben said. "We had a good time."

"Alright. No need to be so defensive."

"I'm not defensive," Ben said, realising too late that he sounded exactly that. Jez's raised eyebrow told him the same. "Stan is...."

"Different?"

"You've been talking to Tone."

It was a simple matter of fact, not an accusation. Ben turned and opened the fridge, extracted jam, scraped the mould off the top before smothering it over his toast.

"All Tone said was that you were seeing the hottest nongirl he'd ever seen in his life."

"Stan isn't transgender. At least, I don't think he is. He's just a guy who looks like a girl."

"Ben." Jez grasped his bicep and squeezed. "If this guy makes you happy, I don't care if he dresses in drag to dance a hula every Saturday night."

"We're nowhere near that yet." Ben shrugged off the hand that was still gripping his arm.

"What, dancing the hula?"

"No," Ben said with a laugh. "Him making me happy."

"Oh."

Ben took a big bite of his toast and crunched on it while Jez finished making cups of tea for them both. He hadn't asked for one—Jez was just like that. Officially, Ben didn't have anything to do until later in the day, then it was back-to-back tutoring sessions for nearly six hours, with only a short break to dash across Hampstead from one appointment to the next.

They had done the planning for the sessions weeks ago, and the two families he had appointments with were fairly chilled. One, the first family, always invited him to stay for dinner, and he had a good relationship with the three sons he tutored. Ben had given his lunchtime shift to Tone, since he didn't want to have to leave early for his second job, which meant he had nothing to do for most of the afternoon.

"What time is it?" Ben asked. The clock on the oven had never shown the right time, not since they'd lived in the house.

"Uhh, twelve thirty," Jez said with a grin. "You got plans?"

"Not really. I might go down to Russell's and piss about on his guitars."

Russell was an old friend, their relationship forged on a mutual love of heavy metal and Russell's relaxed attitude about letting Ben and his friends sit around his shop and try out the instruments Ben thought he'd never be able to afford.

If Russell's place was close to one of Ben's favourite clothes shops, then that was just a fringe benefit.

"Don't forget rehearsal tonight. Starting at ten. Summer wants us to work on this song she wrote."

"Is it shit?" Ben asked around a mouthful of toast.

"Dunno yet. I guess we'll find out later."

STAN ROLLED his shoulders and finally pushed himself away from his desk. For the first time in hours he looked up and almost did a double take at the time. The day had run away from him.

As was the nature of things in journalism, he'd been pulled in to help out a project for the past few days, meaning his day-to-day work had slipped. He had pages of notes, scribbled in his favourite notebook at the launches he'd been invited to by designers. Those things weren't easy to get into, and Stan was eager to get his article written up and submitted to Victoria for approval.

The London fashion world was such an interesting place to work. Although the haute couture scene existed and operated in pretty much the same way it did in other major fashion cities, the underground, indie artist scene was another world entirely. That world was capturing Stan's imagination in a way nothing had for a long time, and he wanted to shine a light on the designers working in garages and basements and, in one case, his mother's attic. Unlike in haute couture fashion, these designers were creating incredible garments with no money, little training, and hardly any facilities. It was fascinating.

Stan reached for his phone and thumbed in his password to scroll through the list of messages and notifications. At least three missed calls were from Ben, and one "call me" text.

Stan grinned to himself and hit the button to call Ben back.

"Hey," he said, answering after the first ring.

"Hello. Sorry I missed your call. I've been busy."

"No worries. I just wanted—I was supposed to be tutoring tonight," Ben said, slightly breathless. Apparently the mere fact of the phone call was raising his heart rate. "But they called it off last-minute. There's a band playing at the venue, at the back of the Buck Shot, and I've been dying to check them out, if you wanna come with?"

"Oh," Stan said. "Um…."

"I know it's last-minute, but I thought you could just come over straight from work. I can make sure we both get dinner too."

"Um, Ben—"

"I'm sorry. I know you're probably busy at work."

"Ben!" Stan exclaimed, laughing. "I cannot answer you while you are talking."

"Sorry."

"Shh. I'd like to come. But I don't have time to go home and get changed."

"That's fine. Wear whatever you went to work in. No one will care." Stan was quiet for a moment. "Stan?"

"I'm wearing a dress." He sounded oddly defiant, even to himself.

"Oh. I don't care. Wait—I meant—"

"I know what you meant," Stan said. "Others might not be so generous, though."

"Stan. I want you to come. If you're not comfortable, that's fine. We can do it another time. But please don't think that what you wear makes any difference to me."

"Um. Okay."

"Great."

Stan said his goodbyes and put the phone down on his desk, then smoothed the silky fabric of his dress over his knees. He wasn't self-conscious. He'd worn dresses plenty of times before. It was just Ben's friends—a lot of them worked in the pub, and they hadn't been introduced officially yet. They probably already thought he was weird.

For the rest of the afternoon, he answered emails and did research for an article he was working on. He was supposed to be booking models for the shoot that would accompany it, but the photographer kept changing his mind on what he wanted, making the job much harder than it should have been.

He logged off and waved goodbye to his colleagues at four, wanting to make it across to Camden in time to get some dinner with Ben. Once again, he'd been surviving on green tea all day and his stomach was reminding him—loudly—that it was empty.

A man on the Tube stared at his bare legs for the entire journey. Stan stood, feeling more in control like this when the trains were busy than he did squashed between people on the seats. With his oversize bag hanging elegantly from one elbow, black, heeled ankle boots on his feet, and big, buggy sunglasses holding his hair back from his face, Stan felt decidedly glamorous. The guy was still a creep for staring, though.

Stan tossed his hair over his shoulder and nudged his sunglasses down onto his nose as he strode out of the station. Ben was outside the pub, leaning against the wall across the road where the smokers congregated. His mouth dropped open as Stan walked up. Flattered, Stan added a little wiggle to his hips as he sauntered over.

"Holy shit," Ben muttered. He dropped the cigarette butt and ground it out with the heel of his boot. "You look incredible."

Stan laughed. "Thank you. You look pretty good yourself." He put both his hands on Ben's chest, spreading his fingers over the soft cotton of the cut-up T-shirt. He leaned in and kissed Ben's cheek in greeting.

"Yeah, but seriously…." Ben frowned. "Tone is going to perv on you all night. I hope you know that."

"What does 'perv' mean?" Stan asked, rubbing away the faint lipstick mark from Ben's cheek with his thumb.

"It's like… to be all lecherous. Looking at you like he wants you."

"Well, he can't have me," Stan said with a little smile.

"Good. I'll make sure he knows that."

"What time do the bands start?" Stan asked, secretly liking when Ben reached for his hand and laced their fingers together.

"Not for half an hour yet. The first one is rubbish, though. I don't mind if we miss them. Did you eat yet?"

Stan shook his head.

"Okay. We should do that."

"We don't have to," Stan said, even as his stomach growled again at the mention of food.

"Stan, I need to eat. I don't mind if you don't, and I don't mind if you want to sit in the bar without me. But I haven't had anything since breakfast, and I'm starving."

"Me too," Stan said in a very small voice. Ben didn't acknowledge the admission and instead squeezed his hand.

"So, I was talking to Lena, who's one of the regulars, and she said there's a good place down at the Lock, if you're willing to risk street food."

"Sometimes street food is the best you can get."

"I completely agree with you," Ben said, leading them away from the pub and down towards Camden Lock. "Do you mind things that are spicy? This is Thai."

"No, I like Thai food. Sounds good to me."

Ben squeezed his hand again and swung their joined hands back and forth as they walked the short distance to the rows of food stalls, the smell of a hundred different cuisines mixing in the early evening air.

The food was served in foil containers, rice piled with some kind of vegetable curry that was made with coconut milk and spices. Instead of traditional seating areas, the Lock was lined with static mopeds and a long bar, so once Ben had collected—and paid for, at his insistence—the food, Stan took a seat gingerly, opting not to swing his leg over the wide leather seat.

"Are you wearing anything under that?" Ben asked cheekily, wiggling his eyebrows as he pushed one of the foil containers and a fork over to Stan.

"I'm sure you'd like to know," Stan told him with a smirk. He dug into the food, gasping at its heat. "Oh wow. This is good."

"Mm."

As well as being hot, there was a subtle chilli heat to the curry, which left Stan's mouth tingling. It was delicious—delicately flavoured with lemongrass and ginger and another flavour he couldn't quite put his finger on.

"Do you like it?" Stan asked. It was a mostly redundant question—Ben was shovelling the curry into his mouth with great enthusiasm.

"Yeah. This is good. We should come back here."

Stan laughed and delicately speared a snap pea with his plastic fork. Ben was so unashamedly interested—it was nice to be with someone who wasn't into playing games.

By the time they'd finished the food and cleared their table space, the sun was starting to set over the city, and Ben once again took Stan's hand as they walked back up towards the pub. They were both quiet, reflective, and Stan wondered just what it was about this man in particular that made him feel so light, so alive.

A small, fairly unenthusiastic crowd of people had gathered at the pub, spilling between the bar and the music venue, which had thrown its doors wide open.

"Ben!" someone yelled, and Ben turned just in time to avoid being barreled over by Tone, who was wearing a Cult T-shirt and a wide grin.

"Alright, Tone?" Ben mumbled.

"And, Stan, right?" Tone asked, holding his hand out for Stan to shake.

"Yes, hello."

"You're far too good-looking for Ben. If you fancy a bit of rough, I'm sure you can figure out where to find me."

"Fuck off, Tone," Ben said with a weary sigh and threw his arm around Stan's shoulder.

Stan laughed and turned his face against Ben's chest for a moment, hoping to hide the heat in his cheeks.

"Ah, you're alright, me babber," Tone said, giving Stan a hearty slap on the shoulder before ducking back behind the bar.

"What on earth does that mean?" Stan whispered as Ben guided them over to the bar, his hand slipping from Stan's shoulder to the dip in his lower back.

"It's Bristolian," Ben said with a laugh. "You learn to speak it after a while. It's an affectionate thing, from what I can figure out."

Tone let them skip the queue and poured two tall glasses of ale, charging them staff prices even when Stan insisted on handing over the money for the drinks. Ben had paid for dinner.

"Would you watch mine for a moment?" Stan asked after taking the first, refreshing sip. "I just want to go freshen up."

"Of course. The loos are over there."

He pointed to a door in the corner, and Stan nodded, quickly moving through the crowd.

After ducking into the female bathroom, Stan carefully set his bag down on the side of a sink and dug out his make-up bag. Things weren't too bad, since he'd touched up his make-up before leaving work.

Instead of reapplying his lipstick, Stan rubbed it away with a tissue and replaced it with a little touch of concealer, blending the colour to hide the rawness on his lips from the curry. If they were going to have a few drinks tonight, and maybe kiss a bit too, Stan didn't want to have to worry about the colour rubbing off.

He quickly fluffed up his hair, spritzed himself with a light cologne, and checked the dress for any marks or stains. It was a shift-style T-shirt dress, made with a fairly stiff satin fabric. Over the white background, huge brightly coloured flowers competed for space. It was one of Stan's favourite dresses, one he'd been given by the designer after he'd worked on a shoot for them.

A girl came into the bathroom behind him, nodded, and ducked into a stall. He nodded back, making eye contact in the mirror, then washed his hands and left. For a while now, he'd felt safer using the female bathrooms when he was out in public. Most of the time, the girls didn't mind him being in there, even when they could see that he was a boy.

The men, on the other hand, too frequently took exception to how he dressed.

Ben was looking slightly worried when Stan eased himself back into the space between Ben and the bar. Instead of saying anything, not when these words were still so unfamiliar to him, Stan leaned up and pressed a small kiss to Ben's cheek.

"You look incredible," Ben said, leaning down to whisper the words into Stan's ear.

"I think you told me that already."

"It bears repeating." He straightened and tucked a lock of Stan's long blond hair back behind his ear. "The next band is starting in a minute. Do you want to go in?"

Stan nodded. "Yeah."

"Okay. Come on."

The second band was good, the third very good, although Stan found himself spending an equal amount of time watching the musicians and the man he was with. They stood off to the side, and Ben kept a part of his body in contact with Stan's nearly all the time. It was affectionate, yet not overwhelming, and Stan felt himself relaxing against Ben's slim torso.

By the time the venue started to empty out, it was creeping up to eleven o'clock, and Stan, who had been awake since five that morning, was yawning.

"Let me walk you back to the Tube station," Ben said.

"Okay." It was easy to agree. Stan led the way this time, out onto the main road, where cars whizzed past at breakneck speed. A light rain had just started to fall over the city, and they ducked into the cover of the Tube station.

"Thank you so much for bringing me out tonight. I think I needed it."

"Anytime." Ben hesitated, and Stan wondered if he was going to be invited somewhere else again, so quickly after their date. "I'll give you a call soon, yeah?"

"I'd like that."

He let Ben kiss him goodbye, a sweet, lingering kiss with fingertips that gently clutched his hip bones. Stan forced himself to leave before Ben offered something more... something Stan wasn't sure he would be able to refuse.

The Tube journeys had become meditative already, even after such a short time in the city. Stan tuned out and got lost either in his imagination or in the echoes of music that filled his head while he reclined on one of the narrow seats, long legs stretched out in front of him.

Thoughts of the evening lingered in his head—the thick, cloggy air in the music venue, the thumping bassline he could feel through his feet, the warm reassurance of Ben leading him through the very new experience. This was so different to anything he'd had before. Not even in New York, where he'd discovered his independence and lost his virginity, had he felt so alive.

It took a little over half an hour to complete the journey, forty-five minutes by the time he walked past Bow Church to his apartment complex. Heavy-lidded and with aching limbs, Stan forced himself to take the stairs instead of the elevator and slipped inside his precious flat.

In here, things were just the way he liked them, his little cocoon safe from the world. Stan kicked off his heels, leaving them by the door, and padded barefoot through to the kitchen to make his habitual last cup of tea before bed.

It was much later than he would normally stay out, especially since he had work in the morning. Something about this kind of spontaneous night out felt very London—throwing caution to the wind and doing whatever he liked.

With the radio providing background noise, Stan took his tea through to the bathroom and showered with the cup balanced on the edge of the bath. Eyes closed, Stan let his hands trace the contours of his body, mapping out what each bone felt like under its thin covering of skin. This was how he measured himself, not with a tape or clothes or on a scale, but what his body *felt* like. He was putting on a little weight, around his middle and on his hips. He tried not to care and sipped some more of his tea before thoroughly washing his hair.

Without any encouragement, Stan's dick rose and filled until it was pressing against his hip bone, hard and insistent. He was good at ignoring it though and turned the temperature down to give his hair a nice shine as he rinsed the shampoo from it, letting the water do a secondary job of quelling his erection. Growing up in a strictly Russian Orthodox Christian family, he was used to suppressing his sexual urges, and even though he'd learned to express his gender in a way that felt natural and beautiful and right, finding a way to exert control over his sexuality was still lagging a way behind.

Stan stepped out of the shower and roughly towel-dried his body, then padded naked through to his bedroom with his tea. He turned the radio off, pulled on a pair of boxers, then crawled between the cool sheets on his bed.

Before settling down for the night, he set the alarm for the morning, then felt his stomach flutter when the phone vibrated in his hand with a message. From Ben.

Goodnight. Sweet dreams. x

Feeling giddy, Stan put the phone on his nightstand and turned out the light. When he rolled over and pulled a pillow to his chest, he couldn't help but bury his face in it and grin like a schoolgirl with her very first crush.

CHAPTER FOUR

BEN WOKE to the sound of someone thundering down the hall and groaned. He was always bitching at the others about making noise on the rickety old stairs. His room was next to them, and any noise woke him straight up. Especially since his curtains were paper-thin and let in all the light.

He rolled over and checked his phone—it was a little after nine in the morning. He'd got to bed around four, after working until two, closing up, staying for a drink with the others on shift, then sitting on a night bus for far too long to get him home.

Because he, unlike the others, was a considerate bastard, Ben hadn't had a shower when he got in, not wanting to wake Jez, whose room was next to the bathroom. The shower too made plenty of noise while it gurgled to life. This meant Ben hadn't scrubbed the cloyingly sweet smell of alcohol from his skin, and in the early morning, combined with sleep and sweat, it made him feel sick.

There was no way he was going back to sleep now.

Ben threw off the covers onto the floor and sprawled on the pale blue sheet, feet hanging off the end of the bed. A long crack ran along the length of his textured ceiling. No point in reporting it to the landlord. He'd only be ignored again.

With a heaving sigh, Ben dragged himself out of bed and grabbed his towel from over the wardrobe door. He padded bare-arse naked down the hallway to the bathroom and prodded the old, rusting shower to life.

The water was freezing, which was a strange blessing—it shocked his body into wakefulness when the process usually took plenty of time. Ben had no idea whose shower gel he grabbed—it didn't matter really—and scrubbed it over his body, then used the same stuff on his hair. The mohawk had been up last night, but he wasn't going to bother with it again today, so he needed to get all of the sticky hairspray out.

After a few minutes, during which his balls retreated all the way inside his body, Ben shut off the water, rubbed the worst of it out of his hair, then wrapped the towel around his waist to go back to his bedroom.

The light coming in from the window was tinged a sickly pink from the curtains, so he threw them wide open to let the bright sunshine inside. It was going to be another hot day in the city, one of those that left him sweaty and gross after a short time outside and made the Underground pure hell.

With the faintest of breezes coming in through the open window, Ben sat back down on the edge of his bed and grabbed his phone. In the time he had taken to shower, a text message had come through from Stan.

Good morning x.

Ben grinned and his thumbs hovered over the keypad, not really knowing how to respond to that. It was an opening, for sure, but Stan was so hard to read.

Morning. What r u up to today?

The response was almost instantaneous.

Not much. It's a beautiful day, I don't want to stay inside.

So he was definitely angling for a date. Ben scratched at his chest and checked the diary on his phone. It was the only way he could keep track of his shifts at the bar, his tutoring appointments, and band rehearsals.

I'm rehearsing two til six this afternoon. Do you want to come with? It's really chilled.

Okay.

Ben arranged to meet him at Monument Underground Station, where they could both switch lines to go around to Notting Hill Gate, where Geordie lived. That still gave Ben a few hours to mess about, so he pulled on a pair of boxers and gathered up an armful of dirty clothes to stuff into the washing machine downstairs.

The ground floor of the house was quiet at this time in the morning. Ben set his washing on, then found a tin of tobacco on the kitchen table and swiped it.

It wasn't yet insanely hot outside, and to be fair, Ben wasn't wearing any clothes. They had more of a tiny courtyard than a garden, but it was an outdoor space where they could smoke without sitting on the side of the road, so he considered it a bonus.

Many, many years ago, someone had planted a few bushes around the edge of the courtyard, but these had long since died and all that was left were skinny, bare branches. The remaining cracked plant pot was used as an ashtray, filled with dirty, cigarette-butt-strewn water. It was rank.

Ben sat on the edge of a raised plant bed and quickly rolled a cigarette. When it was lit, he tipped his head all the way back to try to tempt some of the rays of sun onto his face. The hum of traffic from the other side of the house wasn't quite so loud here, and a few birds were cheeping from the other side of the fence. The family who lived behind them kept their garden slightly tidier, so actual life was sometimes tempted in there.

"Mornin'," a voice drawled from the kitchen door. Ben grunted in response and shielded his eyes to look up at Tone. "I wondered where me baccy had gone."

Ben threw him the tin. Tone caught it deftly and started rolling his own cigarette. He was wearing saggy boxers and a loose, holey T-shirt. A lot of people made the assumption Tone was fat, when he wasn't, not really. He had absolutely no idea how to dress himself beyond jeans and a T-shirt, and had been known to cry when one of his favourite items of clothing literally disintegrated. Most of his shopping for clothes was done at the supermarket.

This meant his T-shirts were either too big or too tight, stretched over his belly, which was, to be fair, slightly round. The rest of his upper body was toned, though, his arms and shoulders muscled from years of drumming. If he laid off the cider for a while, he might actually drop a few pounds, but that wasn't really likely.

Tone lit his rollie, adjusted his genitals, and offered the tin back to Ben.

"Nah, I'm done, thanks, mate."

"You're up early."

"Jarek woke me up when he decided to prance down the stairs like a herd of fucking elephants on parade."

"Wanker," Tone said sympathetically. "What are you up to today?"

"Rehearsal," Ben said, reminding him. "Stan's going to come along."

"Oh, is he now. You seem to be spending an awful lot of time with young Stanislav."

Ben laughed. "How do you know his name?"

"Facebook-stalked him, din't I?"

"You're such a creep, Tone."

Tone shrugged, unaffected by the insult. "He's, like, famous and stuff, Ben."

"Is he?"

"Yeah. He's got a blog, about fashion, and about fifty thousand followers on Instagram."

"Bloody hell." Ben stubbed out his cigarette and tossed it into the plant pot.

"It didn't say how many followers his blog has, though."

Tone contemplated the lit end of his cigarette, then turned to Ben, as if he expected a response.

"What?" Ben asked.

"Nothin'."

"I knew he worked in fashion," Ben said, feeling like he needed to fill the gap. "I guess that sort of thing matters in the industry he's in."

"Yeah."

"Have we got a Twitter account for the band?"

"I think Summer was sorting something out."

Ben shook his head. "It's a bloody miracle we get anything done half the time. We couldn't be more disorganised if we tried."

"Ah, it's only a bit of fun, right?"

"I guess. I'm going to go… get dressed." Ben stood, and Tone slapped his ass. "Wanker," Ben muttered as he walked away.

FOR THE rest of the morning, Ben did the things he hated having to do on the weekend—cleaning his room, washing his clothes, tidying the fuck up. Then he played two hours of ArcheAge and took a power nap before getting up again and getting dressed, ready to head over and meet Stan.

It took another ten minutes to get Tone out of the house—he couldn't find his drumsticks—and Ben made him carry his second guitar. He wasn't normally such a poser. Most of the time he only took his battered old Samick electric to rehearsals, but he wanted to take the acoustic today as well. It was nicer for jamming sessions, more mellow.

The Underground was, as expected, hotter than the ninth circle of hell, and Tone grumbled all the way to Monument, where they met Stan on the platform. He was wearing a loose cut-off T-shirt—which exposed his smooth, pale stomach—skinny jeans, and flip-flops. Ben couldn't help but stare, transfixed, at the tiny, fine line of hair that danced from Stan's bellybutton down under the waistband of his low-slung jeans.

The train wasn't due for two more minutes, so Ben leaned in to steal a kiss.

"No," Stan said, placing his palms on Ben's chest to keep him at a distance, then leaning in and pressing their lips together in the briefest peck. "I am truly disgusting. It's so *hot* down here."

"I know," Ben said. "Tone has been telling me. Repeatedly."

"I'm going to go buy some of those short-shorts," Tone said. "You know, the ones where your bum cheeks fall out of the bottom of them."

"Tone, I am regarded as an expert in the field of fashion," Stan said, mock serious. "And I speak for all of us when I say, please don't."

Ben laughed and grabbed Stan's hand, squeezing it once before letting go.

They waited for a Circle Line train, because those had been recently refurbished and were now, blessedly, air-conditioned, making for a much more comfortable last leg of their journey. The train pulled into the station and conversation was temporarily abandoned as they moved through the crowds to the exit. Ben tucked his Oyster card safely back into his bag once he got to the other side of the barriers and stretched his neck, looking for Tone and Stan, who had fallen behind.

"Fucking tourists," Ben muttered as they emerged onto the bright street.

"I have no idea how you find your way around," Stan said, finally letting Ben reach for his hand and thread their fingers together now they were outside.

Tone laughed. "You get used to it after a while. I figured out the Tubes first because that's all colour-coded, so you pick it up quicker. The buses are a fucking nightmare. The numbers don't make sense at all, so I kept getting lost."

"And Tone refuses to walk anywhere," Ben said, teasing.

"Fuck off," Tone said lightly. "I walk everywhere. Used to when I was back home too."

"Home is Bristol?" Stan asked.

"Yeah. Born and bred. Lived in Briz 'til I was twenty, then got dragged up here."

"If you ever get lost in London, you can tell where you are by looking at the bins," Ben said as they started down the road towards Geordie's house.

"Apparently we are in 'Litter,'" Stan said, teasing.

Tone made a choking noise, spluttered, then burst out laughing. "Fuckin' hell," he snorted. "Not that bit, mate—the other side."

"I know. I was joking," Stan said, sounding pleased he'd made Tone laugh. Tone laughed a lot, and it was a nice sound.

It only took a few minutes to walk to Geordie's house, along a street that was much brighter, and cleaner, than where they'd come from. The door to one of the houses was flung open as they approached.

"Who's this, then? New recruit?"

Stan smiled at the slightly curvy lady, with her big hair and bright lipstick. "Hello," he said.

"This is Stan," Ben said. "The guy I was telling you about."

"You weren't telling me anything," she said with a salacious grin. "You were mooning over the boy."

"Shut up, Sherrie," Ben muttered as Tone guffawed.

"Nice to meet you," Stan said and Ben pulled him away, down the stairs, before Sherrie could say anything more embarrassing.

The rest of the band were already assembled in the basement, but it didn't look like they'd made any attempt to set up. The drum kit was still stacked in one corner and a pile of guitar cases lay unopened in a corner.

Ben rolled his eyes, flopped into a beanbag, and tugged on Stan's hand until Stan relented and sat down on his lap.

"So, what do these little social occasions involve?" Stan asked, his voice low as he murmured into Ben's ear.

Ben grinned. "Smoking. Talking. Gossiping. Sometimes one of us will break out a guitar."

Stan laughed at that and tried to wriggle away, but Ben held on tight around his waist. "I'm afraid I'm not very musical. I'm not sure what I can add to the conversation."

The others settled down, and Stan leaned back against Ben's chest, seemingly content to watch the small group of people.

The on-again, off-again relationship between Summer and Geordie seemed to be very much on, again, and Stan turned away as Summer straddled Geordie's lap and started to slowly grind.

"Get a room," Tone called as he finished rolling a thick spliff and twisted the end closed. "Or I'll get Sherrie down here and ask her to give me a lap dance."

"That's my mum, you dick," Geordie said over Summer's shoulder. Tone just grinned.

"Are we just waiting for Jez?" Tone asked. "Or is Wiltshire turning up too?"

Jez had disappeared earlier that morning, braving central London in his hunt for something or another. He'd promised to be back in time for rehearsal and was now ten minutes late.

"Dan Wiltshire sometimes plays keyboard for us," Ben said for Stan's benefit. "He's really good but totally fucking unreliable."

Stan snorted. "Why do you keep him, then?"

"Because he's *good*. He doesn't like practising, though. He just wants to turn up and play gigs."

"Which means, when we get him on stage, he sucks," Summer added. "Come on, let's get started without them. Jez can pick up what he missed when he gets here."

Stan shuffled off Ben's lap and dragged one of the other beanbags closer, then sat back down on it with crossed legs. For a few minutes, Ben's total attention turned to his battered old acoustic, one of the first things he'd bought after he'd moved to London. It had history, this guitar; he could feel it in the wood and the strings and the noise that came out of it.

His thumb gently caressed the strings, teasing chords out of them. Due to the age of the guitar—it was made some point in the sixties—it often needed retuning. Ben was familiar with it, though, and quickly adjusted the tuning keys.

"What shall we start with, then?" Tone asked. "Shall I get me bongos out?"

Stan snorted with laughter.

"Don't be filthy, Stan," Tone said, winking at him.

"I'm not!"

"Let's start acoustic," Summer said. "Pick up where we left off on Wednesday?"

As they worked through the first song in their repertoire, Ben was acutely aware of Stan next to him, watching quietly. His voice felt a little rusty, probably from shouting at people over the noise in the bar last night, and he let Summer lead on the vocals for a few songs until Jez turned up. She had a nice voice, not quite as rough as most rock singers, but with a soulful growl that blended with Ben's voice well.

Jez arrived after they'd finished the second song, his face flushed with annoyance as much as the heat. "Fucking Underground improvement works," he muttered, grabbing his guitar and sitting down on Ben's other side to match their tuning to each other.

They played one more song before Ben stretched his arms over his head, letting his spine pop out. He chanced a look over at Stan, who was grinning at him.

"So?" he said.

"You're good," Stan said, nodding. "I like how you all start off doing your own thing, almost, then after a few minutes you start to blend. It's like watching you all learn to share."

Ben barked with laughter and leaned over to press a kiss to Stan's temple. "I'm never going to get bored of your way of looking at the world," he murmured, too quietly for the others to hear. Stan grinned and ruffled his hand through Ben's hair, then leaned back in his seat to listen to the next song.

AFTER ABOUT half an hour, Summer nudged Ben up to go get them all snacks, claiming it wasn't fair Geordie always did it.

"I'll go," Stan offered, unfolding his lean body from the beanbag.

"I don't mind," Ben grumbled.

Stan just grabbed Ben's wrist and led him out of the basement room. As soon as they got halfway up the stairs, he backed Ben up against the wall with a firm palm pressed against Ben's chest.

"Do you have any idea how sexy it is to watch you strumming on that guitar?" Stan asked in a low voice. He'd been focused on Ben's bitten-down fingernails for far too long now and wanted to kiss each raggedy nail. That was probably disgusting. He didn't care.

"What can I say," Ben said, smirking, "I'm good with my hands."

Stan laughed and leaned in to press their lips together, just softly at first, then taking things hot and fast with a slick tongue when Ben gripped his hips.

"Later," Ben said, breaking first and gently pushing Stan away. He laughed ruefully. "You're going to kill me one of these days."

Stan felt something hot curl in his belly and smiled, reaching up to push Ben's hair out of his face. "Okay," he said, then slipped his hand into Ben's to be led up to the kitchen.

Geordie's mum sat at a tall island, a steaming mug of coffee at her elbow and a book unfolded in front of her. The room was deliciously air-conditioned, and Stan lifted his face to the cool breeze coming from the unit above the door.

"We drew the short straw, got sent up for drinks," Ben said as Sherrie looked up.

"Help yourself," she said lightly. "Didn't mean to embarrass you earlier, Stan love," she added. "Me and Ben take the piss, you know?"

"It's fine," Stan said with a laugh. "I'm getting used to that."

"Where you from, love?" she asked, leaning her elbows on the island and closing the book. Stan glanced at Ben, who was pulling a selection of canned drinks out of the fridge and setting them on a tray. He clearly didn't need help.

"Um, Russia," Stan said, turning back to Sherrie. "My family live just outside St Petersburg."

"Ooh, cold there, innit?"

"Yes, especially in the winters."

"Little whisp of a thing like you, not surprised you left. Not that London's much nicer, though. It gets awful cold here too."

Stan nodded, then turned as a small person of unidentifiable gender toddled into the room.

"Emily!" Ben said and swept the child up into his arms, making her laugh. She babbled away, apparently pleased with this turn of events, only every third word intelligible to Stan's ears. "This is Sherrie's youngest," Ben said, coming over to introduce the little girl. "And my favourite," he added in a whisper.

"How old is she?" Stan asked. He liked kids. There were always plenty of them around when he was growing up. The very youngest ones were scary, though. So breakable.

"Dunno. 'Bout a year and a half, Sher?"

"Yeah, twenty months now," Sherrie said. She looked at Ben fondly as he sat Emily down on a counter and styled her hair up into a mohawk.

"Is that a...?" Stan asked.

"Wu-Tang Clan T-shirt?" Ben finished. "Yeah. I bought it for her."

Emily started poking Ben in the face, so he handed her back to Sherrie and returned to his rummaging, grabbing a few sharing-size bags of crisps and adding them to the tray.

"Okay, we better get back before Tone starts eating people," Ben said. "Thanks, Sher."

"No problem, love," she said. Her daughter had put her head down on Sherrie's shoulder for a cuddle, and Stan's heart clenched. He'd always loved watching mothers and their children interact.

"Stan," Ben said softly, and he startled at being caught, and walked out of the kitchen too quickly.

They made their way back downstairs in silence, though Stan shot Ben a worried look when the sound of raised voices met them halfway down. Ben just sighed and nodded for him to keep going.

"Farage is a twat," Tone said emphatically. "Protest vote, my arse. It's a Tory vote, and you all know it. If you want to protest vote, go Green. At least they're mostly harmless, unlike those Nazi wankers."

"Tone," Ben said sharply as he set the tray down. "No politics at rehearsals. You know that."

"He started it," Tone said, nodding at Jez, and pouted as he reached for a can of Irn-Bru.

"Well, I'm stopping it," Ben said. He stood up sharply and shook his head. "Fuck me, I sounded just like my mum then. Never mind. Go back to whatever it was you were arguing about."

"Protest votes," Summer said.

"No," Geordie groaned, pushing his hand through his curly mop of straw-coloured hair. "Please, no politics."

"That sounds like a great song title," Stan said as he sat down and helped himself to a Diet Coke. He was joking, but Summer looked at him and smiled widely.

"It does," she said. "Hang on, Geordie, where's that chord progression you wrote down the other night?"

"You mean, after we had that amazing sex?" he said as he rifled through a notebook.

"Oh, fuck off," she muttered.

Stan watched quietly after that as Geordie demonstrated the chords on his bass and Ben switched over to his electric guitar and started to pick up a melody to go over the top. He'd wondered how the hell this band ever managed to achieve anything; they seemed to communicate in arguments and were eclectic as friends, let alone as people coming together to make music.

Watching the song develop, though, seemed to change his opinion. "No Politics, Please" was a song about their differences, and when Tone broke out a kazoo for the chorus, Summer started laughing so hard she fell off her beanbag. Ben choked and tears streamed down his cheeks. That was Tone. Kazoo, bongos, and backwards trucker baseball hat, breaking down the song so it turned into "All About That Bass."

"How do you even know that song?" Summer asked him, breathless.

"Hey, I too am super curvalicious," Tone told her, completely straight-faced, causing Summer to collapse in giggles again.

It took about two hours for the group to polish up the new song, and then they played it slowly so Jez could write it all down, making sure he had the beats, lyrics, and chords recorded in his notebook before they put the instruments down.

"So, that's it, Stan love," Tone said. "That's how the magic happens."

"I'm impressed," Stan said seriously. "You're all very talented."

"Don't, you'll make me blush," Tone told him and made "aw, shucks" gestures.

Stan watched as Ben carefully set his guitar back in its case and stretched his fingers, cracking the knuckles. When he turned to Stan, his smile was beaming—gut-meltingly handsome, the childish features stretched into an expression of pure joy.

"Come here," he said quietly, and Stan couldn't resist him; he allowed himself to be pulled onto Ben's lap. "I really like that song," he said when Stan was settled.

"It's fun," Summer agreed. "I think it'll get people on our side. We should put it pretty early in the set."

"Agreed!" Tone said loudly. "I'll have to go and get more kazoos."

"Why?" Jez asked as Summer started to giggle again.

"I'll chuck 'em out into the audience, get people to play along with us," Tone said, as if it were the most obvious thing in the world.

Ben dropped his head to Stan's shoulder as he started to laugh, then kissed Stan's neck. As Stan settled back into Ben's arms, noticing that no one seemed to care at all that they were being affectionate in front of the others, he realised this was the happiest he'd been in a very long time.

CHAPTER FIVE

IT HAD been one of those very long, very tiring days that wasn't anywhere near over yet. Stan had picked up takeout sushi on his way home and resumed work on his laptop as soon as he got there, a rapidly cooling green tea at one elbow, the half-eaten tray of sushi at the other. A quick glance at the clock told him he'd been working for close to twelve hours.

So when his phone rang, Stan seriously considered just letting it go to voicemail. Anything urgent would be emailed to him, he knew that much. The magazine had a huge photo shoot planned for the upcoming weekend, and somehow he'd been pulled onto the team in charge, even though his job was reporting the trend rather than creating it.

He glanced down at the phone, saw it was Ben, thought for a moment about how much he still had to do tonight, then answered it.

"*Pronto?*"

"Do you always answer the phone like that?"

"Old habits are hard to break." Stan lifted the cup of tea to his lips and sipped. "It's how everyone answers in Italy."

"Oh. What are you up to?"

"Working, still."

"Really? It's late, Stan."

"It's seven thirty."

"What time did you start this morning?"

"Six," Stan admitted.

"Close your laptop and back slowly away," Ben said in a dramatic voice. "Stop working. Now."

"I have," Stan said, laughing. "I'm talking to you, aren't I?"

"Good point. I was going to see if you wanted to come to the pub. But I'm guessing it's not a good time for you."

"Would you like to come over?" Stan asked, holding his phone between shoulder and ear as he flicked through a model spec. "I'm really too tired to come out tonight."

"Are you really working?" Ben asked.

"Yes."

"Then I'll leave you in peace."

"What if I could use a distraction?"

Ben was quiet for a moment. "Okay. You'll have to give me directions, though. I don't know where you live."

"Bow Quarter," Stan said, then gave the name of the apartment complex and told Ben how to get there from the closest Tube station.

"Give me… half an hour?"

"Sure. I can get this finished by then."

He hung up and looked around the flat. Fortunately, he kept it tidy most of the time, and it was clean, thanks to the cleaning service that came with the building. With his priorities now reshuffled, Stan pushed his laptop to one side and quickly gathered up the small pile of *stuff* that had accumulated around his preferred end of the sofa.

Precariously balancing everything in his arms, Stan took it all through to the kitchen and put things into various out-of-the-way places so the flat looked a little tidier.

He checked the bathroom, rifling through his plastic tub of grooming products to check the stash of condoms he'd left in there were still where he thought they were. He had four and decided that was plenty. Just in case, of course.

In his bedroom, Stan straightened the covers over the bed, then stood back and surveyed the room like an outsider might. It looked, in all honesty, like a teenage girl's room. All he needed to do was tack some posters on the wall and the look would be completed.

Clothes spilled from his wardrobe, over the chaise he'd picked up at a street sale, and a few things—scarves, mostly—draped over the wardrobe doors. His dresser was covered with face products, hair products, make-up, and several different types of brushes for both make-up and hair. Hairbands, bobby pins, that thing that allowed him to twist his hair up and hold it in place. He didn't know what the name was.

Stan had neither the time nor the inclination to start tidying that particular nuclear bomb site, so he turned, closed the door, and forced himself to forget about it.

He still had time before Ben was due, and the impending deadline helped him focus for the next twenty minutes, selecting half a dozen models and sending the request through to the agency, copying in Kirsty so she could go through the finer details in the morning.

He was in the middle of typing another email when the buzzer for his phone-entry system broke the silence. The phone was mounted to the wall next to the door, and Stan smiled stupidly as he went to answer it.

"Hello?"

"Mr Novikov?"

"Yes." Stan leaned back against the door and grinned into the phone. "This is he."

"There is a strange, degenerate sort of man asking to see you," Ben said in a silly, low voice. "Should I permit Mr Easton to enter?"

"Please do. That degenerate man is with me."

"I'm shocked, Mr Novikov. You seemed like such an upstanding citizen."

"Get up here, you dork," Stan said, laughing. "Follow the path all the way round 'til you get to block three. I'm on the second floor. Number 3240."

"Got it. I'll be there in a sec."

Stan replaced the phone on the hook, then paced his flat for the long minutes it took Ben to find his way through the complex. People got lost here all the time. The blocks weren't laid out in a logical order, though it was still light outside, so not so much chance of him falling in the pond.

When Ben knocked on the door, Stan nearly jumped out of his skin, then tripped over his feet as he rushed to answer it. Ben was leaning seductively against the door frame, his black jeans ripped in several places, clunky boots on his feet, a grey T-shirt with the NASA logo stretched tight across his toned chest.

Hair that Stan always had to resist running his hands through fell in a swoop across his forehead, and Ben grinned and smoldered at Stan until Stan grabbed his wrist, laughing, and pulled him inside.

"Hi," he said, leaning around Ben's slim frame to push the door closed. "Aren't you a sight for sore eyes?"

"Am I?"

"Yes."

"Should I take my boots off?"

Stan was barefoot, a pile of his own shoes next to the door.

"Do you mind? This place isn't mine. It belongs to the magazine, so I feel like I have to take extra-good care of it."

"No problem at all." He toed off the boots easily—apparently the laces weren't tied—then pulled his socks off too and shoved them into the boots. When he straightened again, Stan realised how close he was standing.

"Hi," Ben said softly. "Can I kiss you now?"

"Yes."

He took his time about it, shuffling even closer to Stan, putting his hands on Stan's slim hips and running his nose up and down the bridge of Stan's own before lightly brushing their lips together. Since he'd been admiring Ben's chest, Stan put his hands there, flattening his palms over the place where he knew Ben's nipples hid and tilting his head to the side, letting the kiss soothe and tease his lips open. Their tongues met slowly, then danced together as their bodies swayed, learning how different this could be when no one else could see.

Ben broke away first and pressed their foreheads together.

"I… uh… I just realised how this must look. I didn't come over here for sex."

Stan laughed softly and kissed Ben again, if only briefly.

"Okay."

"I mean, I do want to have sex with you. Eventually. But tonight I genuinely wanted to just spend time with you. I didn't mean to come in here and start grinding on you like a horny—*mmph!*"

Stan pushed him back against the door, and their laughing mouths met again in a funny sort of kiss, one that ended too soon, with Stan's head on Ben's shoulder, Ben's hands on Stan's ass, a familiar, comforting hug.

"Would you like the grand tour?" Stan asked as Ben groped and kneaded his ass.

"Go for it."

Showing Ben the bedroom seemed presumptuous, especially after Ben's fumbling explanation that he didn't come over for sex. Stan wouldn't have minded if that was where the night was headed, but there was something sweet and almost chivalrous about Ben wanting to wait, so he took sex mentally off the table. For tonight, at least.

The living room connected to the kitchen, and Stan lingered there, knowing people felt more comfortable in kitchens than he did and wanting to make Ben a drink, anyway.

"Tea?" he offered. "I don't have any beer in, I'm afraid."

"Tea would be great. I'm giving my liver a rest after the other night."

"What happened the other night?" Stan asked, fussing with the water and the kettle and finding two nice cups.

"Tone ordered gin online from some bloke who makes it in his shed, or something. It's good shit, but fuck me, that stuff is strong. I was drinking it with tonic, rather than straight like Tone was, and it still gave me the worst hangover I've had for a long time."

Stan huffed a laugh. "I like gin."

"One of them was rosemary-flavoured. It was good."

"Sounds... interesting."

Stan felt Ben step up close behind him, then strong hands settled on his waist, and Ben peppered soft kisses over Stan's neck. It was delicious, and Stan arched into the sensation, all thoughts of tea abandoned.

"You even taste good," Ben murmured.

"Um...."

Stan's mind had gone blank. He gripped the edge of the counter with straining fingers and fought the urge to grind his hips back against Ben's groin.

The kettle clicked, announcing it had boiled, and Stan blinked and forced himself to carefully pour the water over the two teabags.

"I have soy milk, if you'd like some."

"Yes, please."

Ben's breath was hot on Stan's neck, and he shuddered again before delicately moving out of Ben's grasp. When the tea was doctored to both their personal tastes, Stan led Ben back through to the living room and took his preferred end of the sofa.

"There's so much I don't know about you yet," Stan said as he shoved his laptop and the binder of model specs out of the way. "You're from New Zealand, right?"

"Yeah." Ben wriggled down on the sofa and grinned over the top of his cup. "Not many people can place the accent."

Stan shrugged, but smiled at the same time.

"I was an only child when we moved here when I was ten. We moved over the summer so I could start secondary school at the same time as all the other kids."

"You said your dad moved back?"

Ben nodded. "Yeah. My mum came here with him, because he got a job in Oxford. But they got divorced three years after we moved, and Mum refused to take me back to Auckland and disrupt my education again. She met Mark when I was in my last year of secondary school, and they got married a few years later. Then she decided she wanted more kids." Ben rolled his eyes. "At forty-two. Obviously she couldn't, so they did IVF, and she ended up with triplets."

Stan's eyes widened. "Three? Oh wow."

"Yeah." Ben snorted. "Huey, Dewey, and Louie."

"You aren't serious."

Ben laughed. "No. They're affectionate nicknames. Those kids are fucking terrors, though. They're four now. Probably the reason why I hardly ever see Mum anymore."

"That's sad. What about your dad?"

"We keep in touch," Ben said with a nod. "Skype, FaceTime, you know. It's alright."

"He doesn't come here?"

"No. And I don't go back there. It's a twenty-two-hour flight, and… I could only go for a couple of weeks, tops, because of work. It's just not worth it, really. When did you leave Russia?"

"It's a long story," Stan said with a little laugh.

"I've got time." As if to illustrate his point, Ben stretched his legs out in front of him. Stan smiled and leaned back into the couch. He wondered how far he could push this lazy indulgence with Ben, and snuck his feet over towards Ben's lap. Just as he'd hoped, Ben pulled them onto his thighs and gently stroked Stan's bare arches. "You told me you moved to America," Ben prompted.

"Yes. My mother's sister is a photographer, and she got a contract to work in New York for a year. I begged my mother to let me go, begged and begged her, and she said no for the longest time. I was too young. Then Ava—that's my aunt—was told she could take an assistant with her, but she didn't have time to hire someone, so she convinced my mother to let her take me."

"Is your family close?"

"What do you mean?"

"Well… my family is sort of spread out all over the place. It's hard to stay in contact. But some families—like Geordie's—they're all super-close with each other."

"Oh. I suppose… I think we're a typical Russian family. Russian Orthodox. Lots of children all over the place. Ava is something of the odd one out because she doesn't have any."

"Mm." Ben rubbed his hands over Stan's feet again. "So, you went to New York. I'm jealous, by the way."

"Oh, don't be," Stan said, rolling into the touch like a cat. "I spoke almost no English, and I had to go to school where I was looked at like I was a freak. I had to learn a whole new language, a new school system, make friends… and Ava would pull me out of class all the time to go help her. I learned more on photo shoots than I ever did in a classroom.

"Her contract was extended, so that happened for two and a half years. Then I graduated with my high school diploma—on time, with good grades, which is a miracle really. Ava wanted me to work full-time as her assistant then, unpaid, of course. I said no, went to one of the magazines, and asked for a job."

"You've got balls, that's for sure," Ben said with a laugh.

"I do," Stan said solemnly. "That was a few years ago, when fashion blogging was just taking off. But I'd had a blog all through high school, with pictures of myself and some I'd taken on the street. I've got a lot of followers, and one of the people there, at the magazine, had heard of me. So they said yes. The pay was horrible, but they sent me to Italy after about a year. Then Giovanni, he… what is the word? Hunted me?"

"Poached you?"

"Yes! That's it. Giovanni poached me and got me the job at *Vogue Italia*."

"That's one hell of a story."

"It's all true."

"Oh, I don't doubt that."

It was maybe more complex than Stan made out. His family had never really been happy with him moving away, but even at fifteen he was an "unusual child," and his father, at least, had recognised that Stan would have more of a chance in a more liberal country. Their society's easy homophobia, gay-bashing, and life-ruining accusations were something Stan's father couldn't protect him from, even if they weren't views he held himself. America was maybe Stan's only chance to thrive.

Stan's father was an imposing man, by most people's standards, but turned into the softest of giants around his kids. The ache of missing his family had been hardest the first few years in America, when everything around him felt strange and wrong. Stan had learned, through force of circumstance, to find family wherever he lived. Those he'd acquired at birth were a foundation, a constant in his life, and he knew he'd be welcomed back when—*if*—he ever returned.

At least now he could Skype with his mother so she could see he was well.

Using Stan's feet as an anchor, Ben leaned in and stole a kiss. Stan smiled as their lips rubbed together and he pressed his hand to Ben's cheek, holding them in place.

"Do you speak any Italian?" Ben asked when he settled back into his indolent slump.

"Of course. Apparently I can learn languages easily. Italian is more like English than Russian, so once I had learned English, it was easier to learn other European languages. Living somewhere helps." Stan reached for his tea, leaning over the edge of the sofa, then balancing it on his chest. "Tell me more about your family? Please?"

Ben sighed heavily, and Stan worried that he'd pushed too far. Then Ben started to speak. "Well, my mum is half Maori—that's Native New Zealander. Her father—my grandfather—he was Maori, and he married a white woman. Granddad died a year or so before we moved here. My mum would have never moved if he was still alive."

"You were close to him?"

"Yeah. I only had him and a grandmother on my dad's side who we never saw. He was this big bear of a man, huge, had all these traditional Maori tattoos all over his arms and chest. That's where this one comes from…."

Ben pulled up the sleeve of his T-shirt to reveal the design that covered his shoulder, part of his chest, and partway down his arm.

"It's a replica of Granddad's tattoo, or as far as we can tell. I only had some old photos to base it on. But it's like his. It was the first tattoo I ever got."

"But not your last."

"No," Ben said with a laugh. "The most recent one was this one."

He pulled up his T-shirt again, this time revealing a slim but toned stomach and an eagle tattoo that started on his sternum, the wings stretching out across the front of his ribs.

"That must have hurt," Stan said.

"Yeah. But it's cool, though, right?"

"I like all your tattoos."

"And this?" Ben asked, flicking the hoop in the corner of his bottom lip with his tongue.

"Yes, that too. For different reasons."

Ben laughed and jostled on the sofa, wrestling with Stan and almost causing the cup of tea to fall. When Stan protested, Ben carefully set it on the floor, then stretched out full-length, covering Stan's body with his own.

"Hi," Ben said softly.

"Hi, yourself."

Stan sighed into the kiss, a soft, sweet connection. Things between them were yet to heat up too far; they had danced around the idea, or even the possibility of sex for a while now, and Stan was starting to feel impatient. He wanted *more*.

"Can you stay tonight?" Stan asked, running his fingers through Ben's messy hair.

"I don't have anything with me. A toothbrush or anything."

"I can lend you things."

Ben wrinkled his nose. "Have you eaten?"

For a moment, Stan considered his day. "Not really," he admitted.

"Let's get some dinner."

They lay on the sofa kissing until Stan couldn't stand it any longer and nudged a recalcitrant Ben onto his side before their erections took control of their brains. With swollen lips, Stan wandered to his bathroom and relieved himself of the pressure on his bladder, although the one on his balls was more persistent.

"I don't want you to have to cook," Ben said, tapping on his phone when Stan returned to his living room. "I've got a list here of vegan places in London that deliver."

"That sounds fine to me."

"Do you want to look at a menu? Or I can just order anything."

"I trust you," Stan said and smiled before going to make more tea for them both.

The food arrived while they were watching a Saturday night talent competition, something Ben had complained he would receive hell for should he put it on at home. Stan thought it was hilarious and had quickly learned that Ben's running, grumbling commentary was almost as entertaining as the television.

"Here," Ben said, shifting his hips on the sofa to reach for his wallet when the buzzer rang. "I've got half."

"No, it's my turn."

"Stan—"

"I've got it," Stan said with a smile, passing through the kitchen to collect some money before answering the door.

Ben seemed to have been raised with old-fashioned family values, which Stan appreciated, even though it made him feel like the girl in the relationship. That wasn't always a bad thing, but occasionally he wanted to assert his independence and masculinity both.

After paying the delivery guy, Stan took the big brown paper bag through to the kitchen and started to unpack the boxes.

"Come and get it," he called in a sing-song voice, then laughed when Ben appeared quickly around the corner. "Help yourself."

"It smells good," Ben said as he pulled two plates from the cupboard.

"Mm. This papaya salad is amazing."

With plates piled high, they resumed positions on the sofa to watch the end of the talent show from opposite corners. Stan couldn't help but look over every few minutes where Ben was inelegantly shovelling food and rolling his eyes at the television. With a little flutter of something in his belly, Stan realised he could easily become accustomed to this.

CHAPTER SIX

BEN DIDN'T stay that night, even though he really wanted to. Nor the next night, when he went to Stan's with dinner he'd made himself—a Thai soup that was just perfectly spicy and spring rolls Stan reheated in the oven that had yet to be used. Ben had to show him how to turn it on.

The next night, Ben had band practice, then over the weekend he was working and Stan was busy with his epic photo shoot that was taking over so much of his working day. For those few days, Ben had to make do with text messages and the occasional phone call. He realised it was maybe more than a normal number of text messages when Tone threatened to steal Ben's phone and read every one aloud in the middle of the pub.

"Fuck off," Ben mumbled. "It's Stan."

"Of course it's bloody Stan," Tone said. "Who the fuck else is it likely to be?"

Despite working all weekend, Stan still had to go back to work on Monday morning, and from the brief conversation they shared on Monday night, Ben got the impression he was seriously tired. Their manic schedules had aligned on Tuesday—Ben wasn't working at the pub and his tutoring job finished at five, so he had plenty of time to head over to Bow and meet Stan as he got off the Tube.

"You look exhausted," Ben said as he took Stan's hand and led them out into the late afternoon sunshine.

"I am."

Stan had dark circles under his eyes that he'd done a good job of disguising with make-up, but they were still there, nonetheless. He looked weary, and Ben wanted nothing more than to kiss that bone-deep ache away. He knew it well.

Instead, he shouldered Stan's leather satchel and diverted them to a gastropub for dinner, somewhere Stan could order a mushroom risotto, and he could get cheesy chips. These sorts of pubs—the ones that tried a little too hard to be posh—were usually the last place Ben wanted to end up. He preferred them darker, grittier, grimier, but this was more Stan's scene. Refined. Sophisticated. Ben could do that. The food was good, Ben begrudgingly admitted, and decided if this became their local pub in Bow, he would probably be okay with that.

The sun was setting as they walked back to Bow Quarter, fingers loosely entwined, and the sky was turning a rich pink, streaked with purple, outlined with blue.

BACK AT the flat, Ben toed off his boots and padded through to the living room. He flopped on the sofa, then opened his arms for Stan to settle into his side. Nuzzling into his neck like a cat, Stan yawned widely, then settled down with his head on Ben's chest.

Ben turned on the TV and found a music channel that was playing a recording of a Foo Fighters gig, and he left it on for background noise. After a few minutes of Ben playing with the long silky strands of Stan's hair, Stan was almost asleep.

"Are you sure you want me to stay?" Ben asked softly. "I can get a cab back home."

"I want you to stay," Stan said. "Please."

"Okay." Ben ran his hands up and down Stan's sides. "I'll apologise in advance in case I do something…."

"Something?"

Ben blushed and laughed to himself. "That you don't want me to do?"

"I want you to do those things with me," Stan said, turning to put his chin on Ben's chest and look up at him properly. "I want that too."

"Are you sure?"

In that moment, Ben realised his hesitance came from his own fears and not any Stan was harbouring. He knew he didn't know everything there was to know about Stan yet; they hadn't been dating that long, and he was okay with figuring things out as they went along. They didn't need to know everything about each other before having sex. It was possible Stan wanted it just as much as Ben did… and that was almost as scary.

Stan kissed away his worry with impossibly soft lips and fingertips that fluttered over his cheeks. As Ben started to let go, to just touch and feel like Stan was, Stan slipped his hand into Ben's and tugged.

"Let me take you to bed."

"But you're tired," Ben said, half protesting, half teasing.

"Not anymore, I'm not."

Ben hadn't been in Stan's bedroom—there wasn't any need for him to. The curtains were pulled, so it was dark until Stan lit a tall lamp in the corner and another on his nightstand, casting the room in a soft glow.

He had a big double bed pushed against the wall and at the end of the room. Next to the window, a dressing table with a large mirror in front of it reflected the light coming in from the street. The sheets were navy blue and neatly tucked around the mattress.

Those impressions were formed in an instant as Stan tugged them towards the bed and shuffled up it, leaning on his elbows, inviting Ben to crawl up his body.

Stan was angles and bones, silky-smooth skin and the finest dusting of body hair. Ben tugged the shirt up over Stan's head and lightly kissed tiny pink nipples that puckered and kissed him back. Stan's hands grasped Ben's shoulders, his biceps, his waist; gently guiding and encouraging with breathy moans.

Ben wanted to take his time with this man, to explore this body that seemed so fragile and delicate under his. They undressed each other slowly, learning shapes and angles, discovering what lay beneath—the truth under Stan's daily illusion.

"You're so beautiful," Ben murmured as he moved his naked body over Stan's, rolling their hips together in a deep, aching grind.

"I'm...." Stan gasped, then laughed as friction caused their cocks to stick together.

"I want you, Stan. Can I be with you?"

"Yes. Oh yes. Please."

Ben kissed down the taught curve of Stan's neck and nibbled at his collarbone. "I'm going to need some stuff, sweetheart...."

"Oh," Stan said again and nuzzled into Ben's chest. "I have that. In my bathroom. I'll be right back."

He rolled elegantly off the bed, and Ben watched, unashamed, as a milky-white ass and incredibly long legs strode purposefully off to the other side of the flat. He had a feeling this was about to blow his mind, and he squeezed his balls, tugging them away from his body to relieve some of the tension building there.

Stan returned quickly, wielding a tube of K-Y and two condoms. He set both down on his nightstand, then lay down on his side and ran his hands over Ben's firm, flat chest.

"I like this," Stan said, tracing the lines of a tattoo.

"I like that you like it." Ben caught the finger and brought it to his lips for a kiss. "You're sure?"

Stan's smile was soft and bemused. "I've had sex before, Ben. I want it with you."

Ben didn't respond, instead leaning in to kiss Stan again. He snicked the top of the lube open and coated his palm with it, then slicked some over Stan's cock and pumped it slowly until Stan was lifting his hips up into the movement. With more lube, his fingers explored farther back, then circled and petted Stan's hole, spreading the silky wetness there.

Stan stretched his arms up over his head and pulled up his leg, planting his foot on the bed. Ben took that invitation and fumbled with the condom, smoothing it over his cock with lightly trembling fingers, then settled between those slim thighs.

He watched Stan's face carefully for signs of discomfort as he pushed inside. For a moment, he thought the distress twisting Stan's beautiful features was from that initial flash of pain, but as he settled into an easier position for them both, he mustered the courage to ask.

"You okay?" He punctuated his words with a kiss on Stan's cheek, another on his jaw.

"I—" Stan's breath caught on whatever he was going to stay, pain stealing the words.

"I'm just going to pull out for a moment," Ben murmured. Stan wrapped his fingers around Ben's arms, gripping hard enough to leave a bruise.

"It's my back," Stan said when Ben lay down next to him after discarding the condom in the bin at the end of the bed. "And I can't spread my legs wide enough without hurting them. I have this problem with my bones, and...."

"It's okay," Ben said.

"It's not. I *want* you, Ben...."

Ben reassured with kisses, an intimacy they both knew, comforting despite their naked bodies and the failed attempt at making love. With Stan gathered up in his arms, held safely from the discomfort of his own body, Ben let those wandering lips tell Stan it was going to be fine.

He groaned when Stan found his cock and wrapped his hand around it, squeezing gently and pulling on the still-hard flesh. After a moment of searching, Ben took Stan's cock and moved his hand in a matching rhythm.

"How about if we tried it," Ben said after a few moments of mutual pleasure, "like this."

He nudged Stan onto his side, facing away so Ben could spoon him from behind. His cock nestled between Stan's plump arse cheeks, a promise of what could come next.

"Oh," Stan said, a little moan of pleasure when Ben reached around to once again take his cock in hand. "This could be good."

Ben kissed his shoulder and smiled, then reached over to take the second condom and carefully rolled it down his cock. Used more lube.

"Tell me if you need me to stop," he said, then fitted their bodies back together again.

It still took a few minutes to work things out—how to kiss, where to touch, how to move to find the pleasure that would course through them both. Soon, though, Stan was crying out with pleasure instead of pain, for him to whimper into the arm pillowing his cheek.

"Ben," he whispered, then gasped the name again. "Oh wow. Oh my God."

Ben pressed forward again, his face tucked into the curve of Stan's shoulder, one hand on Stan's chest anchoring them together, the other wrapped around his cock.

"With me," Ben murmured. "I'm so close."

Words were lost to Stan, it seemed, and he cried out and cursed in a variety of languages as hot come spilled over Ben's fist. Ben grunted as the flash of pleasure chased his own come from his body, and for a moment he was paralysed, held at that point where there was no space between them, nothing at all.

Stan's bone-deep shudder forced them apart, and Ben laughed breathlessly as he once again tied off the condom and threw it away, then pulled Stan back into his arms.

"Better?"

"So, so much better," Stan said, the words muffled by lips that refused to stop kissing. "Oh wow, Ben."

"I'm glad you liked it."

He yawned widely, and Stan took on something of a mother-hen role, clucking and fussing and handing Ben back his boxers to sleep in.

"I'm just going to get cleaned up," Stan whispered, kissed Ben on the forehead, and left the room again.

When he returned, Ben was almost asleep, clutching the edge of the duvet. He cracked an eye open as Stan paused, then dressed in clean boxers and a T-shirt before crawling into bed too.

Ben grumbled unintelligible words and pulled Stan back into the same position they had made love in.

"Are you comfortable like this?" Stan asked in a low voice.

"I can only sleep with something against my chest," Ben admitted. It seemed so childish. He wanted to make sure Stan understood before he let sleep claim him. "I used to have a teddy bear when I was little, but I grew out of that, and since then, I have to be able to hold something or I can't sleep. Most of the time it's a pillow or a… a…." He yawned widely, then settled. "Or a blanket or something. I like it being you, though."

Stan kissed the hand wrapped around his shoulder. "We all have our quirks, I suppose."

For a few minutes, they both breathed deeply, settling into something that was safe. Theirs. Then, just before he fell asleep, Ben said, "I think I'm falling in love, Stan."

"I think I am too."

THE NEXT morning, Stan woke first and crept out of the bedroom, leaving Ben sleeping deeply. He grabbed his gym kit, which was always kept next to the door, and spent half an hour swimming, then half an hour running at the apartment complex's in-house gym.

It was almost nine in the morning by the time he arrived back at the flat, and he expected Ben to be up, maybe to be gone already, despite the note Stan had left imploring him to stay. But no. Ben was still asleep, lying on his back and snoring softly.

Deciding he would have to wake Ben soon, Stan took a shower and carefully washed his hair, then made two mugs of coffee and took them back to the bedroom. He had space on the nightstand for them both, and the little jug of soy milk, but only when he'd moved the bottle of lube to the top drawer.

Stan sat down on the edge of the bed, still wrapped in his towel.

"Ben," he whispered softly. "Ben."

A chink of light spilled through the curtains diagonally across Ben's body, highlighting his narrow hips, broad chest, and the dark tangle of tattoos. Ben's soft, boyish features were a part of his charm, even when the morning brought a soft fuzz on his chin.

"Izzat coffee?" Ben mumbled as he stretched like a cat, kicking the blankets down to his knees.

"Yeah. I'm not sure if you like it with soy milk, or black."

"Mmm… milk, if you've got it. Please."

Stan fussed over fixing the coffee as Ben hauled himself up into a sitting position, scratching his chest, belly, balls.

"What time is it?" Ben asked as Stan handed him the mug.

"Nine o'clock!"

"Really? What are you doing up so early?"

"Early?" Stan repeated with a laugh. "This is late for me." He took a sip of his coffee and hummed in appreciation. A light prickle at the back of his neck told him Ben was watching. "I got up and went to the gym while you were sleeping," he said in a rush, suddenly desperate to fill the silence. "I have some granola if you want breakfast, or we could go out.…"

"Or we could stay in bed all day and you can let me *do things* to you," Ben said in a low voice.

Stan ducked his head to hide his blush. "Or that," he agreed in a soft mumble.

A warm hand wrapped around his wrist, and Stan was forced to set his coffee down next to where Ben had left his, and then Ben tugged and manipulated him until he sat astride Ben's strong thighs.

"God, you're beautiful," Ben said, tucking a wet strand of blond hair back behind Stan's ear.

"I—"

"Please don't argue with me."

Stan leaned in and kissed him softly, mostly to stem the source of those heat-raising compliments he was so unused to hearing. Oh, flattery was easy to give, and to receive, but that wasn't what Ben was offering.

When Ben's tongue flicked against his lips, Stan tilted his head, offering a better angle for a deep, searching kiss where tongues and lips moved in lyrical synchrony and Ben's hands gripped his waist.

"I don't think," Stan said as they moved apart and Ben's lips continued down his neck, "that I can take you inside me again right now."

"I don't need to be inside you to make you feel good," Ben murmured. Stan arched, tilting his neck back and inviting more of those sweet, teasing kisses. Between their bellies his erection started to rise.

With a soft growl, Ben flipped them both over so Stan was pinned to the bed, looking up into sleepy, horny eyes that smiled down at him with unashamed *want*.

"Do you mind if I suck your dick?"

Stan huffed a laugh. "No. Why would I?"

Ben kissed his earlobe, then left a trail of soft, tiny kisses down his neck. "I'm still figuring you out, Stan. I'm probably going to ask a lot of stupid questions until I get there."

"I'm still a boy," Stan said, tugging at the thick mop of dishevelled hair until Ben looked up at him. "I came to terms with that because it's something I can't change. But I like my cock. And I like it when you touch it."

Ben ran his fingers down Stan's body, and wrapped them around Stan's half-hard cock. He rubbed his thumb back and forth slowly, smiling when Stan's breathing jumped in response.

"If you wanted to change, you could, you know."

"I know. I'm okay with who I am, just like this."

"I think you're stunning, you know," Ben murmured, his lips skimming over Stan's neck. "You're possibly the most beautiful man I've ever seen."

"You can keep saying these things to me," Stan said, making Ben laugh. "Okay."

Stan was already naked, his skin slightly damp from the shower, and Ben kissed down it, learning all the angles and contours of Stan's body. By the time his mouth met his hand, Stan's cock was thick and hard, the pink head peeking out from the delicate foreskin.

When Ben took it into his mouth, Stan knew he wasn't going to last long. Very few people had ever done this to him before, or showed his cock any kind of attention. Some men liked to pretend he didn't have a cock at all. With the love and care and very sexy attention Ben showered on Stan's body—all of it, not just the parts that looked good in a dress—Stan was starting to learn everything he'd been missing out on.

After only a few minutes, Stan was bucking up into Ben's mouth and crying out as he orgasmed, stars dancing across his vision as his body curled up tight, then exploded outwards in a shower of sparks.

Ben, Stan thought as the waves of pleasure pulsed through his body. *Ben did that to me.*

CHAPTER SEVEN

STAN'S VISION hadn't quite returned to normal. He sprawled on his back, feeling more sexually satisfied than he had in a very long time, Ben's head on his stomach, looking up at him. Stan lazily wound his fingers through Ben's hair, smoothing the tangles and tugging at the roots.

Sex hair. The words entered Stan's mind without permission, and he grinned.

"I need to go back to my place," Ben said mournfully, rubbing his finger over Stan's nipple. "I need clean clothes."

"Okay. If I come with you, we could go out somewhere after?" Stan batted away the inquisitive fingertip; he didn't have the energy to go again, not so soon after the last time.

Ben pulled a face. "Where I live… it's not as nice as here."

"That doesn't matter to me."

"It's a dive, Stan. Proper grotty."

"What does 'grotty' mean?"

"Um," Ben laughed. "Dirty. A bit grimy. A mess. And falling apart."

Stan kissed Ben quickly on the lips, then darted out of bed before he could be pulled back into something else.

"I'll get ready, and you can go take a shower."

Ben grumbled and did as he was told, dragging himself through the flat to the bathroom while Stan threw the curtains and the window open and started his morning ritual.

With his hair already partly dry, there was no point in trying to make it smooth and straight. With some mousse and scrunching and his hairdryer on a low heat, he teased rough curls from the unruly strands and let the hairstyle lead the rest of his outfit choices.

Slightly mussed was a look he could do. He mentally picked out tight black jeans, high-top sneakers, and a loose, low-cut tank top, because it was going to be a warm day, he could tell already. A smoky eyeshadow and sketchy kohl liner, a quick slick of mascara, all on top of his usual base, and Ben was back from his half drowning while Stan stood in front of his wardrobe and pretended he hadn't figured out his outfit already.

He was naked.

It made him feel very desirable when he cocked his hip to the side and Ben hummed low in his throat, covering the room in a few short strides.

"Hmm?" Stan said as Ben's hands went to his waist, sliding down to his ass, groping briefly before travelling round to his front and gently cupping his soft cock in both hands.

In response, Ben attached his lips to Stan's neck, surely leaving a mark, hopefully one his hair would cover.

"You make me feel—" Stan said, then cut off the thought before he could voice it.

"Tell me."

"So feminine."

Ben gripped his chin in one hand, tilting Stan's head back to devour his mouth.

"We are never going to leave this house today," Stan said with a laugh as they broke apart once more.

"Jesus," Ben moaned as he pulled his hips away from their kissing. He dropped his head to Stan's shoulder and sighed deeply. "I'll behave."

"Oh, don't do that," Stan told him.

Feeling slightly sheepish, Stan turned on the radio and got dressed in silence, only watching out of the corner of his eye as Ben layered up in the clothes he'd been wearing the night before.

"Do you have everything?" Stan asked before they left. Ben still sat on the edge of the bed, lacing up his boots, but he nodded.

"If I've left stuff here, just hold on to it for me. I'll be back soon, I expect."

"Okay. That's good." He didn't say any more, still wary of letting too many emotions show despite Ben's whispered words the night before. He wasn't going to bring up pillow talk the next morning. He wasn't *that* guy.

It really was a beautiful day, and Stan felt guilty for having spent so much of it indoors already. Even if the time had been well spent.

They held hands as they walked the short distance to the Tube station in companionable silence, content to enjoy the balmy summer day London had blessed them with. The Tube, of course, was a hothouse of hell, and Ben took his clammy hand back, surreptitiously wiping it on the frayed knee of his jeans.

Stan noticed anyway and laughed at him.

The house Ben shared with the other boys was a standard mid-terrace in East Finchley, the small garden at the front covered over with paving stones through which weeds insistently poked up. It looked like where they might keep their bins; evidence of split bags littered the small area in a melee of banana peels and teabags.

"It's really not that nice," Ben insisted again as he unlocked the door and pushed at the peeling red paint, eventually kicking the bottom of the door to gain entry.

"It's fine, I promise," Stan said.

He was hit with the smell of marijuana as they stepped over the threshold, and Ben shut the door before any of the hazy smoke could escape.

"I'm home," he yelled in the direction of the room at the front of the house that overlooked the bin area, then immediately started up the stairs.

Stan followed, wincing at the steps with their threadbare carpet and suspicious stains. There was some kind of sticky... *something* on the banister, and he quickly drew back his hand.

At the top of the stairs, there was a bathroom, the sink, bath, and toilet all a pale blue with reddish rust around the taps. The shower curtain had black spots on it. Stan schooled his face into a neutral expression.

There were three bedrooms on this floor and another flight of stairs that Stan guessed led up to another room. But Ben had mentioned five of them living in the house.... He decided there was probably another bedroom on the ground floor.

"This is me," Ben said, stopping at the end of the hall, where the bedroom would look out over the street. "Um, do me a favour and close your eyes, count to twenty or something while I just... sort things...."

"Okay." Stan closed his eyes and heard Ben open the door. Ben took his hands, led him inside, then kicked the door shut. "One... two...."

"Slower than that!" Ben said, sounding panicked.

"Three-four-five," Stan said in a rush, teasing.

Things clunked and Ben muttered curses as he presumably cleaned up the room; throwing clothes around too if the rush of fabric that passed Stan's arm was anything to go by.

"Six... seven...."

"Shit, fuck, bollocks," Ben muttered. "I need to put some washing on."

"Eight, nine, ten...."

"Slower, Stan, for fuck's sake."

"How messy is this room, anyway?"

"I'm not going to answer that," Ben said in a low mutter.

"Eleven...."

Ben continued his tornado-like sweep of the room, and by the time Stan was up to eighteen, the window had been thrown open, letting the summer breeze into the room. He was secretly pleased. The room smelled... like it needed a window opening.

"Nineteen."

Before he could say "Twenty," Ben grabbed him around the waist and dipped him into a Hollywood movie-musical kiss, supporting his back perfectly so Stan could play the damsel in distress and be kissed like his man wanted to kiss him.

It was only slightly spoiled by the fact Ben was still kicking something under the bed when Stan opened his eyes.

"Hi."

"Hi."

Ben grinned. "Take a seat."

Ben didn't really have anywhere to sit, not a desk or anything, so Stan sat on the bed. It was low, and Ben had obviously made a hasty attempt at making it by throwing a duvet over the rumpled sheets.

"This is nice," Stan said.

"Oh, it's not. Well, it's alright. It's mine, so that's something, but it's not... you know... I wouldn't *choose* to live here, if I had any other options." Ben took a deep breath and ran his fingers through his hair. "Okay. I just need to get changed, and then we can go."

"You said you need to put some washing on."

"Yeah, I can do that later."

"If you do it now, then you won't have to wait for it later," Stan said with a grin.

"Fine, I'll put some washing on!" Ben said, laughing. "I'll have to sort it out, mind."

"That's okay. I don't think we're in a rush."

While Ben changed, Stan looked around. The room was on the small side; the bed took up most of the available space because it was a double, and it was pushed into a corner. Even so, the edge of the bed at the head end was right under the windowsill.

Ben had a small chest of drawers with a TV on top and a game station—Stan didn't know what type—with long controllers attached that hung down like tentacles. A built-in wardrobe meant the entrance into the room was extremely narrow, but the wardrobe meant Ben had more storage space with two sliding mirrors on the front.

The walls were painted a strange bluish grey, but Ben had pinned posters to most of the available space—posters for bands and films and one of a girl with very large breasts in a very small bikini, standing in front of a sports car. She was squeezing a wet, soapy sponge down her front.

"Please don't look at that," Ben said, sounding embarrassed. "Tone got it for me as a birthday present, and he gets offended every time I try to take it down."

"Does Tone live here too?"

"Yeah. But downstairs out the back. It's a converted garage, which is great 'cos he can practise his drums and we can barely hear him in the rest of the house."

"Tone, then, and who else?"

"Jez," Ben said, dragging clothes out of the bottom of his closet to stuff into his already overflowing laundry bag. "Laurence, and this Polish bloke called Jarek who lives upstairs. He's alright, but he's a nurse, so we hardly ever see him. He works really weird shifts, so he never seems to be about when the rest of us are."

"All men," Stan said, offhand. While Ben was bent over to get to the dark corners of his closet, his butt was thrust right up in the air, and Stan couldn't help but admire it.

"Oh, it's fucking horrible," Ben said, straightening up. "They smell, and they don't clean up, and they sit around and smoke pot all the fucking time. I've probably got enough for two loads here, but I'll shove it all in. It'll be fine. It's a washer-dryer, so I can set it to dry too. Then I'll have clean clothes when I get home."

"Aren't you pleased I'm here, now?"

"Yeah, actually," Ben said. "I'm a bit scared to take you downstairs, though."

"Why?"

"Well, compared to the rest of the house, this room is Buckingham Palace. I never bring food up here, but I swear the others have plates and mugs that are growing new species of mould in their rooms."

"That's disgusting."

"And annoying," Ben agreed. "Especially when you cook something and there's nothing to eat it off because these fuckers can't clean up after themselves. I end up having to go through all their rooms, grabbing the dirty stuff and washing it up. I'm not their bloody mother."

"So it's not some kind of gay utopia, then, living in a house with four other men?" Stan teased.

"Four *straight* men," Ben corrected. "Four gay men would be great. We'd have an orgy every night. You couldn't pay me to touch these guys, though. I don't know where they've been. Or I do, in some instances, and that's even worse."

Ben looked around the room again, nodded, and threw the laundry bag over his shoulder. He'd changed into clean jeans and another ripped-up band T-shirt that looked strikingly similar to the first. These jeans had rips in the thighs as well as the knees. Stan wondered if they were like that when Ben bought them.

"Come on, then," Ben said. "I feel like I should get you one of those hospital masks." He held his hand over his nose and mouth. "Just in case you catch something."

"I doubt there's any airborne viruses hanging around here."

"I wouldn't be so sure," Ben said darkly.

The kitchen was as disgusting as promised. Ben led them through it quickly, wincing at the pile of dirty plates in the sink, and to a small room off the kitchen that housed a washing machine and shelves of DIY equipment.

Stan leaned against the doorframe as Ben shoved the dirty clothes into the washer—at least it looked like a large one, able to take the amount of stuff Ben was putting in there—and added washing powder and fabric softener before setting the dial, kicking the door closed, and pushing the button to start it.

"Done," he said, looking back at Stan with a proud smile.

"Good boy."

Ben laughed. "Come on. Let's get out of here—I don't want to hang around with the others. They'll only be getting high, and it's too nice to stay in and do that."

"Okay."

They walked back through the house, and Ben once again shouted into the smoke-filled front room and got a muffled shout back. He rolled his eyes and slammed the door shut behind them. Stan took a deep breath of clean air. It was saying something, that he considered the London smog "clean."

"I want to move out," Ben said as they walked back up the road. "I've been saving for ages. It's just so expensive to live around here. If I got a place of my own it would have to be further out, then I'd pay more to get around London."

"A catch-22," Stan said.

"Yeah. Exactly." Ben squeezed his hand. "So, what do you want to do? I was thinking we could go down to the South Bank, walk up along the Thames. It's touristy, but you get to see so much of London, all the big landmarks and things."

"Sounds perfect. I keep promising my mother I'll send her some pictures of London. She wants a photo of me by the palace."

"We can do that," Ben said with a nod. "Have you practised your bored Londoner face?"

Stan gave him his best disaffected eye-roll.

"Perfect. Come on, let's brave central."

They took the Tube down to London Bridge and walked over the famous bridge itself before starting the long walk along the Thames that would take them all the way to the palace. Even though the pavements were wide here, the assembled mix of joggers, dog walkers, and tourists made it a slow journey.

That didn't matter.

"Tell me about before you moved here," Ben said, and Stan sighed.

"Which bit?"

"It doesn't matter."

It was an easy question. It *should* have been, but Stan knew there was a questioning curiosity underneath. Ben knew Stan was hiding stuff from him, or holding back at least. He deserved to know.

Stan took a deep breath and looked over at the Thames, the boats with their loads of people ambling downriver, the huge wheel they called an eye watching peacefully over the capital.

"I'm anorexic," he said. Ben said nothing. "I used to be anorexic," he corrected, using the language he'd been encouraged to use since his recovery.

"Yeah?" Ben's voice was almost airily light, a clear invitation for Stan to keep talking, or not, depending on how he felt.

"Yes. I… when I was younger, I didn't know how to express this. I didn't know what was wrong with me. No one had given me the resources or the words to describe how I was feeling. I thought the way to fix it was to fix my body.

"It wasn't."

A group of children ran in front of them, causing Ben to rise up onto his toes to avoid trampling them. Parents shot apologetic looks, and Ben nodded and took hold of Stan's hand again.

"I could have died," Stan continued. "I almost did. My mother knew what was going on. I know that now but didn't at the time. She never tried to stop me, and I thought that meant I wasn't skinny enough yet. I thought as soon as I got to the point where I was a skeleton covered in skin, she would notice and stop me. It took me realising that she wasn't going to stop me, not ever, to go and ask someone else for help."

"How old were you?"

Stan shrugged. "Young. Thirteen, fourteen. My mother isn't a heartless person, you should know that. She just didn't see the illness underneath it all."

"Who did you ask for help?"

"It doesn't matter now. A friend. I got help, and I put some weight back on, and when I moved to New York with Ava, she got me a proper therapist. By then the damage was sort of already done. My bones didn't form properly because I deprived my body of so many nutrients when I was going through puberty. I don't think my body ever went through puberty properly, actually. Every time I thought about those pictures in the biology textbooks—those men with broad shoulders and hair all over the place—I freaked out. I didn't want to look like that, which only drove me to eat less. And all of those neuroses—I still have them, Ben. I'm still hung up on what I eat and when, what's clean enough for me to put in my mouth and what isn't."

"That's where the vegan thing comes from?"

"The vegan thing is sort of incidental," Stan said. "It was raw food—that was all I'd eat, raw, unprocessed food. I couldn't even eat anything that was cooked or baked, so as soon as someone boiled a carrot, I couldn't touch it. I know I'm still sick, in a way, because there's things I can't eat even if I tried. It's better now, though. I can eat in restaurants and order in and stuff, and I can drink alcohol if I'm careful and I keep track of my blood sugars and things like that. I even had some chocolate a little while back. Just a tiny piece, but you have no idea how much of a big deal that was to me."

"Do you have anyone here?" Ben asked, looking up at the endless blue sky. The gentle, soothing movement of his thumb on Stan's wrist was comfort enough. "I mean, do you need to see someone here to help you keep getting better?"

"I could," Stan said. "I suppose. I haven't been in therapy since I left the US—I sort of just get there by myself. Being around you helps."

"Really?"

"Yeah. I'm not sure why. You make me want to be… daring."

Ben smiled and he pulled them both over to the edge of the pavement where the wall was waist height, perfect for Stan to lean against while Ben kissed him carefully, then thoroughly.

"Daring enough for you?" Ben whispered, kissed Stan's neck, and took them back into the flow of people.

"You're…," Stan said with a laugh.

"Go on, finish that sentence."

"Wild! You're wild."

Ben laughed too, delighted, and pressed another kiss to Stan's cheek. "You make me this way. I'm usually very reserved."

"Of course you are," Stan said with a sarcastic eye-roll. He could feel the tops of his shoulders starting to burn and lamented his lack of sunscreen.

"No, really. It takes me ages to warm up to people. You're a notable exception. I think I'd like it if you had someone to talk to," he said, switching back to their earlier conversation.

"I'll think about it."

"Just because… I know I can't be there for everything for you. Even if I wanted to be. You're so brave."

"For not being anorexic anymore? That's not brave, Ben. That's basic human survival instinct."

"For lots of things," Ben said.

"It's why I don't model," Stan offered, wondering why he felt like he could open up like this when he was with Ben. Normally people had to drag information out of him, especially when it came to food and his eating disorder. "I don't want people to look at this body and idealise it. I don't have a healthy person's body. I'm sick."

"Have people asked you to model?"

"Only, like, twice a day," Stan said. "More if I go on a shoot. They always think I'm one of the models, and I get treated like shit until someone realises I'm actually in charge."

"Charming."

"Exactly. I know what happens to models in this industry, though—you can never be too thin or too pretty. If just one person told me I needed to lose weight, I know that could send me back on that downward spiral, and fuck no, I'm not going there again."

"You won't, because I won't let you," Ben said.

"Thank you."

"Does being able to be yourself help?"

"Sometimes," Stan said with a nod. He brushed his hair back with one hand and held it away from his neck, trying to encourage a breeze across his sweaty skin. "Being a girl brings its own set of problems. I was going to try hormone therapy once."

"Go on," Ben said, encouraging.

"I was seeing the therapist in New York, and she said she was happy to give me a referral to go and get female hormones so I could start transitioning. Being like this was enough to go there. We were talking about the side effects, and I couldn't do it."

"Which side effects?"

"The putting-on-weight ones," Stan said. He grinned up at Ben ruefully and led them to an empty bench under the shade of a tree. "She told me I'd start gaining weight on my hips and ass and chest and that just freaked me out. I got the prescription and everything, sat there with the box on my lap, wondering what the fuck was going to happen to me."

"Are breasts that scary?" Ben teased.

"Yes! Especially when they were going to be attached to me. It was the fat aspect of it. I'd spent years trying to control the shape of my body, and I'd been so successful at it. Those drugs were going to change me, and there wasn't anything I could do about it. All my wishing for a more feminine shape was right there in a white box and my fears stopped me from taking that step."

"Would you do it now? If you had the chance?"

"No," Stan said softly. "I'm in a different place now. It was only a couple of years ago, but I've kind of learned to accept what I've got."

"I like the way you are," Ben said. Stan shuffled over, and Ben wrapped an arm around his shoulders, the perfect position for Stan to drop his head to Ben's chest.

"I don't want to be a girl anymore."

"That's okay. You don't have to be."

"I might like being *your* girl, though."

Ben huffed a laugh and kissed his forehead. "Sweetheart, you can be my whatever you like."

"Okay. I can work with that."

"Come on," Ben said, and dragged Stan to his feet again. "We need to go and see if we can see the Queen."

Stan sighed dramatically. "There's a joke in there somewhere. I just can't be bothered to make it."

CHAPTER EIGHT

WHEN A sharp knock sounded at his door, Stan nearly jumped out of his skin. He had to buzz in anyone who wanted to visit, or so he thought, so he rarely had any unannounced visitors.

He kept the security chain on when opening the door at first, then frowned and opened it all the way to let Ben in.

"Is everything okay?" he asked.

Ben nodded, his face set in a stony grimace. He leaned in and kissed Stan on the corner of his mouth, the action surprisingly tender for the bad mood that was clearly simmering.

"Tea?" Stan offered. "It comes with free sympathy."

"I'll just take the sympathy, please. We're all being kicked out of the house."

"What?" Stan said, shutting and securing the door once more. "Here, come and sit down."

He took Ben's hand and squeezed once in what he hoped was reassurance while Ben toed off his boots, then led them both to the sofa, Stan in his corner and Ben in the other. Ben rubbed his hands over his face, looking tired or angry, or both, and sighed.

"The house has asbestos in the ceilings that no one knew about, and there's a black mould infestation in the kitchen and through most of the back of the house. We think that's why Tone got sick. He's moved in with Geordie for the time being, because Sherrie insisted on it. The letting agency says we all have to get out, and they don't have anywhere else to put us right away."

"Fuck," Stan said.

"Yeah. It's shit. Apparently the bastard landlord says he'll put us up in a B&B, but that's only because he has to give us notice by law. If not, we could sue him."

"Stay with me," Stan said immediately. "You can move in here."

"Stan…."

"No," Stan insisted. "Please. I want you here." He reached for Ben's hand again and squeezed. Ben linked their fingers together and turned their hands over, then brushed his lips over Stan's knuckles.

"It's nice of you to offer. But we haven't been together that long. I don't want to push things too fast too soon."

Stan crawled into Ben's lap and gently cupped Ben's cheeks to draw him down into a kiss. "Think about it," he murmured. "You come home here every night. We can fix dinner together, watch some TV. You can play on your game-station thing, and I can go on my laptop. We hang out together and then go to bed and make love. Every night."

"Make love every night?"

"Trust you to just listen to that bit," Stan said with a laugh. He pushed his hand through Ben's floppy mop of hair. "Yes. We can make love for hours, and you don't have to ever go home for clean clothes, because this would be your home. Here with me."

"Stan."

"Would you move in with me?"

"Okay. Yeah," Ben said. A slow smile lit up his face. "Yeah, that would be good."

"Good," Stan agreed, then kissed him to seal the deal.

Ben rubbed at his tired eyes, then buried his face in the crease between Stan's shoulder and neck. Stan held him there, gently stroking his hair until Ben gave a big, heaving sigh.

"Come on," Stan said, climbing off Ben's lap and not waiting for him to follow.

In the bathroom, Stan turned on the shower and let the water warm up while he twisted his hair up and secured it with a big clip.

"Is this a voyeuristic thing?" Ben asked from the doorway, leaning against the frame with his arms crossed and a smirk playing at his lips. "Or am I supposed to join you?"

"Either works for me," Stan said.

Ben laughed and started stripping off.

It was a comfort thing, Stan decided as he ushered Ben into the shower, not a sex thing. He wanted Ben to stay the night now that they'd made a decision to live together. He wanted to show Ben how good it could be.

Ben dropped his head and shuffled under the wide spray of water. From there, Stan pulled him close so his chest was pressed against Ben's back, and with his hands liberally covered in Moroccan oil, he started to knead Ben's shoulders.

"Oh God," Ben groaned. He huffed a laugh.

"Is that okay?"

"More than okay."

When he was done, Stan switched to shampoo and worked it into Ben's hair, massaging it into his scalp.

"Want me to return the favour?" Ben asked, his voice low.

"No, I'm fine. Come on."

He switched the water off and stepped out of the cubicle, then wrapped himself in a towel and passed one to Ben. It wasn't late, but Stan was tired and Ben looked exhausted, so they went to Stan's bedroom—*their* bedroom—and pulled up a movie to watch on Stan's laptop.

Barely half an hour into the movie and Ben was asleep, his head on Stan's lap, snoring softly. Stan ran his fingers through Ben's still-damp hair and thought maybe, just maybe, this could work.

EVEN THOUGH Ben would have liked to take things slower, time was against them, and his landlord wanted him out of the hazardous house as soon as possible. That meant chucking most of his stuff in black bin bags and whatever boxes he could beg, borrow, or steal from the pub, then hauling it on the Underground over to Stan's place. Some of the bigger things—okay, just his TV—and anything slightly precious went in the final run in a taxi.

Since Tone was still on strict bed rest at Sherrie's, Ben ended up going through all of his stuff too, though he got a taxi over to Notting Hill with the whole lot rather than going back and forth again.

"I could have done it," Tone grumbled as Ben dumped the last duffel bag on the floor in Sherrie's spare room.

"No," Ben said, slightly breathless. "You couldn't. A thank you wouldn't go amiss, you miserable bastard."

"Thanks."

Tone was sitting back on the bed in boxers and a T-shirt, looking fed up and clashing wildly with Sherrie's décor. The room was decorated in pale colours and roses; Tone was dark and surly.

Feeling sorry for the guy who was admittedly his best mate, Ben reached into his backpack and drew out two bottles of beer.

"Aw, mate," Tone breathed. "Sherrie won't let me drink. You're a legend."

Ben laughed. "Bottle opener?"

"There's one on my keys."

Ben found the keys amongst the other junk on the dresser and popped the lids off both bottles, then sat down on the end of the bed and passed one to Tone.

"How're you feeling?" Ben asked.

Tone shrugged. "I feel alright, then I try to do something and I feel shit again. And I love Sherrie, don't get me wrong, but she's fucking scary when she shouts." He shuddered. "I tried to make a cup of tea yesterday, and she practically chewed me a new one."

Ben snorted. That sounded like the Sherrie he knew and loved.

"So what about you and Stan?" Tone asked.

"What about us?"

"You've only been seeing him a few weeks."

"It's been almost three months, Tone."

Tone shrugged. "Same diff."

Ben shrugged back and took a deep pull on the bottle of beer, then wiped his mouth with his arm. "He offered. I don't have anywhere better to go—God knows I don't want to go and stay with my mum—so it sounded like a good idea."

"What if it doesn't work out? What if it *does*?"

"What's that supposed to mean?" Ben said with a laugh.

"Guys like Stan…."

"Finish that sentence," Ben told him, his voice going suddenly dark and demanding.

"Alright, alright, keep your knickers on," Tone said, holding up his hand—the one not occupied by his bottle of beer. "I just meant you shouldn't lead him on. Don't move in with the guy if you're not serious."

"How do you know I'm not serious?"

"Fuck's sake, Ben. I'm not saying you're not." Tone stretched out, and his spine popped loudly. "He's important, then?"

"Yeah," Ben said. He sipped his beer. "I don't want to put a label on it yet. But he's important."

Tone didn't push for anything more, and Ben was grateful for that. It wasn't that he hadn't considered his relationship with Stan and what it really meant—he had, at length. He was from a family of men who didn't talk about their emotions, though, and definitely not about their partners. Ben couldn't remember ever seeing his dad tell his mum he loved her, which possibly had something to do with why they were divorced, come to think of it.

Ben left Tone in Sherrie's capable hands—much to Tone's distress, but when Sherrie got scary and demanded him out, Ben got out.

THE FIRST few hours were strange, as Ben brought a few battered suitcases of his things through the door and started unpacking his clothes into drawers. Stan fussed. He made tea, didn't drink it, then went back to watching Ben doing his thing.

"I've emptied half of the drawers," Stan said, hovering nervously at the door to the bedroom. "I can make more space in the wardrobe if you need me to."

Ben looked up from where he was stuffing underwear into a drawer—not folding any of it. "Then where will your clothes go?" he teased.

"I'll find somewhere."

"This is fine. Perfect. Thank you."

Stan nodded. "Do you want a cup of tea?"

"I'd love one."

After retreating to the kitchen, Stan fussed with the teapot and the kettle and found the right mugs, then rearranged the cupboard where he kept the mugs and cups until all the handles were facing the right way. Ben came in just as Stan was dumping the teabags into the recycling container.

"Thanks, love."

"That's okay. Do you want a biscuit? I bought some for you."

Ben paused in blowing across the surface of the tea to cool it and smiled without moving the mug from his lips. "No, thank you. This is fine."

"Okay."

Ben sipped his tea, set the mug down on the counter, then grabbed Stan's wrist and drew him close. Knowing he'd feel better after a hug, Stan let himself be folded into Ben's embrace and laid his cheek on Ben's chest, sighing heavily.

"If this isn't cool, then you just have to say," Ben told him, stroking his hand over Stan's hair. "We can do this for a trial period, and if it's not working, I can go live somewhere else. The last thing I want is for this to be the beginning of the end."

"I don't want that either. I want you here, Ben. I promise," Stan said, squeezing Ben tighter around his waist. "I'm just… scared, I suppose."

"Don't be scared. We'll be okay. What happened to promising to make love every night?" Ben teased. He pulled away enough to duck his head and press his lips to Stan's. Stan let himself be kissed, moving his lips slowly and parting them when Ben licked at his tongue.

"We can still do that," Stan said.

Ben grinned and kissed him again.

THE TRANSITION from boyfriends to live-in partners came smoothly, more smoothly than Stan had expected. He'd never lived with anyone other than family before; even when he was in Italy, he'd had a small, boxy studio flat he didn't have to share with anyone else.

He had a worry in the back of his mind that things would be different for them once Ben moved in, that his possessions would be moved around, and Ben would keep strange foods in the fridge and not do his share of the housework. Or, at the other end of the scale, that Ben would feel like the flat in Bow Quarter wasn't his own, that he was a guest or a lodger rather than a partner.

For the first few nights, they danced around each other; Ben had his routine, and Stan had his own, and they had to try to figure out how to layer their lives until they were seamlessly feathered together. Ben liked to play his guitar for an hour or two every night, either practicing or writing new stuff, or just messing around. He liked to have music or the TV on in the background when he cooked or messed around on his laptop.

Stan was used to the quiet, the only noise in his space being noise he made himself. It turned into a strange sort of comfort. It didn't matter whether he was working at the kitchen counter or in the living room while Ben was in bed, he was aware of there being another person around. It was different… a good different.

Neither of them were particularly competent cooks, though Ben was trying to improve his skills. When their schedules aligned and they were both at home for dinner at the same time, he cooked, an interesting variety of vegan meals from recipes he found online. Some experiments were more successful than others. His vegan lasagne was becoming Stan's favourite thing to eat.

"I'll wash up," Stan said as he cleared their plates to the sink.

"I can help."

"You cooked. I'll wash up," Stan insisted. Ben squeezed past and patted Stan's bum lightly on his way to the living room. Stan loved when he did that, though he would never admit it aloud.

He carefully portioned the leftovers into plastic tubs and left them on the side to cool before he put them in the fridge. Sometimes Ben took lunch with him when he went straight from the pub to one of his tutoring jobs, so these extra meals were useful.

The pan took a while to scrub clean; Stan left it to soak as he wiped down the surfaces and dried the plates, then stacked them neatly back in the cupboard.

"Stan?"

"Yes?"

"Come here."

Stan stuck his head around the door into the living room. "Hmm?"

Ben indicated the space next to him. "Dishes can wait."

"Okay. Two minutes."

"Stan," he whined.

"Two minutes!"

He used his two minutes to wash his hands and twist his hair back into a loose knot. Ben had some zombie show on the TV. Stan had never been particularly interested in television, beyond its use for helping him understand another language. For now, Stan was content to be snuggled.

He took his seat on the sofa, leaned back against Ben's chest and sighed.

"You okay, love?" Ben asked.

"Yeah. I'm good."

Ben kissed his head and ran his fingers gently through Stan's hair, undoing the knot, then started working it into a loose french braid.

"What are you doing?" Stan asked, sounding amused.

"Um. Braiding your hair?"

Stan leaned forward to give Ben more room. "How on earth do you know how to do a french braid?"

"I have a sister, remember?"

"You didn't tell me you had a sister. Only that they're triplets."

"Oh." Ben continued rhythmically folding strands of Stan's hair over and over itself. "Well, there's three of them, obviously. Freddie, Molly, and Sam."

"You've never lived with them, though?"

"No. But I babysit every now and then. It was weird…. I was twenty-three when my mum had them, and I had a girlfriend at the time. I could have had kids myself, you know? So I've never been that close to them. Mum showed me how to do Molly's hair when I stayed with them for a week over Christmas."

He finished off the braid, twisting it all the way to the finest strands of Stan's hair to keep it in place, then kissed the side of Stan's neck. Stan leaned back against Ben's chest and sighed again.

"Do you want children?"

"I don't know," Ben said honestly. "Do you?"

"No," Stan said, his voice low and maybe wistful. "I don't think I could do that."

Ben nodded, understanding, and held Stan a little tighter. Their TV show went to an advert break, and Stan got up and took their empty mugs to the kitchen to dump them in the sink. Remembering they were out of soy milk, he wrote it on the shopping list Ben had brought. It was magnetic and stuck to the fridge, so they shouldn't forget stuff like that anymore.

Since Ben had moved in, lazy evenings together doing absolutely nothing had become Stan's favourite part of his whole day. It had only been a week, but their lives seemed to fit together almost seamlessly. Sure, there were awkward moments, but Ben was a good guy. They worked it out.

Stan padded barefoot through to the bedroom and grabbed his box of nail polishes, then went back to the living room in time for the second half of the zombie program to start. Ben looked over and grinned.

"Time for a change?"

"Hmm. I think so. I have a new blouse I want to wear tomorrow."

"You accumulate new clothes like no one else I've ever known."

Stan shot him a cheeky smile. "Thank you."

"I'll do yours if you do mine."

Stan held up a bottle of electric pink and raised an eyebrow.

"I have no objection to pink," Ben said. "Was kinda hoping you had some black, though."

"I do," Stan laughed. He found the bottle and shook it out, then grabbed Ben's hand and inspected his nails. "You bite these."

"Yeah. Sorry."

"It's not hygienic."

"I know. Those file things freak me out, though." He shuddered. "The noise goes straight through me."

"I won't file them," Stan promised. "The pink is for my toenails."

"Oh." Ben sounded relieved. "I can do that."

"You first," Stan said, running his thumbs over his partner's horrendous cuticles. When he had more time, he was going to give Ben a proper manicure. For now, the black polish would cover up the worst of it.

"Okay," Ben said and leaned forward to steal a kiss from Stan's lips.

CHAPTER NINE

STAN LET himself in the front door, toed off his Louboutins, and admired his shiny, pink toenails. Some kind of amazing smell was coming from the kitchen, and he padded in there, following his nose.

"Good evening," Ben drawled. He was stirring something on the stove that smelled deliciously of onions, garlic, and tomato.

"What's that?" Stan asked and wrapped his arms around Ben's waist from behind.

"Um… it's a caponata. Italian aubergine stew stuff. And I'm making a giant couscous salad to go with it."

"It smells amazing."

"Thank you."

Ben turned the burner off under the pan and moved it to one side, then turned in Stan's arms and placed a slow, precise kiss on his mouth. His lips tasted of tomato and garlic too, and Stan smiled into the kiss.

"Missed you today," Stan admitted when they broke apart with a sigh. "It was one of those slow days—we're in-between projects, and I just know it's going to go crazy in a few days' time, so I'm trying to get all my other stuff done before that kicks off."

"I hate those days," Ben said and kissed his forehead. "Do you want to get changed before dinner?"

"No, I'm fine for a minute."

Stan grabbed placemats from the drawer and quickly set the table while Ben dished up the food, and they hooked their ankles together under the table as soon as they sat down.

"This is good," Stan said after his first mouthful. "I like it."

Ben nodded. "Thanks. There's some leftover, if you want to take it for your lunch tomorrow. You can eat the caponata cold anyway."

"Okay," Stan said slowly, thinking over the idea. Leftovers for lunch. People did that, right? "Okay, I will. Thank you."

"No worries. You remember I've got work tonight?"

Stan pulled a face. He'd forgotten and had been thinking about a night on the sofa, then early to bed—not to sleep, of course. "What time?"

"I start at seven."

"I'll come with you."

Ben laughed. "You don't need to do that, baby."

"Am I not allowed out for a drink?"

"Of course you are. Of course. I didn't mean it like that."

"I know," Stan said and brushed his foot over Ben's ankle under the table. "I don't want to be cooped up tonight on my own."

"Come with me, then."

They cleaned up the kitchen together, and Stan ducked into the shower to wash his workday from his skin while Ben got changed into a different pair of black jeans and a long, soft, textured T-shirt.

"This is nice," Stan said, standing in front of Ben, wrapped in a towel and gently undoing the buttons on the front of the T-shirt. "It's not black."

"No," Ben said with a laugh. "Sometimes I wear things that aren't black."

"Well, it looks good on you. You should wear non-black-coloured shirts more often."

"Maybe I will," Ben said, and kissed Stan on the nose. "Come on, or I'll be late."

Ben went back into the living room, and after a moment, Stan heard the sound of the Xbox starting up. He quickly found a pair of skinny jeans and pulled them on, with a pair of flat boots, because his feet were still aching from his day walking around in killer heels that looked fabulous but were hell on his arches. He had a loose tank top that was only from Topshop but was nice enough for an evening at the pub, so he pulled that on and tied his hair back in a knot at the nape of his neck.

With time ticking, and aware he didn't want to make Ben late, Stan swept loose powder over his face, slicked on lip gloss, and used clear mascara on his lashes and eyebrows.

"Ready," he called out, spritzing on a light cologne before grabbing his phone and wallet as he rushed into the living room.

"You look hot," Ben said with a grin, and Stan laughed.

"Thanks. Come on."

As they walked down to the Tube station, Stan shot off a text to Kirsty, who he was sure had said she was out with her girlfriends somewhere around King's Cross for the evening. Camden wasn't so far from there, and she texted him back a few minutes later to say they'd meet him at the pub when they were done with their drinks.

"You can meet my work friends," Stan said, smiling up at Ben.

Ben grinned and threw his arm around Stan's shoulders.

For a Thursday night, the pub was fairly busy, a mixture of the after-work crowd that was yet to disperse and the others who looked like they were settling in for the evening. Ben kissed Stan full on the mouth, earning himself a hoot of appreciation from behind the bar, then ducked down into the cellar to lock away his wallet and grab his key fob that worked the till.

Since Tone was working, Stan hopped up onto one of the stools at his end of the bar and whistled at him between his teeth.

"Cheeky cunt," Tone said with genuine affection. "What do you want?"

"Vodka, please," Stan said, laughing. "With soda water and lime."

"You got it."

Tone fixed the drink quickly and slid it across the slightly sticky bar, waving away Stan's money. "Nah, this one's on me. How are you?"

Stan nodded his thanks and sipped the drink, which had been made with plenty of ice, just how he liked it. He could sit and talk with Tone for hours. He was an easy person to get along with, and they chatted amiably until Ben came up from the cellar, his arms full of a huge box.

"Thought I'd bring these up," he said, dumping the box on the floor with a clatter of bottles. "Refill ready for tonight."

"Thanks, mate," Tone said.

Stan had packed his iPad in his backpack before they left—his designer, tan leather backpack, not the scrappy thing Ben often used—and pulled this out to entertain himself, not wanting to distract Ben while he was working. Coming out to the pub was one thing, being a pain in the arse was another.

It didn't take long for Kirsty and her friends to arrive. They were slightly merry, and Kirsty was still wearing the same thing she'd had on at work, telling Stan she'd likely been out drinking since they finished at five.

"Stan!" she exclaimed as she skipped into the bar. Two other girls followed—one tall and dark with a pixie haircut, the other shorter and plump with gorgeous, glossy curls pulled back from her face with an Alice band. Stan grinned and slid down from his barstool to pull Kirsty into a brief embrace.

"This is Lara and Becky," she said, pointing to each girl in turn.

"Nice to meet you," Stan said with a nod. "Drink?"

He waited patiently at the bar while the girls ordered shots and cocktails, internally wincing at their choices but ultimately deciding not to comment. He'd pack extra painkillers in his bag for tomorrow, in case Kirsty needed to soothe a headache.

A booth had freed up while they were waiting, and it was much more sociable to sit and drink around a table rather than standing at the bar. They ended up talking shop for a couple of hours—Lara worked for another magazine, and Becky was a pattern cutter, so they had plenty in common.

Stan stole glances at Ben working as often as he dared. Ben had a way of moving around the bar that was oddly similar to how he played music; he was fluid and graceful and smiled a lot, even when the customers weren't particularly polite.

"Your boyfriend works here, doesn't he?" Kirsty asked, when she caught Stan looking.

He nodded. "Yes."

"Which one is your boyfriend?" Lara looked over at the bar, where Tone was doing some fancy tricks with a bottle of vodka to impress a group of girls.

Stan smiled at her. "Close your eyes and find the most beautiful man in the room. That one's mine."

The other girls sighed in unison, and Stan laughed. "He's the tall one behind the bar. With the dark hair."

"The guy with the beard?" Kirsty asked, sounding confused.

"No! That's Tone. He's a friend. The one with the undercut."

"Oh. He's lovely."

Stan nodded. "He is."

THE GIRLS couldn't stay long, only for a couple of drinks, and Stan air-kissed them goodbye before settling back into his booth. A moment later, Tone slid in next to him with another vodka and soda and a pint of something for himself.

"Hi," Tone said. "Just finished, thought I'd keep you company. Your friend is fit."

"I'll make sure I tell her," Stan said, amused.

Ben looked over from his place behind the bar, worry etched into the lines of his face. Stan smiled in what he hoped was reassurance. Ben turned away to serve another customer before Stan could figure out if he got the message or not.

"So, I wanted to ask you. Did you leave Russia because of all the gay stuff?" Tone asked.

"No, I left a long time before Putin brought in the law. But Russia has never been a particularly gay-friendly place. I wasn't out when I was living at home."

"And now?"

"You couldn't pay me to go back," Stan said honestly. He lifted his glass, slippery with condensation, to his lips and sipped the bitter liquid.

Tone snorted. "Don't blame you. So…."

"You can ask me anything, Tone. I'm not easily offended," Stan said with a grin.

"Alright," Tone said, obviously summoning bravado. "Are you a girl or a boy? Not your body, I mean. Like, your mind."

Stan couldn't help the rush of affection for this man who was trying so hard. He wasn't the big, offensive oaf the others seemed to think he was. Okay, so his phrasing wasn't great, but he cared enough to ask, and that mattered.

"This is going to be a long answer," Stan said with another laugh. "Are you ready for it?"

"Go for it, my love," Tone said, leaning back in the booth with his cider.

"Okay," Stan said, cricking his neck back and forth and wondering how the hell he was going to find the right words for this. And in English. He sighed, then continued. "So, for a long time we've accepted that sometimes things don't go according to plan when humans are developing. Babies are born with physical disabilities and have been for pretty much all of history. About a hundred and fifty years ago, doctors started to understand that sometimes things go wrong *inside* the body too, genetic or congenital deformities."

"Right."

"For about forty or fifty years, we've accepted that sometimes people are born with differences to their minds—not their physical brains, but their psyche or sense of self. Freud was pretty good at unravelling that stuff."

"Like someone being born with their body not matching who they feel they are," Tone said. "Transsexuals."

"Transgender," Stan corrected with a small smile. Tone nodded. "It's taking time, but a lot of Western countries are starting to accept that these differences in the mind are not fetishes or psychoses, but a part of who a person is. Just like we accept that some people's bodies develop differently and they look physically different to normal—whatever normal is—society is starting to accept that some people's minds and gender identities aren't 'normal' either."

"We're redefining 'normal,'" Tone said.

"Yes. We're trying. It's not easy. In my motherland homosexuality isn't accepted. To be myself there would mean opening myself up to all sorts of prejudices.

"And I don't fit neatly into the label of 'transgender,'" Stan said, reaching for his drink again. "I don't have any issue with trans people, but the whole concept of transgender relies on the given that there are two genders. A person might be born physically male and transition to be female. It's a very masculine view on the situation, if you'll excuse the generalisation—'oh look, she was born wrong, we can fix her.' And they do."

"Right," Tone said. "Are you saying that's wrong?"

"No, not at all. For some people that's exactly the right thing. But if you accept that sometimes a person is born the wrong physical gender, it's not such a huge leap to see that sometimes a person might be stuck between the two. Not male, not female, but a combination of both."

"And that's what you are?"

"Sort of," Stan said with a grin. "I'm still working it out. I'm a boy, Tone. My body is a boy's body and that's okay. It's more than being femme, though. I'm a boy with a lot of feminine traits, both in how I feel from day to day and how I like to dress, to present myself. I'm a boy and a girl both, in different ways. Some people call it gender-fluid."

"That's not easy to get your head around," Tone said.

"No. Because it doesn't follow the transgender narrative that the media likes. That 'wrong body, fix it, right body' storyline—it becomes a success story. But that's not me. I wasn't born the wrong sex for my gender. There is no easy, fix-it success story for being stuck between two genders, so it's not a story people hear very often. Gay men don't like me because I look like a girl. Straight men don't like me because I'm physically male."

"But Ben...."

"Ben is an exceptional human being."

"Nah, he's a bit of a prick, really," Tone said affectionately.

Stan grinned. "He sees the girl and likes her, and can touch the boy and like him too. He doesn't try and make me 'fit' into any tick-box category. He just lets me be."

Stan trailed his finger up and down the condensation on the side of his glass and considered his next question carefully. Tone sipped his pint and waited.

"Tone, can I overshare?"

"Yeah, go on, then. I might make you buy me another pint afterwards to help me forget, though."

Stan laughed. "I don't have anyone to talk girl talk with here."

"There was loads of bloody girls here earlier!" Tone protested.

"I know, but I work with one of them, and the others I've only just met."

"Oh God," Tone said. "Go on, then."

"He's just… the sex is so good," Stan said on a rush, dropping his arms to the table and his forehead to his hands. "I've never had sex that good before."

"Has he got a big cock?" Tone asked. "I'm just curious."

"You can't make fun of him, Tone."

"I won't."

Stan looked up to see Tone making a zipping gesture across his lips, then scratching at his beard. "He's perfect. I've been with other men before, but it's all been a bit…."

"Wham, bam, thank you, ma'am?" Tone suggested.

"Yes," Stan agreed with a laugh. "I used to just accept it. Most of my previous partners were older. And they liked to call me a 'tranny' or 'shemale,' or those sorts of things. I just accepted it, even if I didn't like it."

"Pardon the expression," Tone said, "but that sucks."

"Yes. Very much so. I never really understood how it can be like… like… two people together, you know? Not one man taking all the pleasure and the other lying there wondering what the fuss was about."

"You could always go and be the man taking all the pleasure for himself. Just sayin', you know."

Stan gave Tone a horrified look. "Oh no. I couldn't do that."

"So you're the girl in the relationship?"

Stan laughed loudly, and from the bar, Ben looked over with a questioning expression. Stan smiled at him in what he hoped was reassurance.

"If you like," he said.

"Should I call you 'she'?" Tone asked.

"No. 'He' is fine."

"I don't think I understand it all," Tone said, leaning forward to rest his elbows on the table.

"That's okay. You're listening. Most people don't even give me the chance to explain, so you're doing something very amazing by that fact alone."

"You're a nice guy. And a mate. And a really hot girl, which is confusing, but I won't make a pass at you 'cos Ben would knock my teeth out if I tried."

"Yes. He probably would. He's quite protective."

Tone drained his pint and nodded to Stan's now-empty glass. "Another? Vodka, right?"

"Yes, please," Stan said. "Ben knows what I like."

"I bet he does," Tone said with a lascivious wink.

Stan only laughed.

BEN GLANCED up from his game when Stan shuffled into the living room, then did a double take and almost dropped the controller.

"Holy shit," he murmured.

"Do you like it?" Stan asked, stretching one arm up the side of the doorframe and sticking his hip out.

"Holy *shit*," Ben said emphatically. Stan laughed and walked over to the sofa, his long legs easily eating up the distance.

"Do you need to stop your game or anything?" Stan purred.

"No... no. It's *Assassin's Creed*. I've played it before." Ben was captivated by the delicate lace covering Stan's almost-naked body. It was red, a deep, dark red that contrasted with the creamy paleness of Stan's skin, and fine enough to show plenty of that skin through the fabric. Ben reached out automatically, wanting to run his fingers along the line where the soft, scalloped edges of the lace rolled over Stan's hip, then pulled his hand back. "Is it... I mean, can I.... Can I touch?"

Stan smiled, his whole face lighting up. "Yeah. Of course."

Ben cupped those slim, angular hips in his hands and leaned in to nuzzle Stan's belly. The action was almost painful—he was hard already, his dick straining against the seam of his jeans.

"Fuck, you're gorgeous," Ben murmured.

Stan chuckled softly and ran his fingers through Ben's hair, gently tugging at the roots. "I wanted to look pretty for you. To try to look pretty for you."

With a gentle tug, Ben forced Stan off balance and neatly caught him again, then dragged him down until he was straddling Ben's thighs. They looked at each other for a long moment, lust burning between them, and then Stan leaned in and caught Ben's tongue between his own red-stained lips.

The kiss was as soft and sensual as Ben had come to expect from his lover—nothing was rushed, nothing was forced. Stan put it out there and Ben, well, he had no choice but to go with it. To ride whatever wonderful, exhilarating ride Stan was taking him on.

"Be with me again," Stan murmured as he kissed down Ben's neck. "I want you to fuck me."

"Uh-uh. No."

"No?"

"I'll make love to you. Someone like you...." He pulled back to push Stan's long hair out of his eyes, tucking it carefully behind his ear. "You don't get fucked."

"Okay. Then make love to me. Please."

Ben ran his hand down Stan's spine, feeling the bumps under the soft skin. He tugged his own T-shirt up, off, tossed it somewhere, and completely forgot it existed. Stan was smiling, a light in his grey eyes that Ben thought was possibly one of the most beautiful things he'd ever seen.

Stan pressed his hands to Ben's chest and kissed him again, rolling their hips together in a sensuous grind. Ben had spent years priding himself on being a pretty damn good lover—he liked sex, liked making other people feel good with their bodies. But Stan... Stan was something else.

With an almighty surge of effort, Ben grabbed Stan's ass and hauled them both up, grinning at Stan's squeal of protest, then his laugh as Ben carried them both through to the bedroom. He laid Stan down on the bed gently, then stood up and shucked off his jeans.

Stretched out on the bed like an offering, Stan threw one arm up over his head and trailed the fingers of the other lazily over his belly. Ben pressed his palm to his own erection and kicked out of his socks.

"Mmm," Stan hummed.

"Okay. I wanna make you feel good."

Ben knelt on the bed between Stan's spread thighs and pulled at the edge of the lace underwear, tugging it down until Stan's cock sprang free. Ben couldn't help but smile and nuzzled his cheek into Stan's belly, kissing and licking at the sensitive skin, then down over Stan's hip bones. Each little gasp and whimper poked and prodded at Ben's arousal, nudging him forward.

Instead of pushing the lace underwear all the way down, Ben carefully pulled Stan's cock and balls out and left the panties around his thighs. The skin on Stan's cock was as pale as the rest of his body, and he'd removed all of the hair from the area, so Ben knew this for certain.

The only change in colour was the head of his cock, which was a deep, blushing pink. Ben studied it for a moment, then tugged the foreskin all the way back and licked the tip.

"Fuck," Stan gasped. His fingers wound into Ben's hair, tugging hard enough to make Ben gasp and get the picture.

Ben kissed one hip bone, then the other, then sucked as much of Stan's cock into his mouth as he could manage. It only took a few bobs up and down the length for him to be able to take it all the way into the back of his throat, and Ben pressed his hands to Stan's hips to keep him flat on the bed.

"Ben," Stan gasped. "Ben. Ben! Stop, stop, stop...."

Ben pulled off with a gasp. "Okay?" he rasped.

"Yeah. I want... I was gonna...."

"You can come in my mouth if you want."

"Fuck," Stan groaned and rubbed a hand over his eyes. "No. I want you to fuck me."

Ben huffed a laugh and reached for the lube on the nightstand. "I can do that."

With one of Stan's ankles on Ben's shoulder, Ben had perfect access to Stan's hole. He watched Stan's face carefully as he pressed one lube-slick finger into Stan's body, then two, then started to fuck him slowly with both fingers. A shiny pool of pre-come started to gather on Stan's belly, just under the incredibly pink head of his cock.

"Ben," Stan said again, a new way of expressing his tortured exasperation. "If you do not fuck me in a minute, I will get down there and fuck *you*."

Ben laughed, delighted, and pressed his lips to Stan's belly as he carefully pulled his fingers free of Stan's body. His lips danced over the smooth, flat muscles, then he blew a raspberry on the delicate curve of Stan's ribs, making him squirm and squeal.

"What are you doing?" Stan demanded, laughing manically.

"Roll over," Ben said, laughing too and reaching for a condom. He kissed Stan's shoulder, rolled the latex over his cock, then used more lube as Stan kicked the lace underwear off, rolled onto his side, and hugged his knees to his chest.

Stan sighed heavily, and Ben shifted forward, finding a good angle to press his cock into Stan's body, pausing for a moment, then pushing all the way in. Ben propped himself up on his elbow, the best possible angle to watch Stan's face while they made love.

With his eyes screwed tightly shut, Stan scrabbled blindly for Ben's hand, found it, then drew it around his body to press a firm palm against his chest. Ben picked up a slow, even thrusting back and forth, back and forth and cupped his hand over the lace cropped top, thumbing Stan's nipple.

"Worth the wait?" Ben asked, his voice low. "God, you feel good."

"Yeah." Stan laughed softly and squirmed. "Yes, it's good for me too."

Neither could last long like this; not with Stan's cock aching against his belly and the tightness of his body gripping Ben's cock as he eased slowly, purposefully in and out. He reached up and pushed Stan's long, fine hair back from his neck, and pressed his lips to the shell of Stan's ear.

"I'm close, baby. Can I come inside you?"

"Yes. Oh God, Ben."

Stan cried out as Ben nudged against his prostate, and with Ben's gentle fingers tugging his cock, he shuddered and came. For a second, Ben rode the high with his partner, completely entranced by the beauty of Stan's body mid-orgasm. Then his own body demanded release, and with his face pressed against Stan's shoulder, he lost control and came hard.

For a long moment, the silence in the room was deafening, and Ben was sure his ears were ringing. Then Stan let out a choked laugh, Ben shuddered, and carefully pulled his cock free of Stan's still-twitching hole.

"Fuck me gently with a chainsaw," Ben muttered, making Stan laugh again. "That was…."

"Incredible," Stan finished for him. He rolled over, kissed Ben's chest, then rolled back and got carefully out of the bed. "I'm just going to go… clean up."

Ben nodded and used his discarded underwear to wipe at his crotch. By the time Stan returned a few minutes later, blissfully naked now, Ben wasn't sure where the red lace cropped top had gone, but he hoped not too far. It was incredibly hot.

"Come here," he said on a yawn, lifting his arm so Stan could snuggle into his side. Stan's skin was cold, like it always was, and Ben tugged at the duvet until it covered them both. "You okay? I didn't hurt you?"

"No." Stan let his fingers trail over Ben's chest and yawned widely. "I'm fine. Thank you."

Ben pressed his lips to Stan's hair. "Okay. Good. G'night, baby."

"Goodnight."

CHAPTER TEN

STAN'S ALARM beeped chirpily far too early in the morning, considering how late they'd been awake doing *things* the night before. He slapped it until it silenced, then rolled back into Ben's embrace for a few final minutes of warmth and comfort before the day dragged them away from each other.

Ben threw his arm around Stan's waist and grumbled unintelligibly as he buried his nose in the back of Stan's neck. These early morning moments were short but precious, and Stan let himself savour the warm peace for far longer than he should have before leaning back, kissing Ben's temple, then rolling out of bed.

Not so long ago, he would have considered this a late wake-up, but since Ben had moved in, their mornings were getting later and later. He couldn't blame Ben for it, not really; Ben worked late, especially when he closed up at the pub, and it took him a little while to unwind once he got home. Stan understood and didn't mind, even if Ben almost always woke him up when he finally came to bed.

Stan brushed his teeth while waiting for the shower to warm up, then enclosed himself in the glass cubicle. In his dream house, they'd have a tub—maybe one of those claw-footed tubs with antique-style taps. For now, though, the cubicle was fine.

After a minute or so, the bathroom door swung open and Ben stumbled in—his hair a hilarious mess, the black boxers he'd worn to bed riding very low on his slim hips.

Stan smiled and turned away as Ben proceeded to pee—loudly—grunting and grumbling to himself as he pushed his hair back with his free hand. Moments later, Stan felt a chill on his skin as Ben let himself into the shower.

"Good morning, Sunshine," Stan said, grinning, as Ben wrapped his arms around Stan's body.

"Mornin'," Ben huffed. He rocked them together back and forth under the water, his lips gathering up the little drops of water on Stan's neck.

"How come you're up so early?"

"Came to see if you'd soaped your balls up yet. Thought I could help."

Stan let a silly grin spread across his face, content that from behind him, Ben couldn't see it. He grabbed Ben's wrist and dragged it down his body, then cupped the hand around his cock and balls. Ben snorted with laughter into Stan's neck.

"Need soap?" Stan asked innocently.

"I never know what half the potions in here do." Ben let go of Stan's package and stretched both arms over his head, making his back crack. "I'm scared to touch them."

"Good," Stan said, poking him in the chest. "They're expensive."

He took Ben's palm and poured some of his silky, body-oil conditioning wash into it, then gestured for Ben to rub his hands together to lather it up. Ben took his time massaging the rich foam into Stan's skin, his palms skimming over Stan's chest and back, down his arms, then slowly rubbing his shoulders.

"You still sore from last night?" Ben asked, his fingers dancing down Stan's spine and skimming over his ass.

"I'm okay." Stan's cock was growing, throbbing gently, but he really, really didn't have time for this. "But I have to get to work."

Arching his back, Stan shot what he hoped was a sultry grin over his shoulder. "Maybe tonight you can fuck me like this."

Ben grabbed Stan's hips and rutted his own hard cock against the soft cheeks, groaning before pulling away and turning the temperature handle all the way round to freezing cold.

Stan shrieked and jumped back, then hit Ben on the chest. "What did you do that for?" he demanded, half laughing, half pissed-off.

"Because I want you so bad right now I could scream," Ben said, tipping his head back under the cold water. "You have absolutely no fucking idea how gorgeous you are."

Stan huffed, almost placated, got out of the shower, and wrapped a towel around his waist. "You have fun in there," he said and flounced back to the bedroom.

"STAN," VICTORIA said sharply.

Stan looked up from his computer, brushing his hair away from his face. His boss looked pissed, but that was her default expression, and he tried not to wither under her formidable gaze.

"Can I help?"

"We need an article on winter sun-holiday destinations."

Stan nodded slowly. "Okay. Can you email me a brief? And a deadline?"

"I'm going to need you to turn it around quickly. There's a gap in the layout. We had to pull Helen's smoothie article. It was…." She trailed off and shook her head. "Not good."

"I can do that."

"Okay, good. I know you have a life outside this place—sure, we all do, but for the next week, you live, eat, sleep, fucking breathe this thing. Don't let me down."

"I won't."

Victoria turned on her sharp heel and stalked off back down the hall. If he weren't used to working for women like this, with demands like this, and the blatant disregard for work-life balance, it would upset him. Or at least throw him off his game. Victoria wasn't as badass as she liked to think she was, though. He'd worked for worse people in Italy.

With a little regret, Stan saved the blog post he'd been working on and emailed it home to himself. It was going to have to wait. After a moment's hesitation, he picked up his phone and shot off a message to Ben.

Don't bother cooking tonight. I'll be late. Something came up. Love you.

A few moments later, he got a reply.

Love you too. Please make sure you order some dinner.

The mother-hen thing irked him sometimes, even though Stan got the impression that was just Ben. He did it to everyone.

In the old days, having his job take over his life didn't mean so much to Stan. His work was his life; there hadn't been much outside it to mess up. These days, though, it was different. Throwing himself into turning out a new article, including sourcing appropriate imagery and the research behind it, killed his social life. *Killed* it.

In the week it took to finish the article, Stan had to turn down Tone's offer of dinner one night when Ben was working, he missed band practice on Thursday night and the gig Ares played on Friday. He worked Saturday too, so he couldn't go down to the South Bank with Kirsty and her friends to mooch along and watch the world go by.

By six on Saturday, it was almost done, the layouts approved, and all he needed to do was get Victoria's sign-off on Monday morning and they could draw a line underneath the whole bloody thing. It had been a good project, in hindsight, and if he'd been given four weeks instead of one, he probably would have enjoyed it a lot more. As it was, his back ached, his eyes were itchy, and he'd gone to work that morning in jeans and one of Ben's band T-shirts. At least it was the weekend, so no one was around to see him looking so scruffy.

Stan let himself into the flat, dumped his bag next to the door, and toed off his shoes. It was quiet, even though he could tell the balcony doors were open, letting in the late afternoon breeze.

Ben was asleep on the sofa.

He had his hands pillowed under his cheek, bottom lip pouting as his chest rose and fell with each slow breath. Stan smiled and padded over to the sofa, then perched on the space made by the curve of Ben's body.

"Hey," he whispered softly, pushing Ben's hair back from his face. "Sleeping beauty."

"Hmm?" Ben smacked his lips and screwed up his face.

Stan giggled and leaned over to press a kiss to his forehead. "You all done?"

"Yep. Well, as done as I can be, for now."

"Good."

Ben pulled Stan's arm, knocking him off-balance and shifting onto his back with Stan on top of him.

"Well, that was inelegant. You could have just asked."

There was something about the way Ben pressed his face to Stan's hair, breathing deep, then laughing softly. It had become a warm, familiar gesture, something that encapsulated their relationship in one sweet moment.

"I missed you this week."

"I'm sorry," Stan said automatically.

"You don't need to apologise. I know you're busy. And your job is important."

"I work for a fashion magazine, Ben. It's not exactly life-or-death."

"It's important to you," Ben said, then yawned. "So it's important to me. Doesn't mean I don't miss you when you go AWOL, though."

"It doesn't happen very often."

"That's true."

"Are you working tonight?" Stan asked, pushing himself up onto his forearms so he could look down at Ben's sleepy face.

"No, I opened up earlier. Worked ten 'til five."

"Oh."

"What time is it now?"

"Almost seven."

Ben reached up and tucked Stan's hair back behind his ear. "You wanna do something tonight?"

"If by 'something' you mean watching a movie, ordering in dinner, maybe cracking open a bottle of wine… then yes. I want to do something."

"I actually picked up a bottle of that Pinot Grigio you like on the way home."

Stan leaned in and kissed him loudly. "I knew I kept you around for a reason."

When Ben squeezed his ass, Stan squealed with laughter.

"So, I have news," Ben said when he was done making Stan laugh and they had righted themselves into a seated position. "Sorry I didn't tell you sooner, but you've been busy…."

"No, that's okay," Stan said, tucking his hair behind his ear again. "Tell me now."

"We got offered a gig," Ben said with a rueful smile.

"Oh? That's good. Where is it?"

"It's more of a tour."

Stan gave him an even look, cocked his head to the side, waiting for an explanation.

"Okay, so it's a tour. For six weeks to start with, maybe more."

"Oh."

"Please don't look at me like that," Ben implored. "Please. I said I didn't want to go, but if I back out, then no one else can go either, and I can't be the one to hold them back. They'd never forgive me, and they're my friends."

"You have to follow your dreams," Stan said gently. "I know that."

"It's not my dream, though," Ben said with a harsh laugh. "It's theirs."

"You'll have fun. But what about work?" Stan asked.

"We'll get an allowance," Ben said. "It's not great, but we get a percentage of ticket sales too, so it really pays for us to do loads of promoting and stuff. Racket City is fairly well established now, so they've got their fan base. We're hoping they'll draw in the crowds. I know we're sold out in a couple of places already."

"That's great."

"Yeah. The kids break up for summer holidays next week, so my tutoring work always slows down this time of year. There's only a few parents who are hardcore enough to keep their kids in tutoring over the summer. I've called all of them and let them know, told them I can give them recommendations for other people if they still want a regular service."

"And the bar?"

"Oh, they don't care," Ben said, waving it off. "They'll get a load of temps in for a few weeks, Australian backpackers or whatever. The turnover in there is so high, anyway, they won't miss us."

"I'm sure they will."

Ben shrugged. "We've got our jobs still when we get back. That's the main thing."

"Yes."

"Stan."

"Hmm?"

"Tell me what you're thinking."

"I'm thinking…," Stan said slowly. "I'm thinking I'm going to miss you."

Ben dropped his forehead to Stan's. "I'm going to miss you too."

STAN HAD hesitated for days before deciding to follow his instinct and buy Ben the gift he'd been thinking about. It had come to him in a dream, or in the very first moments of being awake, when he was aware of Ben's strong arms around his waist and little else.

Ben had told him about liking being able to hold things close to his chest when he slept. So Stan wanted to buy him a teddy bear.

He already had a speech planned, mostly to direct at Tone, but also to anyone else who would be around. They weren't to make fun of Ben, not at all, because this was something Stan wanted to do for him. If he couldn't be there every night to give Ben something to hold, he wanted to pick the substitute.

After a little bit of research, he'd headed into Hamleys on a weekday afternoon. He was on his lunch break officially, and Stan knew no one would mind if he took a bit longer than an hour.

The store was busy, as he'd expected, but not horrendously so. After a few minutes of wandering around aimlessly, finding himself distracted by the flashing lights and music and pretty colours on the ground floor, he took the escalator up to the younger-children department.

Apparently it wasn't going to be as easy as just picking up a teddy bear.

The section was huge, stretching away with rows and rows of bears and bunnies and caterpillars and dinosaurs and monkeys and strange dolls with glassy eyes. Stan avoided those.

Slowing his pace, he started to wander down the aisles, letting his fingers trail over the different fabrics, wondering what Ben would like best. Not that Ben was the sort of guy who would ever consciously seek out a toy to cuddle at night. That was why Stan needed to do it for him.

He paused in front of a display of soft, *soft* animals. He was immediately drawn to a giraffe, one with a long neck and a baleful expression and fur so soft it was silky. Stan gently smoothed the fur over the giraffe's head and smiled to himself. He was just about to pick it up, when another animal caught his eye.

It was a bunny rabbit, one he'd initially dismissed. But this one was inky black, with long ears and a tiny, very pale pink nose.

"You'll do," Stan murmured, pleased with the weight of the toy, thinking of how well it would fit nicely snuggled up against Ben's chest. A black bunny rabbit. Very rock and roll.

The pretty girl on the desk offered to wrap it for him, and Stan nodded, delighting in the crinkly, red tissue paper that kept his rock-and-roll rabbit safe for the journey home. Stan tucked the shopping bag inside his handbag and nodded his thanks to the girl who had taken such care with the rabbit. It had an important job to do.

There weren't many weeks between Ben finding out about the tour and it actually happening, and the time seemed to fly by. Stan caught himself watching the clock constantly, at work, on the Tube, in the evenings when they curled around each other on the sofa and he put his fingers in Ben's hair and tried not to cling.

The bus was leaving from the pub, which made sense because Tone kept his drum set there, and it was empty in the mornings, and the pub had space to park the beast of a vehicle. No one in the band, and pretty much no one associated with the band, was a morning person.

Except Stan.

Stan hadn't slept the night before, too aware of the open suitcase in the corner of the room with piles of black clothes shoved into it. Even with Ben's arm around his waist and Ben's soft snores at his back, Stan couldn't find the soft slip into sleep. He was grieving already.

"Have you got a minute?" Stan asked as Ben finished hauling some big case into the tour bus's underbelly.

"Of course."

They slipped around to the other side of the bus, where no one could see them, and Stan slipped off one shoulder of his leather backpack.

"This is kind of stupid. But I got you something."

"Yeah?" Ben's face lit up with the prospect of a present, and the raw sickness in Stan's belly rolled again.

"Here," Stan said, pulling the red-tissue-wrapped package out of his bag. It had been hidden under his bed these past few weeks.

Ben kissed Stan's cheek, then tore into the paper. When he pulled the rabbit out, he laughed.

"Aww."

"It's because… because you like holding something when you sleep," Stan said quietly, hoping his voice didn't crack.

"Jesus, I love you," Ben murmured as he hauled Stan in close. The bunny was trapped between them, and Stan pressed his face to its fur, wanting the comfort it offered as much as Ben's arms.

"I got you something too," Ben said and reached into his pocket. For a moment, Stan was confused, and then his breath caught in his throat. "I can't offer you much," Ben said, "but I can promise you a lot. I want you to know that when we figure out whatever *this* is"—he waved his hand between them—"I'll make it happen. When we figure out what our family and our future will look like, I'll do whatever it takes to make that real for us."

He held out his hand, the thin gold band sitting in the centre of his palm. "Would you wear it?"

"Yeah. Yes. Of course. I don't understand, though…."

"I wasn't sure if you'd like diamonds," Ben said with a smile. "I know they're a girl's best friend and all…. I'll buy you diamonds one day. Until then…."

"Okay," Stan said, understanding now. He took the band—it really was incredibly delicate—and slipped it onto his finger. Suddenly his throat felt thick, and there was a stinging behind his eyes. Stan wasn't a crier, never had been, and he ducked his head to hide the emotion that was surely just singing out from his face.

"It suits you," Ben said.

"I wish you didn't have to go."

Stan threw himself back into Ben's embrace, letting the familiarity of being held soothe his frazzled nerves. He hadn't expected anything, least of all *this*, and it was a little overwhelming.

"Me too, baby," Ben said softly and buried his face in Stan's hair, holding him close so they could both disguise their tears.

"Ben?" someone yelled, making Ben squeeze Stan harder.

"What?" he yelled back.

"Need help with these fucking amps."

Ben silently pressed a kiss to Stan's temple and slipped away.

Stan sniffed, straightened up, and told himself to shake it off. When he followed Ben's steps back around the bus, Tone was leaning against the wall with a cigarette dangling from his fingers.

"What was that Ben had?" he asked. "He just took something into his bunk."

"You can't say anything mean to him, Tone," Stan said in his sternest voice. For some reason, his accent sounded thicker like this. "Please. I bought it for him, and I don't want it to be hidden away because he's too scared you'll make fun of him."

"What is it?" Tone asked, the edge of mischief dancing in his eyes.

"I'm not telling you," Stan said. "This is important to me, Tone. Do it for me?"

The burly Bristolian leaned down and enveloped Stan in a surprisingly gentle hug. "Ben has my back, and I've got his," Tone whispered. "I'll look after him for you. And don't worry—whatever your secret is, it's safe with me."

"Thank you," Stan said and squeezed Tone a little harder. "That means a lot."

"You got it."

Tone kissed Stan lightly on the cheek before pulling away and wandering off to check how the loading was going. When Stan looked up, Ben was standing on the steps of the bus, watching him with a curious expression.

"You want to see inside?" Ben asked.

"Yeah. Yes, please."

"Come on," Ben said, offering his hand.

The tour bus was long and narrow, with the sleeping area mostly upstairs and a line of couches on either side downstairs. There was one more fold-out bed at the back of the bus. Apparently this was Summer's area—she had claimed it as the sole girl on the tour. Stan didn't blame her for not wanting to sleep with the boys.

The bus had bunk beds upstairs, for both the band members and their small crew. They looked narrow to Stan, especially considering how tall Ben was.

"This is mine," Ben said, stopping at the bunk at the top of the stairs. A small curtain encircled the bed. "I already put Hades in there."

"Hades?"

"Yeah. That's what I named him."

Stan pressed his lips together. "You named your bunny rabbit after the Greek god of the underworld?"

In response, Ben kissed him hard. They walked back outside in silence.

"It's a nice bus," Stan said as they emerged in the bright sunlight again. He nudged his sunglasses back down onto his nose.

"Yeah. Sherrie saw the one we had hired to start with and said there was no way she was going to let us loose in that death trap. So she paid for an upgrade."

"I like Sherrie."

"Me too. You should stay in contact with her while we're away. She'll be worrying about us, so you could keep her company. I'm sure Geordie would appreciate it."

Stan heard the subtext—that Ben wanted Sherrie to keep Stan company too—and didn't call him out on it. Sherrie was nice. He could spend some time with her if it kept everyone happy. It wasn't a chore.

"I'm going to miss you so much," Ben said, wrapping his arms around Stan's shoulders.

"Please," Stan murmured. "Please don't. I don't want to cry in front of your friends."

They kissed instead, finding a shady spot to hide and make out until Jez started yelling about the fact they needed to go if they were going to get to Brighton in time to set up and sound check, and Ben was torn away from him, off for weeks of fun on his own.

Stan didn't cry; he rubbed his thumb over the ring Ben had given him and thought of Hades and didn't cry. He watched the bus disappear down the road and walked back to the Tube station and made it all the way back to the flat and onto the bed, with its sheets that still smelled like his lover. Then he cried.

CHAPTER ELEVEN

WHILE BEN and the band went from Brighton to Bristol to Birmingham, Stan threw himself into his work. He'd always kept long hours at the office anyway, and he was getting obsessive and ridiculous until Sherrie called him and said Ben had called her and he was worried.

That was enough to make him stop, to take stock and wonder exactly what he wanted. He still had weeks more until Ben came home. It would be too easy to work himself into the ground, rising up through the ranks at the magazine, but where would that leave him when Ben got home? He couldn't just abandon it all again as soon as his boyfriend moved back to London.

There was the small matter of his blog too.

He had started it when he was still living in New York with his aunt, and even though he was only a teenager, back then he was already honing his sense of style and what made him tick. At school, he didn't dare dress nearly as fashionably as he did now. Being Russian, not speaking English too well, and being a slight, slim boy who was very definitely not heteronormative was hard enough, even in New York. He wasn't about to wear a dress to prom and wreck the thin veil of normality he draped over himself each morning before school.

The one place he'd felt free to let go and be himself was in his own room, alone, with the computer he'd saved and saved and begged for. It was his prized possession, his window into a community where he was assured people like him existed all around the world.

He wasn't a freak, or a disaster, or a fag, or any of the other names that got hurled at him at least once a week.

The blog started as Stan's outlet, his way of trying to piece together the things he knew about himself and the possibilities of what he could be in the future. It had grown, over the years, and when Stan started working in the fashion industry, he found himself in a place where he could talk, with real knowledge and passion about a hobby and a love that had become a career.

Even though his job at the magazine demanded long hours, Stan still spent a few hours every week putting articles together and releasing them on a semiregular schedule. His following was growing, and while Ben was away, he'd started to experiment with making video blogs along with his written and photography posts. His sketches too, made their way online, when he had the time to do them. Stan had always loved experimenting with designing clothes on paper. He was a disaster at the sewing machine, though, so his designs always remained purely hypothetical.

"Tea run?"

Stan looked up from his desk to where Kirsty was hovering in the doorway to his office, wearing what looked like last year's menswear shirt over a very short dress. He decided he liked the look and grinned at her.

"Yes, please. Peppermint. That colour is good on you."

She glanced down at the dark red and smiled back at him. "Thanks. I'll be about half an hour, okay?"

"No worries." He rummaged in his bag—okay, it was more than a bag; it was a Chloé, but he got it on sale and no one needed know—and handed her a ten-pound note. "Can you grab me a salad too, please? Anything without meat in it is fine."

"Got it," she said with a nod.

"Thank you," he said again, and Kirsty ducked into the next office along.

It was weird, now that they were friends, asking her to run errands for him at work, even if that was her job. One of the reasons Kirsty was so good as the departmental assistant was that really, she had little interest in fashion. She saw it as an industry, like any other, and her job was to make everyone else's lives easier.

If Stan sent her a layout to check, she'd look at it with a critical eye, spot any typos, correct his grammar, and suggest amends to the placement of the photographs if necessary. She didn't try to rewrite his work or change his style, which was, admittedly, pretty unique. Her no-nonsense attitude meant things got *done*, instead of debated or picked apart or critiqued.

His mind was full of florals and menswear when Kirsty returned with his peppermint tea and salad with falafels, which was just perfect.

"Did you get anything?" he asked as Kirsty turned to leave.

"Uh, yeah."

"If you want to eat lunch in here, you can," he said, leaning away from his computer for the first time in what felt like hours.

"Or you could leave," Kirsty said, teasing. "It's a beautiful day out there."

"If I leave, I'll never want to come back," he groaned. "I'd prefer to work through and leave earlier."

"Fair enough. I'll be back in a bit."

This was hell.

He needed a distraction.

THE THUMPING bass of the pre-show music throbbed through the whole building as Stan silently contemplated his reflection in a mirror in the ladies' bathroom. The walls were painted red, giving the whole room a womb-like feel, and other girls chattered and fussed around him.

With a practiced hand, Stan fluffed his hair, then carefully checked his eye make-up and smudged the dark powder on his eyelids with the pad of his pinkie finger. The other girls didn't even register to him.

Ben didn't know he was in Manchester. Tone did—Tone had helped Stan figure out what trains to get and how to make his way to the gig venue from the station. He'd also helped Stan find a reasonably nice hotel, which was only a few doors down from the venue, giving him space to be alone with Ben for a few precious hours.

"'Scuse me, love," a girl said, and Stan obligingly moved aside to let her use the sink. He threw his head back, shaking the sweaty hair away from his neck, and ducked back into the gig.

Ben's band had already been on—they were the support act. Stan had watched from the side of the venue, Ben's side, entranced by the man he adored thrashing around on a guitar like some kind of rock star. It was driving Stan mad to know Ben was backstage somewhere right now, possibly only feet away, not knowing Stan was here.

The main act wasn't due to start for another ten minutes or so, so there was a huge rush at the bar, and Stan couldn't bear to wait for it. He didn't have a bag with him, just a wallet and his phone stuffed into the back pocket of his achingly tight black jeans.

He startled when a hand landed on his shoulder, then almost leaped into Tone's arms.

"Hello," he said, then kissed Tone lightly on the cheek.

"Alright, my lover?" Tone growled, and Stan laughed. He hadn't realised quite how much he'd missed this big bear of a man.

"You were really good," Stan said. "So much better than in London."

"I'd say. Come on. I've got you a backstage pass."

"Really?"

"Yeah," Tone said with a grin. "Ben's going to shit his pants when he sees you."

"I think I am too."

Tone took Stan's hand and led him down the side of the venue to where a couple of large security guards stood by the door that would take them backstage. Tone leaned in and exchanged a few words, gestured back to Stan, and they got let in.

"It's a bit of a maze back here, so don't wander off," Tone said, letting go of Stan's hand when they were safely past the barriers. "The dressing rooms for the big bands are on this floor—we're upstairs."

Stan only nodded. Suddenly he felt sick.

Nearly two months had passed since Ben went off on tour. They had added more dates after the initial reviews had been good, and Stan had heard rumblings of taking the whole thing on to Europe. There was interest in Ares; people liked them, responded to their music. That kind of publicity couldn't be bought.

"How've you been, then?" Tone asked. He didn't get a response, though.

At the top of the stairs Stan caught sight of a familiar mop of dark hair. Ben was wearing his glasses, which told Stan Ben was tired, and his chest was sweaty and shirtless. Gorgeous.

"Never mind," Tone mumbled affectionately.

"Stan?" Ben said, the word barely audible from the other end of the corridor and the sudden rush of noise from the stage below them. Stan dropped all pretences and sprinted down the hallway to throw himself into Ben's arms.

"Oh my God," Ben murmured.

Stan wrapped his arms round Ben's neck, his legs around Ben's waist and *clung*. His cheek still fitted perfectly on Ben's shoulder, and he took deep breaths of slightly sweaty skin and felt like crying.

"I missed you."

"I missed you too," Ben said, his voice thick with emotion. "How did you get here?"

"On a train," Stan said, smiling as he slowly sank to his feet. "Tone helped. I wanted to surprise you."

"I'm surprised," Ben said. Any more words were forgotten as Stan closed the space between their lips and kissed like his heart was breaking. Ben's fingers ran softly through his hair, untangling and messing at the same time.

When Ben flicked his tongue into Stan's mouth, Stan pressed forward, aligning their hips and making a silent promise of more.

"Oi, get a room," someone yelled, and Stan pulled away reluctantly. Ben's hands still clutched Stan's hips, keeping him close enough to disguise their combined arousal.

Stan turned his head enough to see Geordie leering at them from the doorway to a dressing room and elegantly flipped his middle finger at the man he considered a friend. Geordie laughed delightedly and went back into the room.

"I have a hotel room," Stan said.

"Yeah?"

"It's not far away. If you want a night off the tour bus—"

"Oh, do I want that," Ben said with a groan and a laugh. "Yeah. Let's go."

"I also thought that maybe we can go out later." It was only just nine in the evening—plenty of time for them to enjoy the city. "To Canal Street. I want us to go and have *fun*."

"Yeah. I want…." Ben kissed up the side of Stan's neck. "I *need* to get you alone first, though. Give me ten fucking minutes, Stan. That's all it's going to take."

"A little longer than that, I hope," Stan said on a breathless laugh.

"No promises."

Ben grabbed a bag out of the dressing room while Stan stood in the doorway and waved lamely at the rest of the band, who were stretched out over sofas drinking whiskey. He blew a kiss to Tone before they left and got the others to laugh at that.

"I need to grab a few things off the bus," Ben said as they approached the venue's stage door. "It won't take me a minute."

"Okay."

More security guards loitered back here, although the area behind the venue was quiet for now, while the main act were playing. Ben ducked onto the bus while Stan stood outside and quickly smoked a cigarette, only now able to ease his fractured nerves.

"Do you still have...?" Stan said as Ben hopped back down and hit the button to close the bus door.

"Hades?" Ben finished for him, running his hand down Stan's arm. "Yeah. Of course."

Stan smiled inwardly. "Good. That's good."

"I wouldn't get rid of him, baby."

Ben slipped his hand into Stan's, and they turned away from the bus, away from the venue, down the street to the hotel and blessed solitude.

The hotel was nicer than Stan had anticipated. It was a chain, which meant he generally had low expectations, but the room was big and the bed was huge, comfortable, with plenty of pillows and a fluffy duvet. It took Stan's shaking hands three attempts to get the door to open, the red light mocking him while Ben's hands encircled his waist and his lips made promises on the back of his neck.

When the door finally flashed green and allowed them entry, Ben dumped his bag on the floor and pushed the deadbolt lock across.

"I don't know if I can make this romantic," he said, the apology clear in his voice. Stan walked backwards towards the bed, kicking off his shoes and unbuttoning his jeans.

"I don't need romantic. I need you."

"I can give you that."

They kicked out of clothes, garments flying around the room while they scrabbled in desperate haste for blessed nudity. Stan cried out as Ben kissed over his collarbone, licked his nipples, then licked up the length of his already straining cock.

"Please," Stan murmured, throwing his arm over his head and spreading his legs wide. "Please."

"We need...," Ben said, kicking his jeans off the rest of the way, then struggling out of his socks. Stan laughed and palmed his own cock, rubbing his thumb over the leaking head and wondering what on earth about this man made him so deliciously wanton.

"Got it all," Stan said. "Right there."

It was, too, a box of condoms and Stan's favourite kind of lube. Ben laughed and reached over, grabbed what he needed, then settled himself between Stan's legs.

"Well, aren't you a sight for sore eyes," he murmured, rubbing his hands up and down Stan's legs a few times before leaning in and stealing a kiss.

"I think about you every day," Stan said as Ben twisted the top off the lube and smeared a little over Stan's hole, then started to stretch him with gently inquisitive fingers. Stan gasped and writhed, and continued his confession. "Sometimes I think about you... you doing this, and I touch myself."

"Yeah?" Ben said, his voice low and dangerous. "Show me."

It felt like the most natural thing in the world for Stan to wrap his hand around his own cock and stroke it languorously while Ben's fingers continued to stretch and prep him.

"I think about you inside me," Stan said, his eyes squeezed closed, his voice sounding different. "I think about that, and sometimes it makes me—Ah!"

Ben pulled his fingers free and fumbled with a condom for too long—too long.

"Roll onto your side for me, baby," he said.

"I want it like this."

Ben kissed his knee. "I don't want to hurt you."

"You won't. I've been going to yoga classes. I wanted to get more flexible so we could... trust me, please, Ben. I can do it."

Leaning in once more, Ben kissed him softly, his gentleness belying the furious need between them.

"If I hurt you, tell me right away and we'll shift about, okay?"

"Yes. Okay. I promise. Please... I've been wanting this for so long."

It was true. Those times when he touched himself at night, Stan was thinking about lying back, just like this, and looking up into Ben's beautiful eyes while they made love. The form and function of the sex didn't really matter, he just wanted to overcome this physical malfunction that made the most intimate part of sex unavailable to them.

Ben scooped Stan's legs up and bent him back, almost in half as he guided his own cock into Stan's waiting body. It was a tight pinch at first, those few moments when the world stopped and the pain was breath-stealing, before the easy slide made everything all right again, and he could do what he'd been dying to do and open his eyes.

"When will you stop being this beautiful to me?" Ben murmured.

"I was just thinking the same thing. Oh my God."

Stan writhed on the bed, any discomfort in his hips forgotten as Ben started the familiar thrust and grind that defined sex between them. His legs were held high, thighs flush against Ben's chest, meaning there wasn't too much pressure on spreading them wide. It made the whole thing easier, and the angle... the angle was perfect for... *perfect*.

"I can't even think straight," Stan said with a laugh. He reached up and held on to Ben's strong arms, the biceps straining to hold his own body weight as he moved with painfully slow, even thrusts.

"Me either. Kiss me, please."

It felt more awkward to lean up like this, to try to let their lips do the talking for them. But Stan tried. And it was worth it.

"I'm okay," Stan said softly. "I promise. Let go. I want this too."

On the next thrust, Ben groaned, a noise that sounded like it had been ripped from his chest and Stan cried out as the head of Ben's perfect cock hit his prostate at just the right angle. It was messy and loud, and Stan was sure he wasn't normally the type to be loud during sex.

Still, Ben made him noisy and unashamed of his body and what it was capable of. This was wicked and delicious—pleasure and pain blending and underneath it all, the safe, undeniable knowledge that Ben loved him.

"I'm so close," Ben said, holding himself at the deepest point inside Stan's body.

"Let go."

Stan watched, fascinated, as Ben rocked his hips a few more times, then threw his head back, gave a silent scream of pleasure as his cock throbbed and twitched.

"Oh," Stan whispered, and the fingers that had been curled around his own cock were suddenly covered with hot, sticky release and the pleasure was bone-deep and muscle-melting.

While Ben pulled away and threw the condom unceremoniously onto the carpet next to the bed, Stan stretched and found nothing hurt as much as he thought it might. On instinct, he rolled onto his side and pulled his knees up to his chest.

"Come here," he said to Ben, who was trying to clean up himself. "We can have a shower in a minute."

"Are you okay?" Ben asked as he obligingly curled his body around Stan's.

"Yes. I feel... amazing."

"Good," Ben said and kissed Stan's shoulder as he kicked the duvet up over them both. "That was incredible."

"I wanted it for a while, so I had to go and do something about it," Stan said around a wide yawn.

"Yoga?"

"Yes. It increases flexibility while developing body and mind."

Ben snorted with laughter, then apologised with kisses. "If it's working, then I can't really complain."

"It is. They showed me how to stretch the muscles in my thighs and build up the strength there to support the problem with my hips. My bones. Make it better. Sorry, my English is terrible right now."

"It's fine."

"You broke my language," Stan murmured.

It was beyond reassuring to be held like this again. Their bodies weren't a perfect fit—Stan was made of too many sharp angles for him to fit neatly against anyone. But Ben had learned how to hold him close without hurting either of them, and it was the perfect position for him to kiss over Stan's neck, which was probably Stan's favourite thing in the whole world.

When Ben took a deep, shaky breath, Stan realised this separation had been as hard on Ben as it had been on him, and Ben probably needed this time as much as Stan did. It was quiet and reassuring. Loving.

"I love you, Ben," Stan said, bringing the hand anchored around his waist up to his lips.

"I love you too."

Wasn't that all that mattered?

AFTER LYING together like that for a little while, Stan dragged Ben out of the bed and into a hot shower, washing away the sweat from the gig and the evidence of their lovemaking. He let Ben wash his hair, fingers working out the knots in the long strands that looked impossibly darker under the water.

"It'll take me forever to dry it now," Stan grouched, even though it was worth it to feel this intimacy again.

"How long are you staying for?" Ben asked.

"I have an open ticket back to London. As long as I travel off-peak, I can go whenever."

Finally clean, they stumbled back into the bedroom, and Stan produced a bottle of wine to share while he got ready, and Ben turned on the TV.

"It's all crap, but I miss watching it," Ben said, sprawled naked on the bed. "Especially like this."

"Not much wandering around naked on the tour bus, then?" Stan teased.

He'd put on underwear and was sitting at the dressing table working the knots out of his hair, ready to blow-dry it into big, bouncy curls. That was the plan, anyway. In the mirror, Stan watched Ben scratch his tattooed belly, the sight of the black ink against the white sheets oddly artistic.

"Too much bloody wandering around naked," Ben said darkly.

"Tone?"

"However did you guess?"

"I like Tone," Stan said lightly. "He helped me figure out how to get here."

"I can't decide if I like the surprise, or if I wish I knew you'd be coming."

Stan shrugged. "I wanted to surprise you. I would have come out weeks ago, but work has suddenly got so busy, and I had to stay and help."

"That's okay. I know you work hard."

While Stan dried and styled his hair, Ben sprawled on the bed and sent text messages back and forth to his friends.

"They're in a pub," Ben said when Stan turned the hairdryer off. "Apparently it's not far from Canal Street, if that's where we're going."

"Yes! I want to dance."

"I'm not sure I'm much of a dancer, baby," Ben said with a rueful laugh.

"That doesn't matter. You can admire me dancing."

Ben grinned. Stan's stomach fizzed at the sight of his boyfriend so obviously happy.

They finished most of the bottle of wine, and Stan forced Ben into the bathroom to shave and get dressed, since he was nearly ready and Ben was still naked. It took great conviction for him to be stern when crawling back into bed together and fucking the night away sounded like such an appealing prospect.

He'd planned this outfit weeks ago, and Stan wriggled into his tight, tight black leather trousers and forced his feet into a pair of very high-heeled, black ankle boots. He didn't have much time to do his make-up, with how long his hair had taken, so it was the standard base to make do and red lips that emphasised his pout, and a reapplication of the already successful dark, smoky eyeshadow.

"What do you think?" Stan asked, striking a pose when Ben walked out of the bathroom wearing a variation on his "band T-shirt and black jeans" uniform.

"Holy crap," Ben said with a laugh. "Aren't you missing something?"

Stan looked down at his bare chest, then winked. "No. It's very warm out, you know."

"You're going to start a riot," Ben said, crossing the room and running his hands possessively over Stan's chest. "You're as tall as me now."

"Mhmm. I like these boots."

"Me too. Are you sure you can walk in them?"

"Of course," he lied.

It was getting late, so Stan ushered them both out of the room while Ben was still patting his pockets, checking for his phone, wallet, keys. This wasn't the night for a handbag, even though his bags were beautiful, and so Stan had been forced to shove his phone in his pocket too, along with a few notes and his ID.

"Do you know where we're going, or do we need to get a cab?" Ben asked as they emerged into the soupy summer heat.

"Honey, I need a taxi. These boots were *not* made for walking."

Ben laughed as he flagged one down and gave the driver directions. In the back seat, they didn't talk much but held hands over the leather. Ben's thumb ran back and forth over Stan's wrist in a warm, soothing gesture.

When they got to the pub, the others had clearly started without them.

"Stan!" Tone yelled from across the room. "Stan, my man. Vodka?"

Stan nodded, grinning stupidly, and gripped Ben's hand tightly as they wound through the tables to the bar.

"*My* man," Ben corrected him affectionately, and Tone pulled him into a hug, then planted a wet kiss on Ben's cheek. "You can get me one too, you bastard."

"Watch it," Stan said, playfully pushing Tone away.

"Aw, I love you both," Tone said. "The others are in the corner, if you want to sit down. I'll bring 'em over."

Stan nodded. "Thank you."

There weren't enough chairs for everyone; it was late, and the pub was clearly popular. Ben grumbled and had everyone shift down in the booth until there was room, then tugged Stan onto his lap.

"Comfy?" he asked, pushing Stan's hair away to murmur into his ear.

"Very."

Tone returned, carting a ridiculous number of drinks and bottles between his long fingers, then distributed them to the group.

"Just there, thanks, love," he said, and a barmaid set down another tray, this one filled with shot glasses.

"Lord, Tone, what have you bought now?" Jez asked as Tone started passing around glasses.

"Vodka. To toast our guest."

Stan lifted a glass and nodded. "Cheers," he said and knocked back the shot.

"Na zdorovje," Tone said in a surprisingly good attempt at a Russian accent. Stan laughed and shook his head, patting Tone on the arm.

"Nice try," Stan told him. "But no."

"Slainte," Summer offered and shuddered as the liquor hit her throat. "Jesus, Tone, are you trying to kill me?"

"Nope, just get you drunk enough that you'll let me feel your tits."

Summer rolled her eyes and apparently decided she wasn't going to dignify that with an answer. As Stan returned his shot glass to the tray, Summer grabbed his wrist, holding his hand up to the light.

"This is pretty," she said, nodding at the ring Stan still wore on his finger.

Ben dropped his chin to Stan's shoulder and squeezed his waist gently.

"Thank you," Stan said softly. He took his hand back and ran his thumb over the ring, feeling strangely protective of it and what it symbolised.

"I can't believe Ben has such good taste," Summer continued.

"Hey," Ben said, pretending to be annoyed. "I have amazing taste."

"Will the bride wear white?" Tone said, leaning back with his pint of cider and grinning at Stan. Stan decided he wasn't being made fun of, so he responded.

"I don't want to wear a dress when I get married, no," he said. "Probably a pair of very well-cut tuxedo pants… and some ridiculously expensive shirt."

Ben grinned. "I wouldn't expect anything less, darling."

"And what will the groom wear?" Summer asked. "You know he doesn't have any dress sense at all, Stan."

"The groom will wear," Stan said and paused dramatically, turning to Ben to cup his cheek in his hand. "Whatever the bride tells him to."

Summer burst into delighted laughter and dropped her head to Geordie's shoulder. He kissed the top of her head, and Stan guessed their relationship was on again.

"Are we doing Canal Street, then?" Summer asked, twirling her hair around her finger. "I think it'll be fun."

"Stan wants to dance," Ben said.

"Then we shall dance!" she declared grandly. "Which way?"

"You're coming?" Ben asked as Tone followed them down the street. He nodded sagely.

"I don't mind the gays."

"Well, I'm sure we're about to run into plenty of them."

"I don't even know where I want to go first," Stan said, skipping alongside them, managing to stay upright by sheer luck alone as he stumbled in his heels. "Not bars, though. I want to go to a club."

"We might not get in anywhere," Ben said. "It's late."

When Stan almost tripped again, Tone swept him up and on to his own back, made warning noises about dagger heels near his balls, and kept Stan in a secure piggyback as they negotiated the cobbled streets.

"They'll let me in," Stan said confidently. "Do they not know who I am?"

"You're a drunk Russian with the best legs in Britain," Tone teased.

"Indeed. They should be honoured to have me in their establishment."

As expected, the line outside the club was huge, but seemed to be moving fairly quickly. Jez and Geordie peeled off, heading in the vague direction of the bus, and Summer shouted obscenities at them until they disappeared out of sight. Ben managed to grab a bottle of water from a street vendor and pressed it into Stan's hands, begging him to drink.

"I get drunk quickly," Stan said mournfully. "I am a disgrace to my country."

Ben kissed him. It was a gentle kiss, sweet and reassuring. Stan smiled into it, reaching up to cup Ben's cheek.

"Come on, you're holding everyone up," Summer grouched, but she was smiling when Stan looked down at her. "You could be a supermodel, you know," she added.

Stan shrugged. "I could," he said. "But I don't want to be."

"Why not?"

"I know I work in fashion, but there are a lot of things wrong with the industry. I love that some photographers are using androgynous models and playing with those perceptions of what male and female 'should' look like. There's always a cost, though."

"Like what?" Summer asked.

She never got an answer—they reached the front of the line, and Stan got leered at by the staff at the door of the club.

"ID," one demanded.

Stan wriggled his identity card out of his pocket and handed it over. It was Italian, since he hadn't got around to ordering a British driving license yet.

The man's eyes flicked back and forth between the card and the man in front of him. Eventually he handed the card back.

"All right. Go on."

Ben insisted on paying the cover charge and kept his hand on Stan's back as they descended into the dark club, noise and heat and flashing lights immediately enveloping them. Apparently he didn't care about the fact Stan was all hot and sweaty.

"Do you want a drink?" Ben yelled.

"No! Dance with me."

Tone nodded and mouthed "go on," and then dragged Summer off towards the long, shiny bar. The club was huge, spanning several levels, but the main dance floor was within sight of the bar. That was good—Stan didn't want them all getting separated.

Lights pulsed from every direction as they joined the mass of hot, writhing bodies, and Stan wrapped his arms around Ben's neck and started to sway to the beat of the music.

"I knew you could dance, really," Stan said, his mouth close to Ben's ear so he'd be heard.

"Only with you."

"Yes. Only with me."

When their mouths met again, it was slower, Stan gripping the curve of Ben's strong arms as they rocked back and forth slowly, completely at odds with the regular thump-*thump*-thump of the music. Ben broke the kiss first, then wrapped his hands around Stan's waist and lifted him high, so his blond hair fell in a curtain straight down. He laughed, then threw his head back and hollered out to the night.

I'm in love!

I'm in love.

PART TWO

CHAPTER TWELVE

BEN WAS bone-deep tired when he finally, *finally* got back to the flat. It had been a long drive from, well, London to everywhere and back again.

After letting himself through the gate, Ben shouldered his bag, ignored all the aches and pains, and crossed the courtyard to the stairs that would take him back to Stan.

The weekend in Manchester had been incredible, but not nearly long enough, and that had been a couple of weeks ago now.

The band had spent the past few days driving down the east coast, stopping for an unscheduled gig in Cambridge. Someone Tone knew had heard about the tour and had booked them in last-minute. It had been worth it, from the band's point of view, but Ben missed his man.

They'd last spoken four days ago. Ben had tried texting to tell Stan about the gig but hadn't got any response. He hadn't picked up when Ben called either. The phone reception had been shit for the past few days, and even when Ben called again, Stan hadn't answered. He told himself it wasn't so unusual—Stan had a way of getting caught up with work, or his friends, or life in general. Ben still missed him, though. A deep, hurting ache, that even the sweetest black bunny rabbit couldn't ease.

"Stan?" Ben called as he let himself into the flat. The air in here was stale, and Ben wrinkled his nose at a bad smell that was coming from somewhere. "Stan?" he tried again. "Baby?"

He didn't get a response. Ben quickly checked the bedroom, which was neat, as always, then made his way back through to the kitchen. He opened the fridge and nearly gagged—the smell was coming from a tub of unidentifiable leftovers that was starting to turn green.

As he was dealing with the ungodly mess, Ben's heart rate started to increase. There was no way Stan would have let this happen. He was too fucking anal about keeping the place clean. Once he'd cleared the tub away, Ben grabbed his phone from his pocket and scrolled through his contacts. His last two messages had gone unanswered, but they were just *Goodnight, I love you*s, so it wasn't something he'd necessarily expected a response to.

Hand trembling, Ben pressed the button to dial Stan's phone. It went straight to voicemail.

He tried Sherrie instead.

"Hiya, Ben," she said, sounding stressed.

"Hey, Sherrie. Sorry to jump right to it, but have you heard from Stan recently? I just got home, and he's not here, and his phone is off."

"Sorry, sweetheart. Emily's been poorly the past week—I told him not to come over in case he caught anything from her. It's just a bug, but he's always looked like a strong wind could knock him over, you know?"

Ben knew.

He wondered if it was too extreme to go down to Stan's office. Probably, but he had a gnawing sort of panic in his stomach now, and he didn't like it one bit. After trying Stan's mobile again, with still no response, he made up his mind and only stopped to change his shirt before heading back down to the Tube.

The office was only a few stops away from Stan's flat, walking distance really, if it was a nice day and no one was wearing high-heeled shoes. Ben thought about that—the maybe forty-minute walk from Stan's flat to his office, and if Stan was on the Tube somewhere. No one got phone reception down here so....

The train pulled into the station, and Ben stumbled off it, headed up through the barriers, and blinked in the sunlight. He was only vaguely aware of where the office was, and it took him a moment, frantically looking around, to get his bearings.

He spotted the magazine's logo before anything else and his heart clenched again as he jogged across the street to the glass-fronted building.

"I'm sorry," Ben said, stopping at the reception desk and pushing his fingers through his hair, aware he was still fairly disgusting from being on a tour bus for the past few months. "I'm looking for Stan Novikov. He works here."

The receptionist gave him a slow, even stare.

"Stan hasn't been here for about a week. He's off sick." Her eyes were piercing, unnatural purple, contrasting with her copper-coloured skin and straight dark hair. Ben got the impression she dressed to intimidate.

He nodded, trying to keep his rising panic in check. "Okay. Well, I'm his partner, and I've just come from our flat, and he isn't there, so I'm getting a bit worried. Can I speak to his manager or something?"

The girl gave him another disparaging look and started flicking through a list of contacts in a laminated file. When she found the right name, she pushed a short series of numbers into the phone with taloned fingernails and waited for a response on the other end before picking up the receiver.

Ben stood back, waiting for the short conversation to be over, not wanting to appear too pushy.

"What's your name?" the receptionist snapped.

"Ben. Benjamin Easton."

She repeated the name to whomever she was talking to, then put the phone down.

"Victoria is on her way," she said. "You can sit down. Over there."

Ben nodded and took a seat on the very white sofa, aware his black jeans were dirty and would probably leave marks.

It didn't take long for a very tall, very slim black woman to appear. She made a beeline for Ben and hovered for a moment before sitting down.

"You're Ben," she said.

"Yes. Victoria?"

"Yes." The woman hesitated again, and Ben wondered just how bad it could possibly be. "Stan's in the hospital."

Pretty bad, then. "What happened?"

Victoria looked down at her hands. Her fingernails were painted purple and filed into points. "I'm not sure how much I should tell you. We have procedures in place to protect our employees' confidentiality."

"Stan's my partner." Ben's chest felt tight; the words came out in a voice he didn't recognise. "I—we—we're sort of engaged. You don't have to tell me everything, but I can't... I can't...."

Before he completely broke down, Victoria nodded and straightened her spine. "Stan collapsed at work a few days ago. We called an ambulance, and they took him into hospital. I don't know many details, but they were having trouble getting hold of his medical records. He has some kind of... mental health...."

"He used to have anorexia," Ben said bluntly.

"Yes," Victoria said and ducked her head. "I don't know all of the details, but it seems like he's relapsed. For lack of a better word."

"And he's been taken to hospital?"

"Whitechapel. The hospital there."

"Who's with him?"

Victoria looked confused. "I'm sorry?"

"Who's there with him? Who's looking after him?"

"Well, the doctors...."

"There's no one there?"

"No."

Ben stood abruptly. "Thank you for your time," he said stiffly. Without giving Victoria a chance to respond, he turned and strode out of the office.

From Stan's office, it was only a short Tube ride to Whitechapel, and the hospital was directly opposite the Tube station, so he didn't have far to walk.

Run.

There was no time to waste, not now that he knew Stan was alone. Something had happened, and he was in hospital, and he was alone, and Ben hadn't known anything about it. The sickness and anger and bone-shaking fear were colliding in his nervous system, making his heart pound and fingers tremble, and something in his belly churned.

Another reception desk, another receptionist. This time an older man with soft, smiling features.

"I've been out of town, and I just learned my partner has been brought in here," Ben said, forcing calm into his voice. "Stanislav Novikov."

He was directed to a third-floor ward, ignoring the signs on the walls that labelled Stan's condition before Ben even got to a doctor. The panic that had been churning in his belly and clawing at his chest almost peaked when he saw the words "Eating Disorder Ward," and Ben forced himself to stop, pressed his back against the wall, and took deep, slow breaths to calm down. There was no point in going to see Stan when he was having a panic attack.

Someone was waiting for him just inside the door. Apparently the nice man at reception had called up for him.

"Ben Easton?" she asked.

Ben nodded.

"I'm Leslie. I'm one of the nurses taking care of Stan."

Leslie looked like his mother. She was shortish, middle-aged, her fawn-coloured hair styled neatly around her face. She had wrinkles around her eyes, just light ones, and her skin looked soft with age and care. She wore a nurse's uniform, and Ben wanted to cry.

"Can you—" Ben choked. "Can you tell me what happened? Can I see him?"

"Stan's condition is critical," Leslie said, folding her arms across her chest. "We're tube-feeding him at the moment, and he's on an IV drip. We're running tests every twelve hours or so, but at the moment, it doesn't look good for his liver and kidneys."

"What does that mean?"

Leslie sighed and led him to the nurse's station. She rifled through a stack of files and pulled one free. "His internal organs started shutting down. All we can do is try to keep him stable at the moment, and once he's out of the woods, we can look at repairing some of that damage."

"Is he going to make it?"

"Mr Easton."

"Ben."

"Ben." She looked over her shoulder, making sure things on the ward were still calm. She scratched at her hair and turned back to him. "We're going to do our very best—"

"Please don't bullshit me," Ben said, interrupting her. "Please. Is he going to make it?"

"I don't think Stan is going to die. However, I don't know what sort of condition he will be in, physically and mentally, when he comes through the other side of this. Look, I'm just a nurse, but I've worked with eating disorders patients for nearly twenty years now. When he gets out of the woods, Stan has to change. He *has* to. There is no more relapsing. If he does this again, he will die, and there's nothing any of us can do to change that."

Ben slumped back against the wall and pressed the heels of his hands into his eye sockets. He felt a warm hand squeeze his shoulder in what he thought was comfort, and then the squeeze got harder.

"Look at me," Leslie said. Ben opened his eyes and sniffed. "If there's one thing I've learned working on this ward, it's that the people who make it are the ones who have something to fight for. Anorexia is a disease that needs to be fought, tooth and nail. Stan has something to fight for, Ben, if you give it to him."

Ben nodded. "Can I see him now?"

"Yeah," she said kindly. "Of course you can."

She led him through the maze-like ward to a small room. Stan was the only one in it, asleep on a bed that looked far too big for him, hooked up to an astonishing number of tubes and drips and monitors.

"Stan is sleeping a lot at the moment," Leslie said softly. "Which is a good thing. When he's asleep, he'll be recovering."

"When will he wake up?"

"I'm not sure. Possibly not while you're here. It's not a good idea to wake him, especially since his mental state is pretty fragile at the moment."

Ben stepped towards the bed and gently stroked the back of Stan's hand with his fingertip. "He's always been skinny," he murmured, almost to himself. "And I knew about the anorexia. He told me about it. He doesn't look...."

"Anorexia is a mental disease, not a physical one," Leslie said. She hadn't moved from her spot next to the open door. "It turns the people you love into liars."

"I only saw him a few weeks ago. He felt so strong then. He was doing yoga, and he said he felt great."

"I don't know what happened. One of the biggest challenges we've had with treating Stan is understanding what has been going on in the past couple of years. We only just got hold of his medical records and they're patchy at best, and in Italian or Russian at worst."

He turned to her and bit his lip. "I talk to him almost every day. I mean, if we miss a day or two, it doesn't matter, we usually text a lot too. I can't help but think if I'd called him, or got someone to check on him, or *something*."

"The 'what if' game will destroy you," Leslie said bluntly. "Don't play it."

"I missed him so much."

"He's not going anywhere. You can stay for a while."

Ben nodded and took a seat next to the bed, reaching out again to touch Stan's skin. It was a funny colour, greyish, though warm. He was alive.

Leslie had backed quietly out of the room, and the door snicked shut behind her. Ben slumped in his chair, exhaustion stealing the last of his energy.

"Fucking hell, baby," Ben whispered, pushing the heels of his hands against his face. "What the hell happened?"

CHAPTER THIRTEEN

THERE WAS something about the smell of an empty venue that Ben had always found intoxicating. Sure, at night, when the place was packed full of people and the lights and the heat and the smell of the smoke machine hung thick in the air—that was magic.

During the day, though, that all got stripped back. With the harsh fluorescent lights on instead of the multicoloured stage lights, the place looked oddly sad. The black paint on the walls was flaking and peeling, thousands of years' worth of cobwebs tangled together on the ceiling, and the smell: stale sweat, the lingering acridness from those smoke machines, the sickly sweetness of spilled drinks.

Ben looked out over the venue, standing on a stage that, a few months ago, he was dreaming of playing on. Now it didn't matter. None of it did.

"Fuckin' hell," Tone said, dumping one of his bags on the stage as he looked out over the empty room. "Bit of a dive, innit?"

Ben turned to him incredulously, then shook his head when he saw Tone was joking. He'd seen enough bands play here over the years that playing the Brixton Academy made him feel like this was it. They had made it. Sort of.

"Okay," Ben said. "Can we do this as quickly as possible? I want to go and see Stan."

The others gathered on stage, dragging bags of equipment and guitar cases. Summer planted her hands on her hips and glowered at him.

"Ben. This is the biggest gig of our fucking lives. You can't half-arse your way through a soundcheck and make it up as we go along tonight. It needs to be good. This gig could launch us."

"If Stan wakes up, I won't even be going to the fucking gig," Ben bit back.

Anger flashed across Summer's eyes, and Tone grabbed Ben's wrist before either he or Summer could start something they couldn't resolve. "Come on," Tone mumbled and dragged Ben off the stage, down to the side door where they could sit on the step and share a cigarette.

"Call the hospital," Tone said simply as he rolled loose tobacco in thin white paper.

"I only spoke to them this morning," Ben said. He turned his phone around in his hand, over and over.

"Doesn't matter. Ask for that nurse—what's her name?"

"Leslie?"

"Yeah. Her. Ask for her."

Ben sighed but dialled the number anyway and waited to be connected to the nurse who was taking care of Stan. A few moments of conversation confirmed what he'd been told earlier—there had been no change since Ben had gone in for the first time a few days ago. Stan was stable but still in a critical situation.

"Thanks," Ben mumbled and rang off, then accepted the cigarette Tone handed him as he thumbed an update text to Kirsty. There was still something nasty clawing at his belly—the knowledge that apart from him, and Tone, and Kirsty, there wasn't anyone else Ben could go to about this.

"So?"

"He's the same as earlier."

"Are you going to come in and do the soundcheck and not be a dick to Summer?"

Ben nodded. "Yeah, alright."

"I get it," Tone said, then exhaled a lungful of smoke, looking at the grimy brick wall opposite the stage door. "I really do. Stan matters to you. He fucking well matters to all of us, mate. But you're the linchpin of this band."

"I'm not," Ben muttered.

"Mate. You so are. I know we've never really put anyone out there up front, and you do more harmonies than lead vocals, but when you get on stage, fucking magic happens. When we take that out of the equation, even when we rehearse without you, it's not the same. This band relies on you."

"Stan needs me right now. I know you guys do too, and you're my brothers, seriously, and I love you. But he's...."

"I know." Tone threw his arm around Ben's shoulders and squeezed him hard. "Let's do this gig tonight, fucking rock the place, then tomorrow we get to figure out what happens next. Okay?"

"Yeah. Okay."

The tension between them still dominated the soundcheck—Ben could feel Summer's eyes burning into his back as he rolled out the antique rug that always denoted his playing area on the left side of the stage. It was a tradition now. He liked the way it felt under his feet, rather than the hard boards of the stage. And it looked cool.

Soundcheck through the first half of the set was a chore, as it always was in a new venue as they figured out levels and what worked with the acoustics of the room. A moment, about ten minutes in, with roadies and noise boys and techs running around was when it clicked for Ben. This was about being a musician. Being a professional, rather than a guy who played a couple of songs in the back room of a pub with his mates.

The people at the venue—those techs and roadies—were doing their job to make him look good, make the whole lot of them sound good. They'd got back from what was supposed to be a short tour supporting a bigger band, and come out of it with the biggest gig of their lives. This was the time for *working*.

If his heart was elsewhere, then, well, Tone was right. Stan was okay for now.

By the time they were working through the second half of the set, Ben felt a strange combination of stress and comfort zinging through his veins. He knew this. Soundchecking had been a regular thing setting up for the gig for each night of the tour. Normally their slot was after the headline act had had their chance to set up, so Ares had a few scrambled minutes in which to make sure the levels were right before they got booted offstage.

Now they were running the entire set, and people were taking them seriously, as artists, not just a bunch of mates pissing about. They had time to run each song, to make sure it sounded good in the echoing space of the Academy.

"Do we have time to run 'Out of Here' again?" Summer asked as they finally finished up the last number in the set.

Ben groaned and ran his hands over his face, then pulled his guitar off and handed it to one of the sound-tech guys.

"You lot can if you want," he muttered. "I've got a headache. I'm going to go have a smoke and sleep before tonight."

Summer went to protest, but Tone said something under his breath that Ben didn't catch as he walked off the stage, out of the glare of the lights.

Technically, they weren't supposed to smoke backstage, but the dressing room smelled like weed, and Ben guessed he wasn't the first one to light up back here. He could hear the others arguing, the sound tinny over the relay, and he decided to ignore them. The gig would be fine, and they could spend hours rehearsing songs they could all play with their eyes shut and one hand tied behind their backs.

A battered sofa slumped in one corner of the dressing room under a large window. The glass was pebbled like the ones sometimes used in bathrooms. Ben pushed open the window, then dug into his backpack for the weed he'd got off Tone earlier in the day.

He skinned up quickly, and as the first drag on the joint hit his lungs, Ben felt himself starting to relax, just a little bit.

The others were still bitching on stage, so he guessed he wasn't going to be interrupted. There was something to be said for being home, even if he was actually pretty desperate to rewind the clock a few weeks and be back in Manchester, when things were amazing, so he could beg Stan to stay with them on tour and not go back to London on his own.

This city was home now, more than Auckland, definitely more than Oxford. This little corner of the world was his, where he fit in, with people who looked like he did and liked the same music and whose thoughts ran in similar directions.

Ben exhaled heavily, knowing the weed was making him philosophical. His headache had eased a little, but he was still bone-tired, unable to rest, the knots of tension coiled around his spine not allowing anything more than a few minutes' sleep at a time.

The sofa stank, when Ben put his head down on the arm, so he pulled his hoodie off and balled it into a pillow, trusting that Tone would come and get him when it was time to move. It was fucking uncomfortable, being curled up like this, and he wouldn't rest. Not really. Not while so much was still up in the air.

Still.

BEN BOUNCED a few times on the balls of his feet, shaking his hands as the lights on stage went down and the noise from the crowd rose into a roar. The tickets for the show had only been a couple of quid on the door, and it seemed the London audiences had caught the buzz from social media and turned up in numbers big enough to pack the venue.

This was undoubtedly the biggest crowd they'd played to yet, and it was *their* gig. Not a support act this time. He didn't have anywhere to hide.

Someone passed Ben a mic, and he nodded his thanks, waited for the signal from the tech that the mic was live before growling into it.

"Ladies and gentlemen... put your fucking hands together and give this bunch of wankers one hell of a welcome home.... It's Ares."

Tone led the way onto the stage, sprinting onto the riser that held his drum kit and smashing at it a few times as the audience screamed. The others all fell into position, and Jez picked up a low reverb on his guitar while Summer plinked a few random keys.

They had this down now, the opening to the show where Ben swaggered out, picked up his guitar, and threw the strap over his shoulder before Tone tapped out the four-four rhythm and they launched into the first song.

This was one they'd written while on the road out of sheer boredom. It had been one of those strange situations where everything seemed to collide at the right moment—the beat and the bass led the song through the first verse, but the melody of the chorus made it good. Better than good. Ben had been humming a note progression for days, and it had come to a head when they were on the bus travelling between Manchester and Glasgow.

He'd been sitting on his bunk, picking out the tune on his acoustic when Tone had found the rhythm, tapping it out on one of the amps. In the three-hour journey, they wrote the whole song, lyrics and all, soundchecked it that afternoon, and debuted the song in Glasgow that night.

It had been reworked and polished a bit since then, but Ben couldn't help but think Ares had really come together with "Out of Here."

"Are you ready for this, London?" Ben screamed into the mic before taking the lead on the vocals. *"Don't know where you came from, don't matter where you been. All I know is, we're gonna get out of here."*

The next song in the set was "London," which made perfect sense, even though the two songs had never been intended to sit side by side. "Out of Here" was about escaping from your home town for the bright lights of a city, and "London" was the band's tribute to the place that had become home, though the story was more about a hooker.

This crowd was completely on their side, and Ben was still baffled that they had managed to gather some kind of underground following, thanks to a few dodgy recordings of their gigs that had been posted on YouTube and social media. That was pretty much what it all came down to—people talking, someone saying they liked a song, downloading it illegally. From that alone they'd built up this small knot of fans, a following that was enthusiastic enough to get the Brixton Academy packed out for a homecoming gig. This was nothing like the night they'd played at the back of the pub, a small thing now, thinking back on it, even though it had been epic at the time. They had changed over the course of the tour, all of them, and Ares too.

Just after eleven the band got off stage, finishing, as always, with their rocked-out version of "Teenage Kicks."

"Do you like the Undertones?" Jez asked the crowd, waiting for their resounding roar before continuing. "Then you're going to be really fucking disappointed because we're about to murder a classic."

Before their audience had the chance to laugh, they launched into the song; this call and response had been perfected in the gigs that had come before. Despite the energy that was always blasted at them from the crowd during this song, for the past few weeks Ben had found it almost impossible to find the energy to go wild, to give it the screaming, raw energy the Undertones deserved. Tonight, though, he drove the song into a new pace, letting every one of his senses take him higher and higher until he was aware of the sweat on his face, the ache in his fingertips, the hoarseness at the back of his throat. The heat, the noise, the soreness in his retinas caused by the bright stage lights. One of his socks was twisted in his boot and it was uncomfortable. All of it.

As soon as he got backstage, Ben crashed.

The others were still buzzing, not that Ben blamed them. It had been the best gig they'd ever played by a long shot, giving their home town audience something truly special. Who knew when they'd get a gig again, especially one of this size, and they'd done it justice. He'd done it.

Instead of going out with the band to celebrate, Ben went home, to the flat he'd shared with Stan for only a few weeks before it all went to shit. He'd only slept for twenty minutes or so after the soundcheck before Tone had dragged him out to get food, and Ben had reluctantly admitted he needed to eat.

He walked around while time slipped away from him. The overwhelming feeling of helplessness was only getting stronger, and he had absolutely no idea how to handle that. He ended up in the bathroom, his back to the bath and his face in his hands.

Half a second later, he shuddered as the breath was stolen from his lungs, and he gasped again, his back seizing with the next convulsion.

In the back of his mind, he recognised this as a panic attack, even as black spots danced at the edges of his vision. His heart hammered in his chest, and his fingertips went numb, then surged back to life with throbbing pins and needles.

Ben stuck his head between his knees, not sure if this would do anything but needing to do *something*. He clutched the fabric of his jeans. Fought for the next breath, then the next one. *Fuck*, this hurt.

He looked up and his eyes fixed on a black lipstick case. Stan's lipstick.

Blinking the tears from his eyes, Ben pushed through the next heaving breath. Then the next one.

His chest still ached, so did his throat, but it was easing. As he finally caught his breath, Ben gave way to the tears he'd been holding back for so long. He finally understood why people said crying was cathartic. All the emotions he wasn't ready to feel pushed up to the surface, and he was forced to feel them all at once, and the only reasonable way to get rid of them was to cry it out.

After a while, feeling pathetic and sorry for himself, Ben stood and turned the tap on, letting the cold water run over his hands, then washed his face.

Even though all he wanted was to go back to the hospital and sleep in one of the awful visitors' chairs next to Stan's bed, he didn't want Stan to see a broken man in place of his boyfriend. No, to be strong for the person he loved, Ben had to be strong himself, and trying to stand up and be there for Stan meant sleeping, eating, showering.

Ben winced and sniffed his T-shirt. It was rank.

He stripped it off and tossed it into the laundry basket. He brushed his teeth, then went to the bedroom and pulled clean clothes out to sleep in. The sheets smelled familiar, another sign of home, and despite the absolute terror still clutching his heart, Ben crawled between the sheets and slipped into sleep as easy as a knife in butter.

THE INTENSIVE care ward had been a terrifying place. Stan hadn't been awake for a lot of it, but he could remember that. Something about the dim lights, the constant noise of machines humming and beeping around him, the stale smell of bodies, the harsh sting of antiseptic made it all so disconcerting. Something about that ward made him feel like he could die at any moment.

That wasn't necessarily an exaggeration.

The eating disorders ward had some fancy title, named after some guy who had donated a load of money to the hospital, according to Leslie. It didn't make the place any nicer, but after almost a week in the intensive care ward, he took what he could get.

Leslie had told him Ben had visited and he'd snapped at her that she should have woken him. Then he'd felt bad, and apologised, and decided he didn't want to see Ben after all. Or, more accurately, he didn't want Ben to see *him*.

The door to his room on this ward wasn't solid; instead it was dominated by a large window. Anyone could walk past and see into his space, which wasn't exactly helping with Stan's anxiety. It meant, though, that he could see when Leslie stepped up and knocked lightly on the glass.

He nodded, and she pushed the door open far enough to stick her head around.

"Ben's here," she said softly.

"Leslie." It was a plea. *Don't make me make a decision.*

Ben made it for him, gently pushing his way around Leslie and into the room.

"Hey," Stan said. He ached all over, but seeing Ben made another ache pang deep in his chest. Ben didn't deserve this. No one did.

"Hi."

"I'll come back in about half an hour to do your feed," Leslie said, then shut the door behind herself as she left.

Ben hovered for a moment, then his shoulders sagged and Stan felt the sickening, hot rush of guilt. He chewed at his lip and blinked back tears, wanting nothing more than to pull Ben into his arms and whisper apologies until everything was right again.

"Are you going to leave me?" Stan asked as Ben hovered close to the door. "If you are, go now. I don't need an explanation. Just go."

"I'm not leaving you," Ben said, his eyes wide, horrified. "Jesus, Stan."

"You want to stay?" Stan said. His voice was scratchy, his throat sore from the NG tube. "With me like this?"

"I'm not leaving you," he said again. This seemed to prompt him into action and he grabbed one of the hard plastic chairs next to the bed and slumped into it. After a second, he reached for Stan's hand.

"You could have called me," he continued. "Anytime, Stan. I would have come home if I knew you needed me."

Stan shook his head and let Ben thread their fingers together. "Not now, Ben."

"Huh?"

"Not now."

Stan tipped his head back, and Ben brushed his lips over his knuckles, and for a while, they sat in silence. Together.

Over the next few days, Ben traded off visiting hours with Kirsty as they took turns to come see him in-between his long periods of sleeping and seemingly infinite meetings with doctors and therapists. Kirsty was a wreck.

"I'm so sorry, Stan," she said for what felt like the hundredth time.

He didn't want to be too hard on her; every night this week she'd raced from the office to the hospital to be able to sit with him for an hour. It meant she'd travelled in the wrong direction and it would take her another hour to get home. She looked as wrecked as Ben and had taken to wearing her awful, old-lady lumpy cardigans again. He wanted to take her by the shoulders and shake some sense into her. If only he had the strength for that.

"Don't be." Her pale green eyes filled with tears again and he gave her a stern look. "Stop it."

"I should have—"

"Stop it," he told her again. "I am serious, Kirsty."

"I'm sorry."

He let out a breathless laugh. "Distract me," he told her, stretching his arms up until his IV line pulled and his spine popped. "Tell me all the horrible things people are saying about each other at work."

He hadn't ever needed to ask her for that twice. She still hesitated for a moment before launching into a scathing review of what someone had said about someone else's choice in footwear, and Stan let the familiar rise and fall of her voice soothe him.

A BLACK bunny rabbit was sitting on the cabinet next to his bed when Stan returned from his therapy session, and a man hunched in the chair under the window. Tone looked fairly content to wait as Leslie helped Stan out of the wheelchair and hooked him back up to the monitor by his bedside.

"I'll come back in a bit," she said, looking over at Tone, then backing out of the room.

"Thank you," Stan murmured. He wasn't sure if she heard him or not.

"Alright, Stan?" Tone asked, his voice light.

"Tone," Stan said and shook his head, the action pulling at the tubes that had been inserted into his nose. "Go home. Please. I do not want you to see me like this."

He reached out and snagged Hades the bunny, then brought it up to his nose. The toy smelled like Ben, like his cologne and the stuff he put on his hair, and Stan's heart ached.

"No offence, mate, but you've got no chance," Tone said in his gentle burr. "I'm a bit pissed off that you didn't call me before now, to be honest."

Stan turned away and sniffed.

Tone was quiet for a few minutes as the beeps and whirrs of the machines, and the constant, quiet hum of the hospital filled the space between them. Stan's fingers twitched and threaded between Tone's in a quiet gesture of solidarity.

"I want to tell you about Kat," Tone said.

Stan turned to him and frowned. "You have a cat?"

Tone grinned and rubbed at his beard. "No. Kat was my girlfriend, when I lived in Bristol."

"Okay."

"She was... she was something else," Tone said with a warm smile, leaning back in his chair and releasing Stan's hand. He rubbed at his scruffy beard, and Stan noticed for the first time the few silvery threads among the darker hairs. Tone's age was almost completely unguessable—he could be anywhere between twenty-five and forty-five years old. "Gorgeous. She had dark hair but she used to dye it loads of different colours. I liked it best when she went red. It suited her somehow."

"What happened?" Stan asked, sure, for reasons he couldn't name, that something terrible had occurred.

"She was hit by a drunk driver," Tone said slowly. "One Friday night in town. She wasn't drunk—just on her way out with friends for a few in the pub where I worked at the time. The guy didn't stop, but he didn't get much further either. He ran off the road and hit a wall. The doctors told me after that, the force of the impact would have snapped her neck. The chances were, she didn't know anything, was probably dead before she knew she'd been hit."

"Oh, Tone," Stan sighed.

"Kat was the love of my life," he said. "I adored that girl. We were only kids—twenty-two—but I knew I wanted to marry her and have a whole bunch of sprogs. That was our plan. I was just waiting 'til I earned enough money to be able to look after her properly. Whenever people would ask when we were getting married, she'd tell them I couldn't afford her. She was teasing, but she was right. I was going to do right by her. Buy a house, get her a sparkly ring, spend our lives together.

"She," Tone started, then rubbed his hands over his face and sighed. "Kat was a beautiful person. On the outside and inside. Someone took her from me, and it broke me, Stan. I broke."

When Stan reached out, Tone let him take his hand.

"I thought, for a very long time, I was going to go after her. Chase her into whatever world she's in now, be with her there."

"You were going to kill yourself."

"Yes," Tone said simply. "As far as I was concerned, a life without Kat in it wasn't worth living. It took someone dragging me to London to sort myself out."

"And now?" Stan asked.

Tone smiled and started to unbutton the flannel shirt he was wearing, revealing pale skin and dark hairs on his chest. On his collarbone was a tattoo of a grey cat, curled up asleep.

"I keep her with me," he said simply.

"Why do you tell me these things?" Stan asked wearily.

"Because I know what it's like to be at rock-bottom," Tone said. "I know what it's like to feel you can't get out of bed, you can't wash yourself or feed yourself or even breathe without effort. I also know the only way you can get out of that absolute pit of depression is with the love of your friends. I had someone take me out of Bristol and get me to somewhere I could start again, not forgetting Kat—never forgetting her—but finding my place in a world where she doesn't exist. There isn't going to be anyone who comes and asks if you want help. I'm going to barge right in and be here whether you want me or not."

"I want you," Stan said softly. "Well—not in that way."

Tone laughed, the sound obscenely loud in the quiet room. "Good. I think Ben might rip my balls off if I come on to you like that."

"You're bigger than him," Stan pointed out.

"True. He could likely still kick my arse, though."

"Was it Ben who brought you here? To London?" Stan asked.

"No. I met him after I arrived. It was someone else."

Stan decided not to push, and let his head drop back against the pillow. The conversation had exhausted him, and he felt sleep taking over.

"Tone?" he said softly.

"Yeah?"

"Thank you."

"Anytime, mate. Anytime."

THE NEXT time he woke, Tone had gone and Ben had taken his place at the vigil point at Stan's side. Stan stretched, feeling his muscles protest at the movement, then sighed as he relaxed back against the pillows.

"Hey," Ben said softly.

"There is no need to speak to me like I am dying," Stan snapped. "I am still very much alive."

"Sorry."

Ben looked like shit. His hair needed to be cut or styled or *something*; it looked like a bird's nest. He had dark circles under his eyes, which were bloodshot.

Stan reached for him and watched as their fingers slowly twined together. Ben brushed his lips over the back of Stan's knuckles, then laid his cheek down on them.

"Are you sleeping?" Stan asked, extracting his hand to smooth it through Ben's hair.

"Not really. I miss you."

His eyes flickered at the sweet attention, dark lashes landing on his cheeks, revealing his blue-veined eyelids. Stan felt a smile tug at the corner of his lips, and he dug his fingernails into Ben's hair, scratching his scalp, making Ben hum with pleasure.

For a long time, all they needed was this. Stan wasn't tired, not really, not even exhausted like he had been for so long. This was so familiar; being quiet together, just existing alongside another person.

When Stan thought Ben might have fallen asleep, he managed to tear his eyes away from Ben's relaxed face and looked around the room. Tone had brought flowers, not ones that smelled too strong, an explosion of bright yellow, pink, and white roses. They sat in a vase to the left of his bed, and Stan smiled at the sight as he brushed his fingers through Ben's hair again.

There was a small table under the window on the far side of the room where someone—Stan guessed Tone, again—had left a bunch of fat green grapes, some San Pellegrino bottled water, and a massive box of chocolates from Hotel Chocolat. For some reason, this made him smile again. Tone didn't care what anyone else thought and probably didn't see anything wrong with taking chocolates to a guy who had been hospitalised for an eating disorder. He'd probably smuggled them in so the nurses didn't know.

Under his hand, Ben stirred, and he twisted until his lips were resting against the pulse point on Stan's wrist. Stan stroked his cheek with his thumb and sighed.

"Tell me about the band," he said softly. "What happened after the tour?"

Ben kissed his wrist again and leaned back in the chair, bringing his feet up until his Chucks were caught on the edge of the seat. He threw his arms up and over the chair's back and stretched, popping his spine.

"We recorded an EP when we were moving around," he said. "I told you about that, right?"

"Bits of it, yeah."

"Well, it's all done now. The whole thing needs to be mixed, but we can't really afford to pay someone to do it for us, so Jez is messing about with it. There's two songs on the website now, and we're hoping to launch 'Out of Here' as a single next month."

"That would be amazing. My boyfriend, the rock star."

Ben grinned then, as Stan had hoped he would. "I wouldn't go that far."

"I would. That's what I'm going to tell everyone around here."

"I don't mind everyone knowing you have a boyfriend," Ben said. He was smiling properly now, not the half-arsed, concerned "how are you" smiles Stan had been seeing from him the past few days.

"I heard you had a pretty good gig at the Academy too. I wish I could have been there."

Ben nodded. "You've been talking to Tone."

"Oh yes. He tells me a lot."

"It's weird how close you are."

"Really?"

Shrugging, Ben blushed and smiled. "He's my best mate, you know? My best mate and my boyfriend." He played with a rip across the knee of his jeans. "Will you tell me what happened?"

Stan sighed and tipped his head back against the huge white pillow. Even though Ben had been visiting for a while, he hadn't asked this. Stan had been waiting for the questioning; it was almost a relief for Ben to have finally caved.

"I wish I knew myself."

"Just talk to me. Everything was so amazing in Manchester."

"It was." Stan smiled at the memory of that night, of feeling so alive, so in love with life and this man. "I got back, and it was just all so… I missed you so much, but I couldn't dwell on that. There was so much to do, at work, and it was all so busy."

The hospital room was always too warm, so Stan kept the window cranked open, knowing he was lucky to be in a room where this was possible. He was always uncomfortable here; stripped of his clothes and his make-up and all the things that made him feel like himself, the rounder, softer person that he'd created. The Stan who had thousands of followers on Instagram and thousands more on his blog, the person with the carefully crafted public persona wasn't allowed to exist in here.

Stan lifted his head and gathered his long hair into a ponytail, wrapping it around on itself to keep it off his sticky neck.

"I wouldn't have thought about it if the doctors here hadn't forced me to," he admitted. "It was how I used to be, all the time, and I suppose I never saw anything wrong with it."

"You don't have to tell me if you don't want to."

Wasn't that just it, though? Ben would always be there, he'd always understand, even when it was hard, even when Stan didn't want to talk because letting this out made him feel more vulnerable than he had ever allowed himself to feel before.

"I used to drink a black tea for breakfast," Stan said with a heavy, weary sigh, "then have some sushi around three or four. Just a few pieces, you know, because the other girls in the office would nag if I didn't eat anything. Then I'd get home around eight, sometimes later, and work on the blog for a few hours. It's going really well—or it was, anyway. Blogging is so fickle. They've probably all abandoned me now. Anyway," he sighed again. "I had a green tea before bed, and that was it. Sometimes a handful of nuts in the evening, if I remembered to eat them."

"Fuck," Ben said.

"It wasn't a conscious thing. I didn't get up in the morning and actively decide not to eat anything. It just happened, you know, I got back into old habits. The way things are when…."

"Finish that sentence."

"When someone isn't there to watch out for me."

Ben was silent for a few moments. "Is this my fault?"

"No! Not at all. Please don't think that. Ben, I... I... I lie here at night and I can't sleep because all I do all fucking day is sleep, and I think about how you hold me when we're in bed together and how you make love to me like I matter. I hate that I'm stuck here, and I hate that it's my fault, and I don't want to be one of those people who is so dependent on their partner that they cannot function on their own. But I need you, Ben, and that scares me even more than the thought of not being healthy." He pushed angry tears away from his cheeks and refused to look over at Ben. Stan sniffed, blinked, and more tears fell. "I love you, but I know I don't want our relationship to be you looking after me for the next fifty or sixty or seventy years. I want to be your partner."

"You are," Ben said. "I... fuck this shit. Come here."

"What?"

Ben pushed himself out of the chair and pulled the heart monitor from Stan's finger. The feeding tube and his IV drip both snaked off to the left of his body, meaning with the heart monitor gone, Ben could get into the bed next to Stan and pull him awkwardly into his arms.

It took a few minutes of shifting and gently moving the tubes and drip out of the way, then Stan was cradled in the safest place he knew; head on Ben's chest, sat sideways on Ben's lap with his arms wrapped solidly around Stan's waist.

"Better?" Ben murmured.

"Yeah."

"Stan?"

"Hmm?"

"Who the fuck brought you chocolates?"

"Oh." Stan giggled and spread his palm over Ben's chest, stretching his fingers so he could touch as much of his boyfriend as possible. "Tone, I think."

"When I see him, I'm going to kick his head in."

"Please don't. I don't mind. He came to see me earlier. He's very sweet."

Ben brushed his lips back and forth over Stan's hair, back and forth, back and forth. "Better now?" he asked.

"Yes. So much better."

It was. Ben's chest was strong and solid under Stan's cheek, his skin warm, smelling of sweat and smoke and fabric softener. His arms held Stan securely, not too tight, but certainly not letting him go anywhere. It was nothing more, nothing less, than absolute security.

CHAPTER FOURTEEN

OVER THE next few days, Stan and Ben proceeded to piss each other the hell off. Ben was bone-tired, unable to sleep without his stupid bunny rabbit or Stan to hold, forcing himself to eat because it seemed grossly hypocritical if he didn't. He went from band practice to the hospital, picking up shifts at the bar when they needed him, then back to an empty flat, and felt hollow and exhausted.

Stan was pissed off about being kept in the hospital when he felt ready to go home. The collapse that had taken him to the Accident and Emergency Department in the first place had been attributed to a urinary tract infection, something that had been cleared up with a course of antibiotics. He wasn't being discharged yet, though. The doctors wanted to keep a closer eye both on his weight and attitude to eating, and monitor his kidney and liver function.

Ben's weariness and Stan's acidic attitude clashed, the resulting friction only smoothed by Tone's creamy baritone and Kirsty's gentle motherly fussing. Tone and Kirsty had jobs, though, and couldn't commit the same time to Stan's bedside that Ben could.

Stan was still too thin. Ben brushed his fingertips back and forth over Stan's wrist, knowing his partner would likely always be somewhere on the scale of "too thin," and that it would be his job to monitor that scale for the rest of their lives. It was a responsibility he was going to take seriously but keep to the back of his mind. Watching Stan like a hawk wasn't going to do either of their mental states any good.

"You don't look at me like you used to," Stan said plaintively, looking down at Ben with big, sorrowful eyes.

"What do you mean?"

"You used to touch me different too. You look at me and touch me like I'm about to break."

"Well, what do you want?" Ben snapped.

"I want you to grab my ass. You used to grab my ass all the time."

Ben sighed heavily and looked away. "It's difficult when you're in a hospital bed, Stan. For fuck's sake."

"You don't want to fuck me anymore."

"No," Ben said, hating the sharpness in his voice. "Not right now I don't, Stan."

"Go away," Stan mumbled, and turned his head to the window.

"No," Ben repeated. "You know what? No. We're going to do this, and I'm going to sound like an utter bastard, but fuck you, Stan. Fuck you. When we're together, it's incredible. I've never in my life felt the way I do when we have sex, because you matter to me. That's why there's a ring on your finger, and that's why I made a promise to you. Because when we make love, it's not about me or you or bodies or getting off, it's about what we are as people, and what we mean to each other.

"Right now I don't feel like your lover," Ben said, slapping his hand on the edge of the mattress. "And I don't feel like fucking you, because even though I love you to the stars and back, and I will do anything for you, this body and this version of you isn't one that turns me on. I don't get hard thinking about you like this. I don't think about bending you over a fucking hospital bed and pounding your ass. I want you to get healthy, come home, and we can make love again. That's what I want."

"What if…?"

"There is no 'what if,'" Ben said, throwing his hands up in exasperation. "I love you. That's it. That has to be enough to make you want those things, Stan. I can't give you any more than that. I love you. Please. If you love me too, the only thing I want you to promise me is to never take the man I love away from me. Never take the man who made my life complete away. I would never be able to forgive you if you did that."

"Ben," Stan said, and when Ben looked up, tears were rolling down his cheeks. Ben pushed his palms over his own wet cheeks, sniffing. "Take me home. Please."

"I'll get you there," Ben said. "I promise."

STAN'S NURSE was all in favour of the feeding tube coming out, which was the first step in the process to getting Stan out of the ward and back to the flat. It was uncomfortable, worse than it going in, somehow, as they gently extracted the long, flexible tube from his nose. Ben held his hand and scowled at Leslie while she spoke soothingly to Stan as she completed the procedure.

Almost as soon as it was out, Stan started to feel better. He'd be kept in the hospital for a while longer, for observation on the eating disorders ward, but Leslie was confident they were working towards letting him go home.

"Soon?" he pressed as she passed him a meal-replacement shake for his dinner. It was too soon for him to go back to solid foods, not after he'd been tube fed for the past two weeks, and the shakes meant high-calorie, high-nutrition meals.

"It's up to you, love," she said. "Find your reason to get out of here, and you'll get there quicker."

"I'm going home to live with my partner," Stan said decisively. "To be with Ben."

"There you go, then. Drink it."

He did, sipping and wrinkling his nose at the artificial sweetness.

Ben had brought Stan's laptop and some clothes—real clothes, that he was allowed to wear now he'd been upgraded and taken off high-level observation. Stan was encouraged to interact with other patients on the ward, though he often found himself depressed by their stories and preferred to sit in his room and work.

The blog he'd been running for years had continued without him with only a very small blip in his posting schedule. Stan had warred with himself for a few days on whether or not he was going to come clean and admit why he hadn't been responding to messages, comments, or tweets for a few weeks. In the end, he gave an edited version of the truth and wrote an article that danced around his personal experiences while discussing eating disorders in the fashion industry as a whole.

In the past, Stan had written about gender identity—at times at length—plus-size fashion, LGBT issues, and more, so his readers were used to his own particular brand, which combined his insider industry knowledge with things that affected him personally.

When he woke up, acutely aware Ben wasn't next to him, and the rabbit in the crook of his elbow giving only a small amount of comfort, Stan knew things were changing around him. The constant, annoying beep of the monitors was gone now that he'd been moved to a new ward. He had been given a room of his own—a luxury, and he knew it—because of some argument around his gender. Putting him in a room with another boy or a girl was fraught with too much politics for the hospital administration staff to handle.

That meant no one asked about Hades, and even though his day was regulated in terms of meals and activities and group therapy and individual therapy, he was allowed to get up and turn on his laptop and work on things that were important to him. And that was important.

After about half an hour, Stan flipped the lid of the laptop down and stretched, then rolled out of bed and padded through to his bathroom. When he'd first moved into this room, Stan thought it was almost like a hotel. That was, until he noticed all the little things that were a constant reminder that he was being watched, all the time, and he was still in hospital.

He didn't have a shower so much as a wet room, with handles on the walls and a flip-down seat for when the person using it didn't feel strong enough to stand. That had shocked Stan, after he was admitted here, how he didn't feel strong enough to stand up on his own. He'd been running between his flat and work in *heels*, on the Underground, lugging around his laptop and a huge bag, and he'd been fine. Then, after he'd collapsed, he couldn't even stand up on his own any more.

It was like he had been running on a combination of grief and fury, and once that emotion was sucked from his body, he didn't have anything left.

There wasn't a mirror in the bathroom. Stan knew why.

He turned on the water and shed his clothes, then stuck his hand under the shower to wait for it to warm up. Kirsty had gone out and bought Stan's favourite type of shampoo and shower gel. Even though the shampoo was expensive, she didn't say anything or ask for the money back. She'd found the conditioner that went with it too and scowled at Stan so hard when he tried to say something about getting some cash out to cover it. Kirsty was the sort of friend people had talked about, Stan had read about, but hadn't really known existed.

He ducked under the spray and sighed, letting the warm water be its own kind of comfort. A few minutes later, a light knock sounded from the doorframe. He wasn't yet allowed a door between the bathroom and the bedroom.

"Stan?"

"Yeah?"

"You okay?"

"I'm just taking a shower," he said, trying not to be annoyed. The nurse was only doing her job.

"You should have called for me. I'll just wait in here."

"Fine." And he definitely snapped that word out.

He still took his time, lathering the shampoo through his hair and washing all the suds out before doing it again, then slicking it through with conditioner. Washing his body was harder, but Kirsty had bought him one of those fuzzy shower-sponge things so Stan didn't have to feel all of his protruding bones, a constant reminder of how deathly skinny he was. It helped. A little.

When he was done, he wrapped his hair in a towel turban and pulled a dressing gown around his shoulders.

"Okay?" the nurse asked when he stepped back into his room.

He nodded.

"Good. Breakfast will be in the canteen in half an hour. You think you can be ready for that?"

He nodded again.

She smiled and left.

Being able to pick out his own clothes and put on make-up in the morning had made more of a difference than anything else. This too was monitored, and Stan was often asked to explain the choices he'd made. Why that shirt? Why lip gloss today, when he hadn't the day before? Why this hairstyle?

When Leslie knocked on the door and let herself into the room, Stan had just finished tying his hair up into a loose knot at the base of his neck.

"Can I come in?" she asked. She always asked. None of the other nurses did.

"Of course. Good morning," Stan said, straightening up on the bed.

"Morning. You're up early."

"I suppose."

"Sleep well?"

Stan nodded. "Not as well as if I were at home." It wasn't meant to be rude, just a simple statement. He'd never sleep as well here as he did with Ben. He gestured to the bed, and Leslie came and sat down on the end.

Technically, she wasn't his nurse anymore. She worked on the intensive care ward, but she still came in to see Stan when she was working, usually before her shift started, or just after she'd finished.

"I was talking to Dr Cardwell," she said. "He thinks we should be able to get you home in the next few days. You didn't hear that from me, though."

"Really?" he asked, trying, and failing, to not get his hopes up.

Leslie smiled and nodded. "Yep. I'm so pleased you decided to stay here, Stan. I'm not sure if you see the difference, but I certainly do."

She spoke like this, about Stan's "choices," like he'd been the one to make decisions about himself since he'd been admitted. He hadn't. Things had been done to him—like the feeding tube—decisions made for him.

He reached for her hand and squeezed. Stan thought they both probably knew he wouldn't keep in contact when he left, not with the nurses or the therapists, or anyone else from the hospital.

"Thanks," he said. "I have to be at breakfast in a minute."

"I'm going that way. Let me walk with you." She brushed her hand over Stan's shoulder, silently admiring the cut of his shirt. "Your hair looks nice today."

"Thanks," he said, and smiled.

TONE SET the pint down with far more force than was necessary, and Ben nodded his thanks without looking up. Then he set down two shot glasses of clear liquid.

"Oh, fucking hell, Tone," Ben grumbled. "I'm not in the mood for getting hammered."

"Too late," Tone said. "Drink up."

Ben did the shot—*tequila*—and shuddered, chasing it with his beer, which made his stomach turn.

"Good boy." Tone took his own shot neatly, then pushed the two glasses to the edge of the table. They leaned back in the comfy booth, the surroundings of the pub familiar, even though so much had changed over the course of one short summer.

"I'm really not in the mood for this," Ben said.

"I know, mate. I know."

"Why does he talk to you and not me?" Ben heard the petulant tone to his voice, did nothing to hide it.

"Uh, rude," Tone drawled. He sipped his pint and grinned. "Dunno. Me and Stan… in a parallel universe, we'd make beautiful babies."

Ben laughed once, hard, the sound unfamiliar in his ears. "That's so fucking weird," he said on another laugh.

They were quiet for a few moments, not an uncomfortable silence; they knew each other too well, and had done for too long, for this to matter.

"Tell me what's going through your head," Tone said simply.

"I don't even know myself. Stan is so… he's… he needs me. And that's so fucking weird, because I don't think anyone has ever needed me before."

"What about me?"

Ben laughed softly. "Yeah, alright. You need me to haul your fat arse home after a night out. But with Stan—I'm starting to realise we mean more to each other than I thought we did. And before we left on tour, I put a fucking ring on his finger."

"Stan's stronger than you give him credit for."

"Is he?"

Tone nodded sagely. "He's got this inner steel, you know? He'll keep fighting."

"I don't know how I can stay in the band," Ben said. He expected some kind of lightness to follow this confession, for it to suddenly feel like the weight had been lifted from his shoulders, and Tone would be able to help him fix it all. Instead, he got an angry, incredulous stare.

"You are shitting me, right?" Tone demanded.

"No. Stan needs me, you said it yourself. He'll keep fighting if he has me, and I have no idea how I'm supposed to keep going and touring and all that shit if it means he gets left at home. He's out of chances now, Tone. You know that. There is no more relapse. Once more means he could die, and I can't let that happen. I can't."

"Why does it have to be one or the other?" Tone demanded. "Can't you have both?"

"Do you know what the life of a touring musician is like?" Ben said, struggling to get his point across. "We're going to be working our arses off now, especially because we don't have a record deal and representation to do all the other crap for us. The band can survive without me. Stan can't."

"It sounds like you've made your decision already. So, what? You're just going to walk?" Tone chugged half of his pint, then pushed the glass away. "Fuck that, Ben. You're what makes us."

"Dude. That sounds so gay."

Tone snorted with laughter but turned away so Ben couldn't see the amusement on his face.

"Ares won't make it without you, Ben," Tone said. When he turned back, his expression was neutral. "We won't."

"The EP is already recorded. You can release it, and—"

"And what? Suddenly our lead guitarist walks away? How are we supposed to handle that?"

"Replace me." The thought burned in Ben's chest. The very last thing he wanted was to see some other twat up on stage playing with his friends.

"No," Tone said simply.

"Tone."

"I'm not fucking around," Tone said. "We'll work something out. You can't walk away from Stan, and you can't walk away from the band. So we'll figure it out."

"I don't know what the answer is," Ben said. "All I know is that I have to give Stan my full attention now. I can't half-arse my way through this relationship."

Tone shook his head. "Do you hear yourself?"

"What do you mean?"

"Stan is good, Ben. He's good. He needs help, he needs support, but he is a strong guy. The hardest thing for you to do now is not to be there for him, but to let him be strong for himself. That's what he needs to build his confidence back up—not someone doing that shit for him, but someone standing right next to him cheering him on. Let him do it himself; just be there while he's doing it."

"For a simple West Country bastard, you do sometimes talk sense," Ben said. "Yeah. Alright. I'll try."

"What's he like in bed?" Tone asked.

"What?" Ben laughed at the sudden change in direction. "Are you serious?"

"Yeah. Is he good?"

"You're such a pervert." Ben drained the last of his pint. "Yeah. The sex is incredible."

"He thinks so too," Tone said.

"We really need to get you laid. The thought of you wanking to fantasies of me and Stan doing the nasty is… nasty."

"Hey, when your boyfriend is that hot, you have to accept people are going to wonder what he looks like naked."

"Right now, even I don't know what he looks like naked. Hey… why are you taking him chocolate?" It had been bugging Ben ever since he saw the care package Tone had put together.

Tone shrugged. "Thought he might fancy some."

"Tone. He's in hospital for an eating disorder."

"Doesn't mean he doesn't like chocolate. Look, Ben. I love you. You know that. But you're missing the point with Stan. It's not about food, or being a picky eater. It's about being in control when you feel like everything else in your life is falling apart around you. You know after Kat died I turned into a total alcoholic. That wasn't because I liked the taste of booze. It was because I had no idea how to cope. This is how Stan is dealing with not knowing how to cope. The food isn't the issue, same as the booze wasn't the issue for me. The issue is control."

"Sorry," Ben mumbled. "I should give you more credit." He ran his hands over his face, exasperated and dejected in equal measures.

"You don't need to be Stan's saviour, Ben. He doesn't need one. What he needs is his boyfriend. Giving him something to get up for in the morning. The food issue… well, I can't speak for him, but for me, sorting my life out made the drinking problem go away."

"What sorted your life out, then?" Ben rubbed the back of his neck, feeling a tension headache starting there.

Tone grinned. "You fuckers. The band."

Shit.

"Look, mate, I'm sorry."

Suddenly Ben felt very selfish. The division of loyalties between Stan and Ares was so much more complicated now. It wasn't a question of Stan's health and a group of people who would survive without him, it was one person he loved or another group of people he loved. How the fuck could he make that decision?

"It's okay," Tone said. "I'm in a better place now. But we have something, Ben. Hardly anyone makes it in this fucking industry, and we have a real shot. We're going to have to work our arses off, but there's a chance. We have to take it, to ride it and see what happens. Not to would be an insult to the good name of rock and roll."

Ben laughed again and nodded to Tone's empty glass. "Pint?"

Tone shook his head. "Nah. I told Sherrie I'd watch Emily for a few hours."

"Since when did you turn into the Babysitter's Club?"

Tone flipped him the bird. "Since I lived with them for weeks, you wanker. Emily loves me. Sherrie has a new man friend who wants to take her out. I don't feel like I can say no to her."

"Fair enough," Ben said. "I'll probably go back and see Stan again."

"Remember," Tone said, sliding out of the booth. "Support him as he builds himself up. Don't do it for him. And if he wants to give me that Kirsty's phone number, I'd take real good care of it, I promise."

Ben got out of his seat and, on impulse, wrapped his arms around Tone in a massive bear hug. Tone squeezed back so hard Ben felt his spine pop.

"Thank you," Ben said. "Seriously. I don't know what I'd do without you."

"Be an even more massive prick than you already are," Tone said with absolute gravity. "I love you, man."

"Love you too."

"This is all a bit gay for me," Tone said, not letting go of Ben, or even loosening his grip.

"Don't worry," Ben whispered. "It's not catching."

CHAPTER FIFTEEN

SHERRIE LOOKED around the table, taking stock of each of them in turn. Ben couldn't help but think something was seriously wrong. For one, he and the rest of the band looked ridiculously out of place in Sherrie's dining room. It was a huge, high-ceilinged, very white space, with a glossy, black table and bright pink printed wallpaper along one wall. Incredibly smart, and shiny, and clean, in direct contrast to the scruffy, messy, or downright dirty group of people who sat at the table. Ben had put his hands down on the tabletop and left smudges—now his hands were tucked safely under his thighs.

"Um," Sherrie started, then looked down at her lap. "Okay, this is weird."

"Want me to lower the tone for you, Sher?" Tone asked, giving her a wink. "'Cos your tits look amazing in that top."

"Tone. That's my mum," Geordie said with a groan.

Ben snorted and at least some of the tension broke.

"I just wanted to talk to you about where you're all living," Sherrie said, sounding self-conscious. She still hadn't looked up. "I mean, Tone's still here, and Ben's with Stan. But he's going to lose the flat, right, Ben?"

Ben nodded and waited for Sherrie to look up before he spoke. "If he leaves his job, and I think he's going to, then yeah. We'll have to move out. The flat is owned by the magazine. We're just renting it."

"What are you gonna do?"

"I don't know yet. We'll figure something out."

"Just tell them, Mum," Geordie said softly. He sat next to Sherrie and reached out to squeeze her hand gently.

"I've spoken to a financial advisor, and I want to buy another house. As an investment thing, like."

"Okay," Ben said slowly.

"I thought I could find somewhere up around Camden where you all work, and you could live there."

"What, all of us?" Tone asked.

Sherrie nodded. "Yeah. I'd work it out so all you lot needed to do was cover the bills. The rent should be pretty cheap."

"Sherrie," Jez said. He'd been sitting quietly at the head of the table. "That's a lot, you know." He shook his head.

"It would be an investment piece, like I said. When you're all grown up and want to move out, I can sell it on. Or my girls can live there. I'll find somewhere with enough bedrooms so you've all got your own room. If you're all serious about making the band work...."

"We are," Jez said.

"Well, then, living together has to be a good thing. We can find somewhere that has rehearsal space too."

"Mum," Geordie said, and she grinned at him.

"Yes, darling?"

Tone snorted. "Darling," he repeated, mocking.

"This is pretty amazing."

"Not really. If I was that amazing, I would have bought you your own house, instead of sticking the money in a trust fund until you turn thirty."

"Yeah, I'm not sure I've forgiven you for that yet. Can I help pick the house?"

"Of course you can."

"Don't make it too nice," Tone said. "I wouldn't feel right living somewhere proper posh."

"Yeah," Summer agreed. "It needs to have.... What do they call it? Character."

"Preferably somewhere a bit dank and miserable," Ben said, teasing now, but Tone was nodding.

"Great," Sherrie said. "I need to find a seven-bedroom house in bloody Hampstead Heath and drop five mil on the place, but make sure it's got some asbestos to make you all feel at home."

"You got it, Sher," Tone said, rocking his chair back onto its two rear legs. At Sherrie's disapproving cluck, he dropped it back to all fours.

"Geordie's right, Sherrie," Summer said, leaning to grab Sherrie's hand. "You don't know what this means to us. It might mean we actually make something of the band."

Sherrie shook her head. "All I've ever wanted was to see my kids happy," she said. "Money ain't got much to do with it really, but sometimes it helps." Her grin turned a little watery. "Not sure when I adopted all you lot, but somehow you turned into my kids as well. I want that fucking band to work just as much as the rest of you."

That seemed to decide it. Ben had to admit, getting them all under the same roof would probably do wonders for the band. They were scattered all over London at the moment, and even though they still congregated at Sherrie's house to rehearse, it was getting harder and harder to coordinate time for everyone to get together. No way could they finish an album the way they were going.

As the others ducked out of the dining room, heading to the kitchen and the promise of snacks, Ben hung back until he was alone with Sherrie.

"You alright, Ben love? How's Stan?"

"He's okay," Ben said. "Doing a lot better actually. He should be coming home soon."

"Maybe he can move straight into the new house."

Ben rolled his shoulders, feeling suddenly nervous. Sherrie was already doing such a nice thing for them; it seemed incredibly selfish to ask her for more.

"That's kind of what I wanted to talk to you about," he said. He leaned against the doorframe, then remembered it was white and he probably shouldn't. "Stan is…. I mean, he's amazing, but he's got a lot of hang-ups about being tidy and clean and what he eats. I'm pretty sure he'd be up for living with everyone in theory, but in practice?" He shook his head. "I don't want to sound like the most ungrateful prick on the planet."

Sherrie shook her head. "I get it," she said. "Maybe I can look for somewhere that has a flat above the garage for you two, hmm?"

"I can't ask you for that."

"You're not asking," she said, taking his hand and squeezing. "I'm offering. God knows I feel guilty enough for not keeping an eye on Stan while you were away. This is the least I can do."

"No one blames you for that, Sher," Ben said. "He wasn't your responsibility."

"No, but he's one of you lot, isn't he? One of my kids."

Ben smiled at her, his throat suddenly thick. She squeezed his hand again, then dropped it.

"You go take care of him, love. I'll make sure you're both okay."

"Thanks, Sherrie."

Ben put off telling Stan about the new house for a couple of days, not wanting to remind him about the realities that were waiting for him outside the hospital room. He was making good progress, Leslie was pleased with him, and the regular therapy sessions were starting to rebuild his confidence. Ben knew Stan's goal was to get out as soon as possible, and he couldn't help but feel torn between his desire to have Stan home and to leave him where he was, with all the professional help that came with his stay on the eating disorders ward.

It took Sherrie and Geordie only a couple of days to find a house that fit all of the requirements that had been thrown at them. Sherrie called it a "fixer-upper" and, checking out the pictures online, Ben had to agree.

The house was in a good area, a short bus ride or a longer walk down to the pub if he had to work, only a few streets away from a Tube station that would take him anywhere he wanted to go around London, and with a huge basement where the band could rehearse without disturbing their—likely very posh—neighbours.

Thought you and Stan could have the attic, Geordie told Ben via text message.

There was only one picture of the attic conversion room on the estate agent's website, but it looked like the space was a recent refurbishment. It covered about two thirds of the house's impressive floor space and included an en suite bathroom.

Ben didn't have any furniture of his own, and Sherrie had said she'd kit the place out, but he had some savings set aside and let his mind wander to how he'd set about decorating the room.

Yeah, thanks mate, he texted back.

He didn't have time to say anything else—he was at the top of the escalators at the Tube station and his phone signal was about to disappear.

Their own sofa, he decided as he finally squeezed onto a train and leaned against a door because there were no seats left. With their own sofa, they could watch TV upstairs on their own if they didn't want to socialize with the others. He'd put Stan's sketches on the walls and get a nice, sturdy bed for the two of them.

It was easy to daydream on the Tube; it was one of those places where he wasn't expected to concentrate on anything or interact with anyone, and his mind could fill in all the gaps and come up with possibilities—solutions, instead of problems.

His face was familiar on the ward now, and the nurses waved Ben through without stopping or questioning. He nodded to Leslie, who was sitting at the front desk, and knocked before letting himself into Stan's room.

"Hi," Ben said with a warm smile, pleased to see Stan sitting in the chair next to his bed with his laptop open. He quickly crossed the room and placed soft kisses on Stan's lips.

"Hi, yourself," Stan said when Ben pulled away. "Did you get a haircut?"

"Yeah," Ben admitted, running his hand over his head. "I think they cut the sides too short."

He'd pulled the length of his hair back and secured it with an elastic, keeping the weight off his sweaty neck. He sat down on the edge of the bed, since Stan was in the visitor's chair, and gripped the edge of the mattress.

"I like it," Stan said.

He was back to looking almost normal, in the clothes Ben had brought in for him. It was just jeans and one of Ben's shirts—a blue one, rolled up to the elbows, with a white tank underneath it. Ben thought he looked beautiful.

"I need to talk to you—" he started at the same time Stan spoke.

"Ben, there's something—"

They both laughed, and Ben inclined his head. "After you."

Stan took a deep breath and snapped the lid of his laptop shut. "I'm going to quit my job," he said in a rush.

"Oh?"

"Yeah. I'm still going to write for the magazine, but freelance, instead of being on the staff. I've contacted a few other people I know too, to ask if I can pick up freelance work with them. I think I can keep a much better schedule if I'm in charge of my own workload instead of constantly being pulled onto other things."

"That sounds good," Ben said, nodding. "I mean, you were working ridiculous hours before. If you freelance, then you should be able to control it all a bit better, right?"

"That's the idea," Stan said. He fiddled with the end of his hair, which had been folded into a long braid. "It means I lose the flat, though. It came with the job, and the magazine is going to want it back. I'm not sure how long I have left…."

He trailed off as Ben started to laugh, then held his hands up in apology. "I'm sorry. I'm sorry, baby," he said, still grinning. "I just—I came here to talk to you because Sherrie is buying a house. For the band. So we can all live together."

"Oh," Stan said slowly.

"I came over to ask you to move in with us. That's what I wanted to talk to you about."

Stan pressed his lips together, trying to hide a smile. "Oh," he said again.

Ben slid off the bed and crouched down in front of Stan, pulling both his hands forward and gripping them lightly. "We have our own room," he said. "Geordie texted me to say there's an attic room that's huge, bigger than the others. And it has its own bathroom, which is separate to the rest of the house. I don't know how you feel about living with other people—especially when those people are my friends, who are fucking weird. But it'll be our space up there. The two of us together."

"You know what I want?" Stan said with a sigh.

"Go on. Surprise me."

Stan grinned. "I want… a night in on the sofa, with some horrible film playing on the TV so we don't have to watch it. I want to wear your pyjama pants and an old T-shirt and snuggle."

"Is that it?"

He laughed. "Yeah, pretty much. I want just the two of us, you know? Me and you."

"Snuggling." Ben said the word like he was testing it out. "Do we do that?"

"Yes," Stan said gravely. "You are a very competent snuggler."

"In that case," Ben said, then brushed his lips over Stan's knuckles, "let's work on getting you home. So we can snuggle."

MOVING STUFF out of Stan's flat and into the new house was something Ben expected to do on his own. He'd moved so many times over the past few months, he was starting to get sick of the sight of boxes, especially when they were filled with his stuff.

This time, though, it was something more permanent. Or so he hoped.

Instead of spending a day trying to move all of Stan's things, and treating shit that wasn't his own with respect, Ben bit the proverbial bullet and forked out for a moving company to do the work for him. The cost of the exercise made him wince when he thought about it, so he tried, very hard, not to think at all.

The upshot was, the entire contents of the flat in Bow Quarter were expertly packed, carried downstairs by people who weren't Ben, transported across London to Hampstead Heath, and carried back up three flights of stairs to the attic bedroom. The boxes were dumped in the middle of the room ready for Ben to unpack, and he was ultimately grateful he'd forked over the cash.

He'd spent most of the day "supervising" as the others moved in in drips and drabs. No one was particularly organised, which wasn't surprising in the least. The only things that were taken care of were musical instruments, set up in careful formation in the basement while boxes of clothes and DVDs were scattered through the rest of the house.

If Sherrie hadn't turned up with boxes of pizza and demanded they "clear their shit up," Ben was sure boxes would have remained stacked in the hall for months to come. As it was, Sherrie was scary, plus she owned this place, and they were all still slightly in awe of the fact she would do something so nice for them.

Now all Ben needed was for Stan to come home.

CHAPTER SIXTEEN

STAN SIGHED and tipped his head back. This was his favourite chair in the common room, the one that had a good angle to see out the window and the TV, if he wanted to watch it. TV use was carefully monitored and only the most bland and untriggering of shows allowed, so they were currently all being lulled to sleep by some gardening show.

They were in fucking London. No one here had a fucking garden.

Stan's therapist—or one of them, anyway—was very insistent that Stan integrate himself into the community here. James wanted him to interact with the other residents, to play cards with them, to pick up a knitting class. James didn't seem to realise Stan was a very social person, that he loved being around people, but being surrounded by other eating disorder patients only reminded him he had his own eating disorder to deal with. Stan didn't want to see suffering and pain at every turn. He wanted to see vibrancy and joy.

Still, the best way to escape was to play the game and make the effort, and to make the progress he really needed to make it in the real world. There was something very comforting about the thought of going to live in a house full of people. He'd never particularly wanted that before, but now, having his friends around him seemed like an appropriate new chapter.

"Stan?"

He looked up to where Leslie was standing in the doorway to the common room. Stan smiled at her and unfolded himself from the chair, then rushed over to give her a hug. Leslie stopped by almost every other day, a bright point in this depressing place.

"I've got some news," she said as they stepped into the hall. "I spoke to Dr Caldwell. They're going to soft-release you."

"Does that mean I can go home?"

"Yes." She beamed at him. "You need to come back for all your therapies, but you're essentially an outpatient."

"Oh my God." Stan threw himself into her arms again and tried not to sob.

"It's going to take a day or so to get everything sorted for you," she said, gently rubbing his back. "And I'd expect you're going to spend a lot of time going back and forth to different appointments, so prepare yourself for that."

"Okay. But I can go home. With Ben."

"You can."

"I need to call him."

"Then we should do that."

STAN NEVER expected it to be easy. Nothing about the past month and a half had been easy. Nothing about the few months before *that* had been easy either. All in all, it had been a pretty rocky year.

Ben turned up with Tone, which was probably a good thing. Tone was the only person who was able to keep Ben's mother-hen instincts under control; while Ben wanted to cluck and fuss and do every little thing for Stan, Tone shrugged, called him a prick, and went for a smoke.

"Partner," Stan said, making loose fists and rapping his knuckles against Ben's chest. "Lover. Not carer. Not nurse. Okay?"

Ben kissed the knuckles. "I'll try. I promise to try."

Stan sighed and relaxed into Ben's arms.

"Kirsty said she's sorry she couldn't come help you get home, but she's busy with work. She's going to come over and see the new house later this week."

"Sounds good," Stan mumbled against Ben's chest.

He had paperwork to fill in—so much paperwork—and an agreement between Stan and his primary doctor that any sign of a relapse would mean he was immediately brought back onto the ward for observation. There were lists and nutrition plans and therapy schedules, and Stan wasn't allowed to miss any of those for the time being either. He had responsibilities and the number of a cab service that worked with the hospital and would turn up at his house to take him to his appointments whether Stan called them or not. It was a good service.

Finally, *finally*, they were allowed to leave. As the automatic doors closed behind them, Stan felt a sudden rush of nerves. He wasn't on his own again, not yet, but this was undoubtedly the first step towards that.

"How are you doing?" Ben asked when they were in the cab. Dirty city rain was pounding at the windows, unseasonable yet strangely welcome.

"Good," Stan told him. "I'm excited to see the house."

"You're gonna love it," Tone said. "The kitchen is huge."

"Are you done decorating?"

"Pretty much," Ben said.

"We've got some bloke coming round next week to put proper lights up in the basement," Tone said. "At the moment, we've just got a bunch of lamps down there. It's the only place we can practise without seriously pissing off the neighbours."

"Sounds good."

"And Summer wants to redecorate the living room," Tone said, scratching his belly. "Something about it being too prissy. There's like, flowery wallpaper in there at the moment. I said she should paint it black and be done with it."

"I can help," Stan offered. "I like doing things like that."

Tone grinned. "You should definitely talk to her."

"How's it all working out? You all living together?"

"Well, we arranged a cleaning service after three days," Ben said. "After Jez threw a plate at Geordie's head because he refused to wash it up."

Stan snorted with laughter.

"We've got a fucking dishwasher, for fuck's sake. Anyway. So now we have a cleaner who comes over three times a week to do the kitchen and bathrooms and the living room. When we split the cost between all of us, it's not too bad and it saves on the arguments."

"Sounds like a sensible plan to me."

The rain had eased off by the time they got back to the house. Stan had spent the past ten minutes plastered to the window, becoming steadily more shocked at the size and opulence of the houses in this neighbourhood.

"We don't really live here," he breathed as the car pulled over.

"We really do," Tone said. He passed the driver a few notes and swatted at Stan's hand when he tried to give him some money back.

"This place is gorgeous."

The ground-floor exterior was painted a pale cream, like the other houses on the road, and the upper floors were all exposed brick. It was set back from the road and had a shiny, dark blue front door and a hedge to offer a little privacy.

So classy.

So very not Ares.

Ben shouldered Stan's bag and took Stan's hand, then gently tugged him up the path.

"I've got your keys inside," Ben said.

He used his own set to open the door, revealing a light, bright, airy hallway and curving staircase.

"This must be a joke."

"Nope," Tone said, shutting the door with a bump of his hip. "Take your shoes off, please. There's a cupboard there for you to put them in."

"Oh shit, sorry," Stan said, immediately toeing at his Vans.

"He's winding you up, love," Ben murmured.

"I'm taking them off anyway," Stan insisted. "I can't believe I live here."

"Want to see our room?"

Stan nodded. "Yeah."

"I'll leave you to it," Tone said. "I'm gonna make some lunch."

Ben took Stan's hand again and led him up, and up, and up. Normally this many stairs wouldn't be a problem, but Stan wasn't exactly at full strength. By the time they reached the attic, he was almost out of breath.

"You okay?" Ben asked.

"Fine." Stan waved it off, not wanting the attention.

"So, um, this is it," Ben said as he pushed the door open. "I've kind of fixed it up a bit."

The attic room was bigger than Stan was expecting. Ben had told him a few things already, that he'd repainted and bought new blinds for the skylights. It didn't seem to matter that the walls were a rich, navy blue; there was so much light pouring in from the windows at the front and skylights at the back, the room wasn't dark at all.

The floors were all exposed wood, rich and textured, and their bed was a beautiful, antique-brass double. Ben had brought over the few pieces of furniture Stan had purchased: a lamp, the coffee table, a colourful textured rug. Some familiar things, to make it feel like home.

"The bathroom is back there," Ben said, coming up behind Stan and wrapping one arm around his waist, dropping his chin to Stan's shoulder. "All those cupboards at the back are wardrobes. I hung your stuff up, but you can reorganise it when you're ready. Oh, and I didn't want to set your dressing table up yet, because I wasn't sure where it should go. It's all here, though, when you're ready for it."

Stan turned in Ben's embrace and wrapped his arms around Ben's neck.

"This is amazing. Thank you."

"I just wanted us to have a space. You know. That's ours. It's not quite a home of our own, but it's our little piece of the world."

Stan tangled his fingers in Ben's hair. "I love you so much."

Ben rubbed their noses together. "Love you too."

"Can we take a nap?"

"Yeah." Ben grinned. "A nap sounds pretty good to me."

STAN WAS woken by one of his alarms. They went off at regular intervals, to remind him to eat.

Ben was already awake, propped up on one elbow with a book between them.

"You're awake," he murmured.

"Mm. I need one of my shakes."

"Want me to get it for you?"

"I can do it," Stan said, stretching. "I kind of want to see the rest of the house too."

"Okay."

Ben leaned over and kissed him very, very carefully. They hadn't been alone like this since—*fuck*—since Manchester. That was a hell of a long time Ben had gone without sex. Stan tugged him down until Ben's familiar, comforting weight was pressing Stan back into the bed. Ben flicked his tongue into Stan's mouth, and, God, they needed this.

"I missed you," Stan breathed over Ben's lips. "So fucking much."

Ben gave him a sad smile and brushed his thumb back and forth over Stan's cheekbone. "You're not cleared for 'strenuous physical activity' yet, love."

"That's okay. I'll just lie here and you can do all the work."

Ben hid his laugh in Stan's shoulder. "Come on. You need your shake."

"Fine," Stan sighed.

Tone wanted a pizza party to celebrate Stan coming home. For a split second after he'd suggested it, Stan thought Ben might actually punch Tone on the nose. He didn't, though, just explained in a tight voice that maybe it wasn't the best idea.

Stan thought the whole thing was hilarious. He sat at the wide kitchen island and watched, amused, as his new housemates emerged from different corners of the building to welcome him home.

He decided it wouldn't take long for this to feel like home.

That night they all piled down into the basement for "band practice." Stan wasn't exactly sure what the rehearsal schedule for the band looked like anymore, now that they all lived together.

Band practice was supposed to start at seven.

They didn't even get instruments out until ten.

There was pizza, too much pizza for the six of them really, but Tone could easily eat one by himself, so they managed. Then there was beer, and Stan waved that away—half a slice of pizza he could just about stomach. Beer on top of that was out of the question.

Then there was weed, which Stan had never been a fan of before he met Ben. He'd smoked it some in the US. It wasn't really as much of a thing in Italy. Italy was where he'd got addicted to cigarettes.

"Right!" Summer said, falling over herself laughing. "We need to work."

"Should I go?" Stan asked. He stretched lazily, arms over his head, aware his shirt had ridden up only because of the look in Ben's eyes.

Three different people said no at the same time, so he settled back into the beanbag.

This basement was a little smaller than the one they had been rehearsing in before, at Sherrie's house. It was good for reasons Stan wasn't able to explain. The dark, moody room with its low ceiling and excellent acoustics made for one hell of a practice space.

Ben pulled out his acoustic guitar and shifted about on his big beanbag until he was comfortable. He'd ordered a whole bunch of custom guitar picks—Stan was finding them *everywhere*—and pulled one of them out of his back pocket.

"Where do you want to start?" Geordie asked, thumbing a few notes on his bass.

The boys all looked to Summer, who rolled her eyes. "Why am I always the one who organises you all?"

"Because you're so good at it, darling," Geordie told her.

She snorted. "Okay, well I want to run 'London,' so let's start there."

To Stan's right, Jez exhaled and passed him the blunt so he could pick up his guitar and plug it into the amp. Stan nodded his thanks and took a long drag on it, making the end smoulder.

"Stan," Ben said softly and Stan turned to him, smiling. "You're hilarious when you're high."

"You're…."

Stan couldn't finish that sentence. Tone had already started banging out the intro to the song on his bongos, which were apparently his rehearsal and song-writing drums of choice.

It wasn't a proper run-through of the songs, more like a way to remind everyone what their musical parts and harmonies were. Proper rehearsals happened with the band playing their instruments all plugged in. Stan had been privy to enough of these sessions to know how they'd work: Summer would pick some songs she thought were rusty, pull a keyboard onto her lap, and nudge them through a few run-throughs.

The house was quiet, apart from their little underground space. They'd rehearsed until about two in the morning, not seriously, just messing around with old songs and new. Getting high. Making out. Teaching Stan the kazoo part to "No Politics, Please." Ben had laughed until he complained his sides were hurting, and it felt like the world was recalibrating. Like they were finding a way through everything that had happened over the past few months.

When they fell into bed, Ben pressed a familiar black bunny rabbit into Stan's hand.

"I don't need him anymore," Ben said, his voice husky from the weed. "I can hold you tonight."

"And tomorrow," Stan said.

"And tomorrow."

CHAPTER SEVENTEEN

THE NEW routine meant Stan was often up, out of bed, dressed, and almost done with breakfast by the time Ben emerged from their room. They exchanged kisses while Ben made coffee, and then Stan skipped out for his outpatient appointment.

Depending on what day of the week it was, he spent between an hour and four at the hospital, meeting with different therapists, doctors, and nutritionists. He had good days and bad days; days when the very last thing he wanted to do was choke down another high-calorie shake and smell the tangy antiseptic of the hospital corridors, others when he ate toast and coffee with Leslie in the cafeteria after meeting with Dr Caldwell.

In the afternoons, when Ben wasn't working at the bar or tutoring, they curled up on the couch in their room and closed the rest of the world out. Just for an hour, maybe two, sometimes to make love, other times to have some quiet space with just the two of them.

It was almost like being back in the flat at Bow Quarter. Only a few months had passed, but to Stan it felt like a lifetime ago.

"So, my dad got in touch."

Stan looked up, surprised. "Yeah?"

He'd been curled up on the sofa, watching *Antiques Roadshow*, with his feet on Ben's lap.

"Yeah. He's, uh...." Ben pushed his hand through his hair. "He's getting married in a couple of weeks. Someplace in the south of France."

"That's a long way from New Zealand," Stan said with a small laugh.

"I know. His girlfriend is from Italy, and apparently her parents own this villa. Anyway, he wants me to go."

"Oh."

"Yeah. I'm really sorry, baby. I think I'm going to be gone for about a week."

Stan's stomach clenched at the thought of being away from Ben again, especially for so long, but he forced his face into a mask and nodded in what he hoped was reassurance. "That's okay. I'll be fine."

"Tone is going to hang out with you. I already spoke to him about it."

"Ben." Stan forced himself to unclench his jaw and shifted off Ben's lap to look at him properly. "I am a grown man. I do not need a babysitter."

"Did I say you did? Tone's not your keeper. He's your *friend*, Stan. I know you don't like it when people take care of you, but we do it because we love you. Okay?"

Stan blew out a hard breath. "Yeah. Okay. I'm sorry."

"Don't be," Ben murmured, pulling Stan back onto his lap. "I won't go if you don't want me to."

"Don't do that. It's your dad. You should be there."

"Yeah. Thing is, he left a long time ago. I'm going to spend the rest of my life with you." He thumbed over the ring Stan had taken to wearing again, now he was out of hospital.

"Are you going to tell him about me?"

"Yeah."

"You don't have to."

"I wish I could take you with me," Ben said, just gently groping at Stan's arse. "The next family thing, though. You'll come, right?"

"Of course. I want to meet your triplets."

Ben hid his grin in Stan's hair. "They'll adore you. Oh my God. You'll have to prepare yourself. I swear they won't put you down."

"Your mum too."

"Everyone," Ben said.

"Okay. Good."

TONE HAD said Ben needed to get away. Insisted on it, in fact. Stan was getting better; they could all see that. He fitted into the rhythm of the house like he was meant to be there, or even more than that, like they needed him to complete the symphony. Summer liked having another "girl" in the house. Tone and Stan got on like a house on fire. Jez and Geordie pulled Stan in with no questions, no hesitations. He was one of them.

Ben knew he hovered, and he definitely knew how much it drove Stan crazy when he did. He wasn't doing it on purpose. The thought of maybe losing Stan again was more than a little terrifying, and Ben wanted to keep him safe.

Okay, he really did need to get away.

He got the train out to the airport to fly to Toulouse, leaving Stan in bed with warm, sleepy kisses. Maybe that would be the worst part of it; not being able to sleep with Stan against his chest for a whole week. They'd only just got that back; it was hard to think of losing it again.

FRANCE WAS hot enough to make Ben irritable, and full of relatives he only knew in the vaguest of terms. It was awkward, being reintroduced to cousins he hadn't seen in almost fifteen years. They looked at him like he was some strange creature, a hunched vampire in black clothes while they breezed around in summer dresses and khaki shorts and baseball caps.

Ben bought a baseball cap from a little tourist shop in the town. It was black.

At least he had his own room.

All the cousins were sharing, but Ben got to stay in the niceish hotel next door to the villa because there wasn't enough room for everyone. His drunk uncle was down the hall, and a few of his soon-to-be stepmother's family and friends. The hotel was small, family-owned, and had probably once been a privately owned villa too.

He left the terrace doors open to tempt a breeze in while he kicked back on the bed and connected to Wi-Fi.

"Ben."

Hearing Stan's voice was pretty much all Ben needed. He grinned and waved at his iPad, feeling stupid and not caring.

"Hey, baby. How are you?"

"Good." Stan smiled, and there was a new kind of light in his eyes. He seemed to be a younger, more carefree person than the one Ben had met back at the beginning of the year. "Tone is cooking tonight. Kirsty's coming over too, but they keep saying it's not a date."

"Oh God. The last thing you need is food poisoning."

Stan laughed and pushed his fingers through his hair. "He's making TFC."

"TFC?"

"Tone's Fried Chicken."

Ben huffed a laugh and shook his head. "What are you going to eat, then?"

"I might try some."

"Seriously?"

"Yeah. I've been working with Amrita on trying new things. Tone says I'm addicted to chocolate now."

Amrita was Stan's therapist. He'd just gone from four sessions a week to two and seemed to be coping well. Ben found himself starting to relax and smiled at the serene expression on Stan's face.

"I've only been gone a few days. What happened to you?"

Stan reached out and touched the screen of his iPad from the other side. "I missed you."

"Missed you too. My stepmum said to pass on her love."

"Bless her. Tell her I said thank you."

Ben leaned back in the deck chair next to the pool and caught Stan up on everything that had been happening. It was a warm day in Toulouse, balmy and breezy, so Ben had huddled himself under a large deck umbrella to stop his skin from burning. He'd done that already—burned—on the day he'd arrived, and now his skin was gross and peeling.

The wedding had happened the day before, but people were hanging around for a few more days before going back to wherever they'd come from. It was years since Ben had seen his dad and uncle, and the two of them had got rip-roaringly drunk early on in the trip.

At the bar, Ben had decided it would be a good time to come out.

His dad had been confused, his eyes, so like Ben's, glazed over from the alcohol.

"You're gay? Like a poofter?"

"Cheers, Dad," Ben had muttered and ducked his head, hiding behind the thick mop of hair that was, once again, not pulled up into a mohawk.

He'd explained about Stan in the best way that his father would understand—that Stan wasn't exactly a masculine sort of guy, that he danced to his own tune, and fuck anyone who didn't like it. Maybe he could blame the French wine, or the late hour, or the fact they hadn't seen each other in so long, but Ben's inhibitions were practically non-existent, and he pulled his phone out of his pocket to show his dad pictures of the two of them together.

"That's a bloke?" Ben's uncle had asked, incredulous. He made the picture of Stan bigger, then continued swiping through the photos. "He doesn't look like a bloody bloke to me."

"I told you. Stan is different."

Ben's dad had shaken his head, pushing the phone away. "Do you love him, Ben?"

"Yeah. Yeah, I do."

"Then nothing else matters."

Ben repeated those words back to Stan, loving the soft blush that rose in his cheeks.

"I have your father's approval, then?"

"I guess so. Not that you needed it."

"Oh, I know. It's still nice."

"Yeah. I'll be home in a couple of days, baby. You're going to be okay until then?"

"Of course. Tone's looking after me."

"I know. That's what I'm afraid of."

IT HAD been hard for Ben to keep his mind away from the last time he'd come home to Stan, when his boyfriend wasn't at home and everything went to shit. He'd called Stan twice since he landed back at Gatwick and had fiddled with his phone the whole time he was on the Underground, annoyed that he had no signal to text Stan again.

He had to force himself not to run down the road to the house, even though a light, misty rain was falling and no one would probably have paid any attention to him.

Finally, finally, he was shoving his key into the lock on the blue door and shouting out for Stan.

"Hi," Stan said, stepping out of the kitchen at the back of the house.

Ben dropped his bag, pushed the door closed, and grinned.

Stan was wearing black jeans and a baggy T-shirt Ben thought might be one of his own. His hair was loose around his shoulders, and he looked good. Stan paused for a moment, his hand on the doorframe, then ran down the hall and launched himself into Ben's arms.

"You like doing that, don't you?" Ben murmured against Stan's neck, appreciating the quick, hard laugh Stan gave him in response. He cupped Stan's ass in both hands and turned them both around, then pressed Stan back against the wall so he could kiss him.

"You've been gone too long," Stan said, his lips brushing against Ben's. "I put on three pounds and masturbated twice."

"Three pounds? Where? Let me find them."

With one hand easily supporting the weight of Stan's body, Ben pushed his other hand up under the T-shirt and dug his fingers into Stan's ribs to make him laugh and squirm.

"I love you," Ben said as he moved his lips to the pulse point in Stan's neck and rested there. "I don't tell you enough. I love you."

"I love you too. Take me to bed."

Ben's mouth stretched into a grin. "It's the middle of the afternoon."

"No one's home. Please, Ben."

"Oh, alright," Ben said with a long-suffering sigh neither of them believed.

It took longer than it should have, stumbling over each other in their rush to get upstairs to the sanctuary of their room. Stan kept it tidy when Ben wasn't around to mess it up, and one of the skylight windows was cracked open, letting a soft breeze into the room.

Ben noticed all of that, even as Stan pulled Ben's T-shirt up over his head and tossed it in a corner somewhere, then ran his hands possessively over Ben's chest.

"God, I missed you," Stan murmured as he kissed from one shoulder to the next.

"Missed you too. Fuck. Take some clothes off, would you?"

Stan was laughing as they stumbled towards the bed, kicking off shoes and wriggling out of jeans that were always too tight. When they were down to underwear, Ben pulled Stan close to his chest and held him there, desperate for the feel of their skin pressed together. Stan ran his fingers through Ben's hair and kissed him slowly, deep and needing.

"Want me inside you?" Ben asked, mouthing softly at Stan's neck.

Stan shook his head. They were building up to that again.

"Just want to feel you."

"We can do that."

Ben kissed over Stan's chest, licking and nibbling, taking both of Stan's nipples into his mouth in turn and lapping at them until Stan was arching up into the touch. His fingers were in Ben's hair, tugging and insistent, pulling him back up from where he'd been licking Stan's hip bones for a slow, sure kiss.

"Off, off," Stan muttered, using his bare feet to nudge Ben's boxers down over his hips.

Ben was laughing as he helped, then kicked the last of his clothes off as he settled down next to Stan, running his fingers over Stan's long, lean body.

"You still want me… even like this?"

Ben ran his fingernails over Stan's ribs. Sure, they still stood out a little. But Stan was so much better than he had been before.

"I want all of you." He skimmed his fingers down again to press his palm to Stan's cock. "I love every part of you. All of it."

Stan whimpered in the back of his throat, and Ben chased the noise away with more kisses, slipping his hand into Stan's tight, black boxers and gently stroking his cock. Stan grabbed for Ben's dick too, making it about both of them, and for long minutes they let slow kisses and frantic hands take over.

"There's lube and stuff in the drawer," Ben said. "You're closest."

STAN WAS a little out of breath already, just from kissing and petting, but oh God, did lube make things better. And he was closest.

As expected, when he leaned over, Ben dove for his ass, kissing and licking his lower back and tugging the boxers the rest of the way off. Stan was giggling when he rolled back over with the tube and let Ben nuzzle into his hip.

"Can I…?"

"Always."

That wasn't strictly true. Being on the receiving end of a blowjob wasn't always Stan's favourite thing, but Ben always asked, and Stan loved that he did. It helped that Ben was really, really good at sucking his dick. He was always so gentle and he did that thing with his tongue and—Stan arched off the bed and a noise he didn't recognise was ripped from his throat.

"Oh fuck."

Ben gently tugged on his balls, staving off the imminent orgasm, and muttered something about lube.

Stan handed it to him blind.

After some fumbling Ben grunted out a curse or two, then his slick hand wrapped around both Stan's dick and his own and *oh fuck*, that was a brilliant idea.

It also meant they could kiss, sloppy and loose, as Ben worked their cocks together, and Stan was on some kind of hair trigger from missing him. That had to be the explanation because he was so close to coming and Ben was panting above him, nipping at Stan's collarbone and it was perfect.

The pleasure trembled through Stan's body, filling him and making his heart ache with love for this man. He curled his fingers around the back of Ben's neck, holding him close, and Ben's kisses were whisper-light over Stan's lips.

"I love you," Ben murmured. "Come with me. I love you."

Stan didn't cry out, didn't buck or thrash like he sometimes did when his orgasm hit like a sucker punch to the gut. His toes contracted and something pulled in his belly and the noise that escaped his lips was a sob.

This lovemaking soothed him, and as they climaxed together, vibrating with shared pleasure, Stan found a part of himself clicking into place. He was a lover. A partner. The two of them together made something, created something, and it was beautiful and unique and theirs.

Ben fell forward as he caught his breath. Stan wrapped both arms around his back, silently begging him to stay close, *please*, just a little longer. His finger stole into Ben's hair, all inky blackness and silky smooth as he stroked it back.

When Ben kissed him again, it was to gather the salty tears from Stan's cheeks, then to share them with his lips.

"Don't leave me, please," Stan murmured. "I missed you too much. I can live without you, but God, Ben, I don't want to."

"Not leaving you," Ben said. His voice sounded thick. "Me and you."

They wriggled for a few moments, Ben cleaning up their bellies with a discarded T-shirt, then rolling onto his back and bringing Stan to sprawl on top of him. Stan dragged the duvet up to cover his naked back and pressed his face to Ben's neck, strangely pleased when Ben wrapped one arm around his waist and settled the other hand on his ass.

They lay together like that for a while, snoozing a little, Ben's hand brushing back and forth over the smooth skin of Stan's ass. This was familiar, loving, perfect; all the things Stan had ever wanted from a relationship.

When they woke up again, the sky outside was almost luminous pink, the clouds reflecting a vibrantly setting sun. Ben started the task of untangling Stan's hair with his fingers; an excuse, Stan always thought, for them to be touching.

"What did you think of me when we first met?"

Ben frowned and pushed a long strand of Stan's hair away from his face, tucking it neatly behind his ear. "What do you mean? When you first came into the pub?"

"Yes. I'm curious."

"Well...."

"I won't think any different of you, I promise. I really just want to know."

"I'm pretty sure I thought you were a girl when you first walked in," Ben said. "I was serving Gary, one of the regulars, and I looked up and saw this long-legged goddess striding through the pub. You walked in and I had to fight Tone to be allowed to serve you."

"Really?" Stan said with a laugh.

"Oh yeah. You know what Tone's like—he sees a pretty girl, and he's all over her."

"He's not a creep, though," Stan said, feeling strangely protective of his newest best friend.

"If you say so," Ben said. "He let me come over, anyway, and I thought you were even more beautiful up close."

"You're just saying that."

Ben laughed and kissed Stan's cheek. "Nope. I realised you were a boy pretty quickly. Then you asked for a beer, and the rest is history."

"You called me."

"Yeah. Well, you were the one with enough balls to leave your number for me."

Stan shrugged. "I figured you could call me, and that would be great, or you wouldn't. London is a big city. I could easily avoid you for the rest of my life."

Ben laughed and pressed a kiss to Stan's neck. "I was scared to call you."

"Why?"

"Because you might have answered."

"You're so silly," Stan said with a long sigh. He let the moment linger between them, fresh air and sweat and spunk, then kissed the shell of Ben's ear. "I'm really glad you called."

"Me too, baby. Me too."

CHAPTER EIGHTEEN

BEN WOKE alone in his bed. He stretched, searching for Stan's familiar warm weight, and met nothing but cool sheets.

That wasn't so unusual. Stan had never really broken his habit of rising early, though Ben was often aware of him slipping out of bed. A quick glance at the clock on the bedside table told him it was only eight thirty, ridiculously early for a Sunday, but if Stan wasn't in bed with him, Ben wasn't interested in being there alone.

With a groan, he heaved himself up and stumbled through to the small en suite bathroom. It took a few minutes for him to feel normal again—face washed, bladder emptied, a pair of boxers pulled on to cover his naked ass. And a T-shirt, after a moment's hesitation.

Ben guessed no one else was awake yet, probably just Stan, pottering around as he liked to do. Instead he found both Stan and Tone in the conservatory at the back of the house doing what looked like yoga.

"Stan?"

"Shh," Stan said softly. He was sat cross-legged on a yoga mat, hands on his knees, spine straight, breathing evenly. Ben couldn't help letting his lips twitch into a smile. Stan's long hair was flowing softly down his back, a shiny waterfall of blond, over the very loose, white tank top he'd put on over tight, grey yoga pants.

Next to him was Tone. Wearing a battered Jack Daniels T-shirt and black boxers, his beard scruffy, he also sat on a yoga mat, breathing deeply.

Ben turned back around and went to the kitchen to make coffee.

It was late September, and autumn was being unseasonably kind to them. For a week or more, it had been warm, midsummer temperature, and Stan in particular was making the most of the last of the sunshine. In the kitchen, the sun streamed in through the low window, and Ben took his time wandering around, seeking out biscuits to go with his coffee, tidying away the last few things they'd used the night before. Kirsty had come over for dinner again. Ben was starting to lose faith in Tone's protestations that they were "just friends."

When the coffee was done brewing, Ben made himself a large mug and wandered back through to the conservatory. He knew nothing about yoga, though he was pretty sure Stan and Tone were doing the "downward dog." Not wanting to laugh at them, he left again and went into the living room, turned on the TV, and muted the sound as he switched it to the BBC News channel.

A few minutes later, Stan came in and planted himself decisively on Ben's lap.

"Morning," Ben said softly.

"Morning." Stan stole his coffee cup and took a sip. Then winced and handed it back.

"What were you doing?"

"Sun salutations," Stan said easily. He took one of Ben's biscuits instead.

"Okay."

"It's a great way to get your blood moving. A good start to the day."

"Why was Tone doing it with you?"

"Because he likes yoga too." Stan kissed Ben on the cheek. "Can we go out somewhere today?"

"Of course."

They stayed like that, curled up on the sofa for most of the morning. The house slowly woke up around them, people moving, the old corners creaking and groaning as people stumbled towards showers to wash away the lingering hangovers.

Ben had pulled a blanket from the back of the sofa and wrapped it around them both. Stan was clearly cold after his workout but refused to leave Ben's lap to go to get dressed. It suited them both just fine to cuddle together for warmth. Ben brushed his lips up and down Stan's neck, gathering the scent and the taste of him, keeping his arms secure around Stan's waist.

"I am so ridiculously in love with you."

Stan turned and gave him one of his most devastating smiles. Leaning in slowly, he bumped their noses together.

"I know."

Summer thundered down the stairs before anyone else. Ben didn't know where Tone had disappeared to after his sun salutations, but he definitely wasn't around the ground floor anywhere. Summer stuck her pink-haired head around the living room door, rolled her eyes at both of them, then headed to the kitchen. After a moment, the radio came on, and Ben shifted on the sofa, stretching his legs out until his knees clunked.

"Do you want some breakfast?"

Stan nodded. "Sure. I think I still have some strawberries left from yesterday."

Ben kissed him again, because he could, and for all the other reasons he was currently unable to name.

On lazy days, no one really got dressed. It was an unwritten house rule. Summer had spent enough time with the guys on tour that she paid absolutely no attention at all to when they wandered around naked. In the kitchen, Summer was wearing what looked like men's pyjama bottoms and a tank top, one that was tight enough to make Tone leery when he reappeared. Whether Kirsty was his girlfriend in the making or not clearly didn't make any difference.

"Mornin'," Tone drawled.

"How are you feeling?" Stan asked, going to the kettle to boil water for tea. Unlike the others, he still preferred green tea in the mornings.

"Not bad. You might be onto something with this yoga malarkey," Tone said with a grin. Stan rolled his eyes, and Ben thought he was making some effort not to do the same.

One by one, the kitchen filled up with the rest of their housemates. Tone lit all the burners on the hob and pulled down half a dozen pans, starting the process of a full English. Ben was thrown a loaf of bread, and he got started on the toast-making process, sat on the counter next to the toaster.

"Here," Tone said, and Ben looked up to see him place a bowl of porridge in front of Stan, who sat at their huge kitchen table. Stan grinned.

"Thanks."

Ben said nothing, just watched as Stan upended his bowl of carefully prepared strawberries on top of the porridge and started eating.

"How come he does that for you?" Ben asked Tone in a low voice.

"What?"

"Eats."

Tone snorted. "Because I don't make a big song and dance about it." The *like you do* was silent, but clearly implied.

Ben still pouted.

"Look, mate," Tone said, going back to the hob and forcing Ben to follow him. "You still don't get it. We joke about those chocolates, but do you know how long it took him to eat them?"

"No," Ben said, looking over his shoulder to make sure Stan wasn't overhearing their conversation. He was talking to Summer, though, not paying any attention to them.

"Over a month. And there wasn't even a dozen chocolates in the box."

"He was a vegan and you gave him fried chicken."

Tone rolled his eyes so hard Ben thought it must have hurt. "Jesus. He ate half a piece and picked most of the coating off. I'm not some magic, anti-anorexia fairy. You spend so much time worrying about shit you don't see the bigger picture."

The next batch of toast popped up, and Ben loaded the pieces onto a plate, burning his fingers in the process.

"Bigger picture," he muttered.

"Yeah," Tone said. "Bigger fucking picture. And chill the fuck out. You want bacon?"

"Nah, just eggs, please."

Tone passed him the huge frying pan, and Ben piled the eggs on top of his toast, then went and sat down next to Stan. "That good?" he asked.

Stan nodded. "Yeah. I know he only does it in the microwave, but whenever I try, it goes all gluey."

"Tone has a special affinity with microwaves," Ben said, pleased when Stan laughed.

"Yeah, he does."

"Hey, hey," Summer yelled suddenly. "Shut up, shut up."

She was frowning hard and Tone looked over at her, worry clear in his eyes.

"What's wrong?"

"Shush." She waved a hand at him demonstratively and reached over to turn up the radio.

"…is a band I saw a few weeks back at the Brixton Academy," the radio DJ said. "They're new, they recently toured with Racket City, and they're really good, amazing live, so go see them if you can. I got sent an advance copy of their EP, and it's pretty awesome. I'm going to play you one of the songs off that record now—this is Ares with 'Out of Here.'"

Ben felt his jaw drop as the first clashing chords—*his* clashing chords came through their little radio.

"Holy shit," he breathed.

"What the fuck?" Tone demanded as Ben heard his own voice start to sing the main melody. "What radio station is this?"

"Radio One," Summer said. She was shaking her head in disbelief. "It's Radio fucking One, you guys."

"I didn't think...," Jez started, then shook his head and pushed his fingers into his hair. "I never thought they'd actually play it."

"You sent them it?" Geordie demanded.

"Well yeah," Jez said. "I sent it to a bunch of radio stations. We finished the mix, and it was sounding good, so I just...."

"Tweet them," Stan said. "From the band account. Quickly."

Summer fumbled for her phone and tapped at it furiously. Ben could feel his heart thumping hard in his chest. They were being played on the biggest radio station in the UK. If they wanted a big break, this was likely it.

"Done," Summer said. "I hope they get it."

"They'll have social media guys waiting for something like this," Stan told her. "Just hang on."

The song ended, and Summer shushed them all again.

"That was Ares and 'Out of Here,'" the DJ said. "It seems like you guys like it. We've had a whole load of tweets and texts about this song, so go check them out if you can—they're an unsigned band creating some great new music. Next up is the news and weather."

Ben shook his head slowly. "Did we just get a shout-out from Radio One?"

Summer looked like she was about to boil over with excitement. Then she broke, jumping up from her spot at the table and into Geordie's arms, squealing and laughing. Geordie laughed and spun her around, then planted a big kiss on her lips.

"Right," Jez said, clearly amused at the affection on display. "Now the real work starts."

IT WAS possibly the last balmy, warm evening of the year. Stan had convinced Ben to stay in bed for a little afternoon delight, while the rest of the band fled the house to start setting up at the Buck Shot. Jez had arranged a gig there, the last one in London before they headed out on tour again, this time with the intention of covering as much of Europe as they could. Festival season was over, but there was still plenty of interest in live music at this time of year, especially as universities started building their weekend gig schedules.

The difference was, this time Stan was going with them.

He didn't quite have an official job within the Ares machine yet, but it was something to do with blogging, social media, industry contacts, tour planning, and making sure none of the band got arrested. The adverts he'd set up on his own blog were turning in some income, and the EP was selling well enough to fund at least part of the tour. Unbeknownst to the band, Stan had arranged for part of the gig tonight to be filmed, and that footage would make up part of their first music video. They didn't know about that yet either.

In the week since the song had been played on Radio One, things had gone slightly mental. They'd gained tens of thousands of Twitter followers, seemingly out of nowhere, and a few other radio stations had picked up the song and played it. The website had been radically overhauled to accommodate the traffic heading towards it, and Jez had figured out how to get the EP onto iTunes. They'd had interview requests. From both magazines and radio stations. And calls from agents. They were still trying to figure out what to do with that.

"You ready?" Ben called.

Stan took a deep breath and fluffed his hair for the last time.

"Coming."

After plenty of internal debate, he'd decided to wear a dress for the gig. The last time he'd worn something feminine was before he went into hospital, and he knew Ben noticed. Unlike Tone, Ben was still dancing around Stan's illness, treating him like he was something precious and fragile. That wasn't necessarily a bad thing. There was room in his life for someone who treated him like a queen, and also for someone who ignored Stan's protests of veganism and plied him with chocolate and fried chicken and porridge.

For tonight, Stan had curled his hair into big, bouncy waves. The dress was a long, black slick of diaphanous fabric that fell to just below his knees. He was wearing his black Louboutin ankle boots, the ones that made him feel powerful and feminine and badass. Plenty of dark eyeshadow finished the look.

"Stan," Ben said, his voice exasperated as he stuck his head around the bedroom door. "Holy shit, you look incredible."

"Too much?"

"Definitely not. If I didn't have a gig to get to, I'd stay home and just take it all off you."

Stan laughed. "Okay. I'm ready."

They caught a cab to the pub—because heels—and they were far too close to bother getting the Tube. The cab dropped them off on the wrong side of the road because it was easier than trying to turn around in Friday night traffic.

Ben slipped his hand into Stan's as they waited at the pedestrian crossing and Stan felt something flutter in his belly, like it often did when he had a chance to be affectionate with Ben in public like this. The sun was just starting to set over Camden. This was when the real fun started in their little corner of London—the sun went down and the boys came out to play.

A young girl was waiting to cross the road, holding hands with her mother. Stan looked down at her pretty face and pigtails and grinned.

The little girl grabbed the hem of Ben's black T-shirt and tugged.

"Alice," the mother scolded. Ben shook his head at her—he didn't mind.

"Is she a princess?" Alice stage-whispered.

Stan did a double take; firstly at the pronoun, secondly at the title. From the look on Ben's face he was trying, very hard, not to laugh.

"Yeah," he said. "She is. But don't tell anyone, okay?"

"Okay," Alice said, then turned back to her mother, an excited expression on her face.

"Sorry," Alice's mum said.

"Not a problem," Stan said softly.

The lights turned, traffic stopped, and Ben pulled Stan into a run across the road.

"Princess, eh?" Stan asked as they came to a stop in front of the pub. Ben laughed, tipping his head back to expose his throat.

"Yeah. My princess, anyway."

Stan let Ben pull him into a long, slow kiss. He reached up to wind his arms around Ben's shoulders, hanging on as they swayed together and Ben's hands drifted down to squeeze Stan's ass. Someone passing by whistled at them and Stan broke away with a laugh, kissing Ben's nose instead.

"You ready for this?" Stan asked. Ben seemed to understand. Tonight was the start of something new for all of them. The end of one era, the beginning of the next one.

"As long as I can do it with my princess, I can do anything," Ben murmured, the words soft against Stan's lips. Stan smiled and pulled himself just a tiny bit closer to Ben's solid chest. "With my beautiful, impossible boy."

AUTHOR'S NOTE

THE IMPOSSIBLE Boy has been quite a journey for me. It's taken me about four years to write this novel, during which time the world has changed a lot. Parts of Camden Market have been torn down to make way for a high-speed train line (the Thai food stall was a real place, though it's now gone). Women like Laverne Cox and Caitlin Jenner have brought mainstream attention to what it means to be transgender. The great trans bathroom debate has risen and fallen. All of this happened after I'd written the bulk of the story.

I've honestly never been so scared of a book the way I am of this one. This is, after all, not my story to tell. I'm not a trans or gender-fluid person, which made me agonise over whether I was telling this story in the "right" way. I expect I always will. It came down to writing something which was true to these two characters and their individual experiences, not trying to generalise or brush over the more complex issues, and letting this story be just its own thing in a growing world of trans narratives. I believe, very passionately, that everyone should be able to read a love story about someone like themselves.

A transgender/gender-fluid romance will always be a difficult pitch, so thank you, dear reader, for giving this one a chance.

ANNA MARTIN is from a picturesque seaside village in the southwest of England and now lives in the slightly arty, slightly quirky city of Bristol. After spending most of her childhood making up stories, she studied English literature at university before attempting to turn her hand as a professional writer.

Apart from being physically dependent on her laptop, Anna is enthusiastic about writing and producing local grassroots theater (especially at the Edinburgh Fringe Festival, where she can be found every summer), going to visit friends in other countries, baking weird and wonderful sweets, learning to play the ukulele, and Ben & Jerry's New York Super Fudge Chunk.

Anna claims her entire career is due to the love, support, prereading, and creative ass kicking provided by her best friend Jennifer. Jennifer refuses to accept responsibility for anything Anna has written.

Second place winner of the 2012 Goodreads M/M Romance Member's Choice Award "Best Musician/Rockstars" for *Tattoos & Teacups*.

Website: annamartin-fiction.com
Twitter: @missannamartin
Tumblr: annamartinwrites.tumblr.com
Facebook: www.facebook.com/annamartinfiction
Goodreads: www.goodreads.com/author/show/5251288.Anna_Martin

When you realize you want to marry your best friend at age six, life should follow a pretty predictable path, right? Maybe not.

As a kid, Evan King thought Scott Sparrow was the most amazing person he'd ever met. At seventeen, his crush runs a little deeper, and nothing seems simple anymore. Scott is more interested in football and girls than playing superheroes, and Evan's attention is focused on getting into art school. A late-night drunken kiss is something to be forgotten, not obsessed over for the next ten years.

When life suddenly brings them back together, it doesn't take much for the flame Evan carried for Scott nearly all his life to come roaring back, and Evan discovers that life sometimes has a strange way of coming full circle.

www.dreamspinnerpress.com

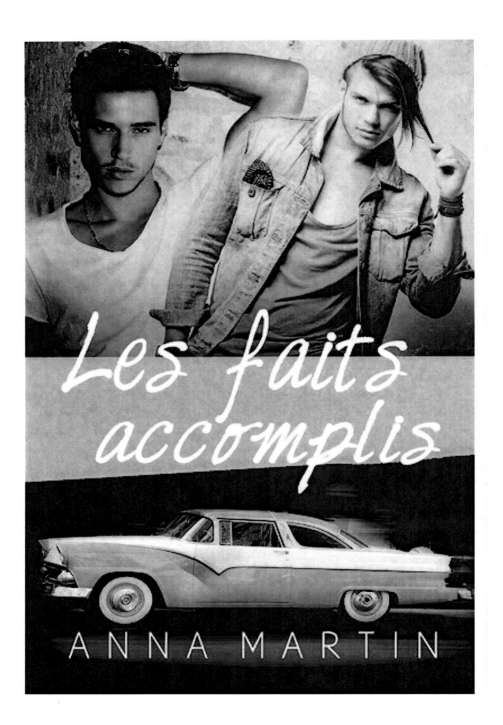

Adam Hemlock rules the elite New Harbor Academy. With his mother in Paris, he throws hedonistic, alcohol- and drug-fueled parties for his equally rich, desperately bored classmates. How's a guy who lives life to the extreme to stay entertained? Take on a challenge, of course, and hope the exhilaration of the play-by-play fallout chases away the indifference. At the big pre-senior-year bash, Adam's offered a dare—seduce the new kid. Adam initially laughs off the idea but changes his mind when he sees Jared.

Jared Rawell has spent the past two years at a Texas military school, where his father sent him to "pray away the gay." He sees the academy in more liberal Washington as a chance to start over and achieve the grades he needs to get into an Ivy League school. When a beautiful but terrifying girl offers Jared a deal—don't sleep with Adam Hemlock and she'll help Jared get through senior year—he sees no reason to say no. But nothing is as simple as it seems.

With layers of hidden agendas, backstabbing, lying, cheating, drugs, and entitled teenage egos, Jared and Adam must navigate a high school minefield while waiting for the inevitable explosion.

www.dreamspinnerpress.com

After growing up in a rough part of town, George Maguire worked his way out of Manchester and to a career as a design engineer. Alexander van Amsberg, an architecture student at the University of Edinburgh, wasn't the sort of guy he normally had explosive, hotel-room one-night-stands with. Alex was charming, classy, and, as George later learns, Prince of the Netherlands.

Fate brings them together again, and Alex makes sure to get his sexy stranger's phone number this time. Despite all the reasons why they shouldn't work, something clicks, and Alex thinks that this time, he might have found the right guy. But Alex's aristocratic ex stirs up trouble in the press for George and his humble family, and Alex realizes he has to get real about having a boyfriend from the wrong side of town.

While George acknowledges his modest upbringing, he doesn't let anyone insult his family. Life's no fairy tale, and regardless of his royal title, Alex might destroy his one chance for happily ever after.

www.dreamspinnerpress.com

After spending most of his life in special schools, Caleb Stone now faces public high school in his senior year, a prospect that both excites him and threatens to overwhelm his social anxiety. As a deaf teenager, he's closed himself off to the world. He speaks a shorthand with his parents and even finds it hard to use American Sign Language with people in his local deaf community. But Caleb finds comfort in his love of photography. Everything he can't express in real life, he posts on his Tumblr.

Struggling to reconcile his resentment for his father's cruelty with the grief of losing a parent, Luc Le Bautillier scrolls through Tumblr searching for someone who might understand his goth look and effeminate nature. When Luc reblogs a photo by Caleb, sparking a conversation, they both find it easier to make friends online than in person.

Luc and Caleb confront their fears about the opinions of the outside world to meet in New York City. Despite Caleb's increasing confidence, his parents worry he's not ready for the trials ahead. But communication comes in many forms—when you learn the signs.

www.dreamspinnerpress.com

FOR **MORE** OF THE **BEST GAY ROMANCE**

dreamspinnerpress.com

CPSIA information can be obtained
at www.ICGtesting.com
Printed in the USA
LVOW10s0855290117
522483LV00029BA/502/P

9 781635 332049